LOST TO LOVE

When Robert put his arms around Deirdre's waist, she moved closer to him. He kissed her softly on the lips several times, before tilting his head and moving in even closer.

His tongue danced with hers as they explored the newness of each other. Her heart raced and her body temperature rose as she wrapped her arms around his neck. The sweet taste of his mouth and the heat of his body rendered her lost in love. It was happening all over again. She was falling in love with Robert, the man, this time. Deirdre lost herself completely in his embrace, enjoying the kiss she'd been waiting for all her life.

Then she heard the faint sound of a child's giggle. She stopped herself and pulled away.

"What's wrong?" Robert asked.

Deirdre pointed at the two smiling faces pressed against the window. Mia and Vita.

"I see we have an audience." He grabbed Deirdre's hand, and they took a bow.

LOST TO LOVE

BRIDGET ANDERSON

BET Publications, LLC
www.msbet.com
www.arabesquebooks.com

ARABESQUE BOOKS are published by

BET Publications, LLC
C/o BET BOOKS
One BET Plaza
1900 W Place NE
Washington, D.C. 20018-1211

First Printing: April, 1999
10 9 8 7 6 5 4 3 2 1

Printed in the United States of America

This book is dedicated to my mother and best friend, Margaret Anderson. Thank you for the note of encouragement that I'll cherish forever. Your unconditional love means more to me than you'll ever know.

ONE

"What the hell is that?"

Deirdre stopped in front of her office door, and tilted her head, trying to read the writing scribbled on the glass door.

Is that blood? The brightness of the morning sun reflected off the glass, obstructing her view. Something was wrong. A shiver ran through her as she reached into her purse for the door key.

A strong urge to get inside engulfed her. She inserted the key and pulled on the door. Her hand slipped from the handle. Locked.

She'd locked the door instead of unlocking it. She found that strange because with all the vagrants in the area, the door was always locked.

After taking a step back, she tried again and slowly opened the door to the silence inside. Why wasn't Susan at her desk with her radio on, as usual?

Once inside, Deirdre closed the door and looked down at the glass again. The scribbling wasn't blood, but paint. She had smelled the strong fumes the minute she opened the door.

The mumble of voices caught her attention. She turned and walked across the small reception area. Her heart raced faster as she contemplated what was going on. Who was in her office? She scanned the area for a possible weapon.

"Deirdre?" Susan called from down the hall. "Is that you?"

Deirdre relaxed. "Yes, it's me. What's going on?"

Susan, a tall woman made up mostly of legs, entered the reception area. "Girl, somebody broke in last night, or this morning, and sprayed that on the door." She pointed at the glass door and read aloud, "Crazies."

Deirdre followed the direction of Susan's finger and finally made out the smeared word.

"Well, ladies, the police should be here any minute now." A deep voice echoed through the hallway behind Susan.

At the sound of his voice, Deirdre's satchel fell from her shoulder. She repositioned it as Mr. Hamel walked into the room.

It surprised Deirdre to see him emerge from her office. She wasn't exactly his favorite person, and the feeling was mutual. As director of the community center, he hadn't wanted a counseling agency connected to the center, but lost out to the board of directors.

Deirdre told herself to be patient and things would soon work out in her favor. Until then, she had to remain civil. However, this was still her office and she didn't like him snooping around inside.

Susan walked back to her desk and sat down, while Deirdre and Mr. Hamel faced each other.

"It seems you had an unwanted visitor." He stood with his hands on his hips.

He reminded Deirdre of Mr. Bookman from the seventies television show, *Good Times*. Short and round with a big belly. Mr. Hamel always showed up when you didn't want him to, and tried to throw his weight around. He had a way of annoying her.

She turned her attention to Susan and asked in frustration, "What happened?"

"When I came in this morning I saw the writing on the front door. I wasn't about to come in here alone, so I went next door to the community center and got Mr. Hamel. When we came in, we found the back door open and a few things gone."

"Like what?" Deirdre asked, looking from Susan to Mr. Hamel.

He didn't answer, but walked behind her toward the front door. "We can't have this type of incident happen so close to the center.

I don't want these children exposed to such crimes." He stopped and looked back over his shoulder.

The hair stood up on the back of Deirdre's neck as she spoke through gritted teeth, "Mr. Hamel, thank you. I can take it from here. I'm sure you need to get back to work."

"Yes, we have a board meeting in a few minutes. If the police need me, you know where to find me." He walked out, letting the door gently close on its own.

"I'm sorry, but I had to get him," Susan explained. "When I saw that door, I didn't know what to do. I was scared to come in here by myself."

"Don't worry about it. You did the right thing by not coming in here alone. Someone could have still been here for all you knew." Deirdre dropped her satchel and purse into a nearby chair.

"Before he saw the need to tell me about his board meeting, you were about to tell me what was taken?"

"Oh yeah. . ." Susan paused for a few seconds. She ran her hands across her secondhand veneer desk. "My good radio desk clock, and some notes I left out." In anticipation of Deirdre's reaction, Susan bit her lip.

It took a few seconds for the words to sink in, then they hit Deirdre like a brick against a wall.

"You left files out?" Deirdre asked in a distressed tone. She couldn't believe it. Susan had keys to lock everything up. She knew better.

"Not whole files, just notes from yesterday's sessions. I didn't have time to type them before I left, and I forgot to lock them up." Susan's voice trailed off as she sank deeper into her chair.

Deirdre picked up her satchel and tried not to panic.

"Is anything else missing?" she asked, looking down the hall toward her office.

"No, that's it."

In desperate need of an aspirin, Deirdre started past Susan, then stopped abruptly. "Whose notes were they?"

"I don't remember, but I think Geneva's and Sheila's." Susan shrugged her shoulders as she flipped through her desktop calendar searching for yesterday's appointments.

Deirdre cringed, then turned and stepped closer to Susan's desk. In six months of employment she'd never done something so careless.

In as stern a voice as she could manage, she said, "Susan, those notes are confidential and extremely private. My clients trust me to keep everything in the strictest of confidence. If those notes get into the wrong hands it can be detrimental for this agency. Don't ever leave notes out again."

She didn't wait for a response, but walked into her office and threw her satchel and purse on the desk. She tested her desk drawer—locked, good.

Susan followed her. "I'm sorry, and I feel awful about this. Believe me, it won't happen again. Anyway, the police should be here any minute."

"Good. How long have you been here?" Deirdre flopped into her chair.

"About ten minutes. Mr. Hamel wanted to look around before I called the police. It looks like they came in through the door that leads into the center. The front door was locked."

Deirdre looked up at Susan with raised brows. "You think some kid from the center next door broke in here?"

Susan held out her hands and shrugged her shoulders. "The back door does open into the community center's kitchen."

Two knocks came from the front door.

"I'll get it." Susan walked back down the hall to the reception area.

"It's the police." She opened the door.

"Ms. Levine?" One officer asked.

"No, I'm Susan Myers, her secretary. Have a seat fellas and I'll get her for you."

Deirdre walked into the room in time to catch Susan running her hands through her shoulder-length hair. A simple seductive gesture, and Susan's way of flirting.

She whirled around to face Deirdre. "Oh, here she is." She

turned back to face the officers. "I'm sorry I didn't get your names?"

The officers remained standing. "I'm Officer Duncan," the older black gentlemen said, then pointed to his younger black partner. "And this is Ray Fields."

"Gentlemen, my boss, Ms. Levine." Susan stepped aside so the three could shake hands.

"Deirdre Stanley." Officer Duncan gave her a sideways look. "I thought I recognized you."

"Hello, Bill, how have you been?"

"Great, just great." He gestured to his partner. "Ms. Stanley and I know each other from high school. Isn't that right?"

"Yes, we sure do," she said smiling.

"How long have you been back in town?"

She sighed. "Six months now."

"Well, it's good to have you back."

"Thank you."

"Well, we received two calls to check out a break-in over at Ms. Levine's counseling office on the river front. Can you tell me what happened?"

"Two calls?" Deirdre asked, creasing her eyebrows in wonderment.

He looked down at his paper. "That's what it says here. Can you tell me what's missing?"

"I only called once," Susan volunteered.

"I don't really know much, my secretary was here first. She informed me of the break-in a few minutes ago." Deirdre looked at Susan, who seemed ready to burst with whatever she knew. "Maybe you can help the officers with the details."

"Oh sure." Susan immediately grabbed Officer Fields by the arm and pointed out the spray-painted door.

"Deirdre, I'll still need a little information from you. It is okay if I call you Deirdre isn't it?"

She waved her hand in a nonchalant manner. "Oh sure. Whatever I can help you with, I will."

Deirdre barely remembered Bill Duncan from school. His

clean-shaven face and serious expression projected a rather in-
tellectual appearance, although, in school he looked more like a
black James Dean. She gave him all the information he asked
for as he checked the offices over.

Once they returned to the reception area, Deirdre looked at
her watch. "I'm sorry, it's almost time for my first client, and I
need to get ready for my session." So much for the fifteen-minute
review she liked to do before each session. This morning, she'd
be lucky to glance at her notes.

"Okay, I believe I have all I need for right now. If you notice
anything else missing, don't hesitate to call the station."

Deirdre hoped the thief had gotten his kicks and wouldn't
return. "Thank you. I won't."

"Excuse me, Ms. Levine?"

She turned toward the sound of a deep, masculine voice. She
opened her mouth to speak, but almost choked when he took her
breath away. Her thoughts transported to the past, as she looked
into the face of her high school prince. Her knight in shining
armor, at least in her dreams. Finally, she managed to spit out a
word.

"Yes?" The word stumbled from her lips.

He extended his hand. "I'm Robert Carmichael, from the
Brunswick Constitution. I came by to discuss the break-in you
had this morning."

Deirdre stood there, paralyzed. She knew who he was; she
used to know everything about him. He still had that youthful,
boy-next-door look, and smooth mocha-colored skin. She even
remembered the little mole over his left cheek. He'd grown a
moustache and small goatee, which added to his sex appeal.

She shook his hand. "Deirdre. I'm sorry, but as I told Officer
Duncan here, I don't know very much. My secretary's the one
who discovered the break-in."

"Deirdre, I don't want to take up any more of your time. I'll
check with your secretary again on my way out." Officer Duncan
walked past Robert and nodded his head as he left. "Robert."

Robert smiled. "Bill, good to see you again."

Officer Duncan joined his partner and Susan outside. When Deirdre turned her attention back to Robert, she caught his profile as he watched Bill. The years had been good to him. He looked so polished and distinguished. He still resembled the prince she dreamed one day would sweep her off her feet.

"They must have a police scanner down at that paper." She said sarcastically, and crossed her arms.

"Yes, I think we have one of those somewhere." Robert gave a chuckle as he played along with her. "However, a phone call lead me here this morning."

"Who called the paper?"

"Maybe your secretary?" he answered, as he clasped his hands together.

"No, I don't think she'd do that." Deirdre tilted her head to the side and peeked out at Susan.

He shrugged and smiled at her. "Okay then, we received an anonymous call, but somebody wanted us to check it out. Was anybody hurt?"

"No, and nothing of value was taken." She wasn't about to tell a reporter that her notes were stolen.

Robert rubbed his goatee and squinted at her. "Don't I know you from somewhere?"

Her heart skipped a beat, then speeded up double-time. She hadn't wanted him to recognize her. Uneasiness washed over her as she adjusted her jacket. "I used to go to school here."

"High school?"

"Yes, Lincoln High." She lowered her gaze, and observed his well-tailored, single-breasted suit and black lace-up shoes that were surely calfskin. Nothing delighted her more than a well-dressed man. He appeared to have done good for himself. Why shouldn't he, she thought. He came from a good family.

He snapped his fingers and pointed at her. "Yes, I remember you. I went to Lincoln too."

She nodded. "I know." So much for her hopes that he had a bad memory. She looked up as Susan reentered the office. In true Susan fashion, she lingered in the doorway while she flirted with the policemen.

Deirdre turned her attention back to Robert. "Here comes my secretary now. She can tell you more. I don't see that this incident even warrants an article in the paper." The last thing she needed was bad press.

Robert nodded and glanced around the office. "So, how long have you been in Brunswick? I haven't seen you around."

"I moved back six months ago." Deirdre tapped her foot against the floor. *Come on, Susan.* She didn't want to get into a personal conversation with Robert.

"So, you're creating an article out of this little break-in?" she asked, hoping to make it sound trivial.

"I'm researching the progress of the Riverfront renovation for an article. You know, you——"

Before he could finish his sentence, the front door swung open. Susan walked in, followed by Damon. He stopped inside the door and looked from Deirdre to Robert.

"Damon, you're right on time," she said, sensing his surprise. "Give me a minute and I'll be right with you." In the small reception area he looked like a Mr. America candidate. Deirdre cleared her throat in an attempt to cut the silence that fell over the room.

She'd always kept her office clear when clients arrived. Many of them were private people who didn't want their counseling public knowledge, like Damon.

He nodded at everyone in the room, then walked over and took a seat. The look in his eyes matched the uncomfortable way he sat on the edge of the seat.

"Susan, can you get Damon's file?" Deirdre made eye contact with Robert, who'd taken a seat across from Susan's desk. "And, Mr. Carmichael from the *Constitution* would like to talk with you," she said, walking toward the hallway. She hoped Susan knew enough to keep her mouth shut about the notes.

"I'll be right with you, Mr. Carmichael." Susan grabbed Damon's file from the cabinet.

"Thank you." Robert sat back and crossed his legs.

Damon stood and pointed to the front door. "What happened?" he asked Susan.

"That's what we'd like to know." Susan answered. She ushered him into the office and closed the door behind them.

Robert couldn't get over how good Deirdre looked. He didn't recognize her at first. The girl he remembered in high school had been reserved and quiet. She dressed in long black skirts and coats all the time. She didn't seem to have many friends, and he never saw her at a ballgame or dance.

The one thing he did recognize were her beautiful hazel eyes. She had always worn her hair low across her brow in school, but her hazel eyes had always stood out. And he always guessed she had a body under all those clothes. Yes, it was all coming back to him now; he remembered her. She transferred from another school in the middle of the year. People whispered about an incident that happened to her, but he never knew the details.

He looked around the reception area and noticed how comfortable it was for such a small place. The furniture consisted of four chairs, a few file cabinets and some large leafy silk plants.

When Susan returned, she glided across the room and smiled seductively. "So, Mr. Carmichael, what can I help you with?"

He moved his chair closer to her desk. When he looked up at her, he remembered the phone call that prompted him to stop by the office. It couldn't have been her; the caller was a man with a muffled voice.

TWO

After a full day of answering the same questions over and over, Deirdre left the office and went home to be with her daughter, Mia.

She pulled into her parents' driveway and killed the engine, all the time wishing she was going to her own home. Here she sat, in front of the same house she'd spent most of her childhood years in.

The front door opened as she stepped on to the porch.

"Come on in, honey. How was work today?" Anna stood in the doorway with a kitchen towel in her hand.

"Mom, you won't believe it." Deirdre gave her mother a quick kiss on the cheek as she leaned in to hug her on the way inside.

Anna stood several inches shorter than Deirdre, who inherited her height from her father.

"What happened?"

"Someone broke into the office." Deirdre closed the door behind her and followed her mother into the kitchen. The smell of fresh garden flowers lingered throughout the house.

"Lord have mercy, did they take anything?"

"Susan's clock radio, and my notes from yesterday's session. I can't see what good they'll do anybody." She set her purse and satchel in a kitchen chair.

"Do you think it's some of those bad kids from the community center?" Anna asked.

"Yes, I do. They broke in through the back door, which opens into the kitchen of the community center. I hate to think some of those kids are behind this, but it sure looks that way."

Anna continued to dry off the dishes while her daughter sat at the kitchen table. "Wash your hands and help me cook dinner. It'll make you feel better."

Deirdre sighed and lowered her shoulders. Things were always better with her mother around. Their cooking ritual had a way of lifting Deirdre's spirits. She remembered with fondness their conversations, and the lessons she'd learned in the process. Not to mention all the family gossip they shared. However, today Deirdre had a lot on her mind.

"I need to check on Mia first. Where is she?"

"She's taking a nap and you shouldn't wake her. That little lady has more energy than any six-year-old I've ever seen. She about wore me out before she lay down. Besides, your father won't be home until tomorrow and I could use a little company in here."

"Where's Daddy?"

"He rode over to St. Simons with Billy Mitchell. They've chartered a fishing boat for the morning." With pouted lips, Anna shook her head.

"What's wrong? You didn't want him to go?" Deirdre asked, knowing how much her father loved to fish. She got up from the table to help her mother cook.

"His fishing don't bother me none, it's who he's with that I don't like."

"Mama, he's known Billy Mitchell for years."

"And I've disliked the man for years." Anna put down her tea towel and busied herself putting dishes away.

Deirdre shook her head. If her mother didn't like you, you knew it. She had never known her to warm up to anyone once she decided she didn't like them.

"I'm going to change clothes. I'll be right back." Deirdre grabbed her things and left the kitchen.

"Okay, I'll get started." Anna opened a drawer and pulled out an apron.

Deirdre scanned the pictures of her and her older sister, Barbara, that lined the walls of the stairway. Every occasion, from their high school graduation to their children's birthdays, were there. She stopped and stared at the picture of her niece and nephew sitting on Santa's lap. Beautiful children, she thought as she looked at them. Too bad she hadn't seen them since the picture was taken, more than three years ago.

At the top of the stairs, she gently opened the door to Barbara's old bedroom, now Mia's room. She eased over to the child's bed, careful not to make a sound and wake her. The soft snore flowing from her daughter reminded her of her ex-husband, William. As she brushed her hand along Mia's hair, Deirdre marveled at how much Mia resembled her father. At the age of six, she had her father's temperament and looks. Comfortable with Mia sound asleep, Deirdre went into her bedroom and changed clothes.

A few minutes later, she returned to the kitchen in a pair of denim shorts and a T-shirt.

"I hope the police find out who broke into the office." Deirdre still couldn't believe what had happened.

"Honey, don't think about work for awhile. Relax your mind."

If that were possible, she'd do it. However, there was too much at risk. How could she make her mother see that?

"Mama, you don't understand, this job is important to me. It's like a stepping-stone to my private practice. I moved here with impeccable credentials, and I can't let anything hurt that." She paced around the kitchen gesturing with her hands.

"If I'm lucky, my clients will stay with me after I purchase the property and open my own practice." She walked over to the refrigerator, and helped her mother pull food out to prepare dinner. Each knew their assigned task and moved about the kitchen as they talked.

"Well, if you don't get that loan from the bank, you can try to get on at the hospital."

Deirdre snickered and shook her head. "I don't want to work for the hospital. I want my own counseling agency. I've already spent years working for someone else, now I'm ready to fly solo.

Besides, the money will be better, coupled with my Internet work anyway."

"If you say so, but I didn't know you went into counseling for the money. I thought you were more interested in helping people, teens in particular." Anna walked to the sink with a bowl of peeled potatoes and turned on the water.

"I am, but I have to be able to support myself. You know William's little child support check only goes so far. Mia and I have to move out of here at some point. We can't keep being a burden on you guys."

"What burden? You know Daddy and I are tickled to death you two are here."

"And you know I appreciate it, Mama, but as soon as I save up the down payment money, I'll be looking for a house."

"You should have gotten alimony from that man."

Deirdre stopped snapping green beans and stared at her mother. "From where?" She asked with a questionable expression on her face.

"You can't squeeze blood from a turnip. William doesn't have any money. As hard as he works in that laboratory, it's all research. The school doesn't pay him for all those hours. I told you the man's obsessed with his work."

Anna merely nodded, letting her daughter talk.

Deirdre shrugged her shoulders and returned to her green beans. "Besides, I don't want or need his money. One day I'll have plenty of money and I won't even need his little child support checks."

"Move your office out into the suburbs with the rich folks if money is your concern."

"As far as real estate goes, I'm in a prime spot. The Riverfront is the best location in town. I know some other people have expressed interest in the community center, but I don't think anyone has acted on it. It's right in the heart of all the new development." Deirdre paused and thought about what she'd said.

"I guess that's why Robert Carmichael showed up today." She

added aloud. A shiver ran through her body at the mention of his name.

"Who's that?" Anna asked, carrying the bowl of potatoes and celery back to the table.

Deirdre looked up, surprised she'd spoken loud enough for Anna to hear. "He's a reporter for the *Brunswick Constitution.*" She didn't dare tell her mother he went to Lincoln with her. No need in bringing all that up again. In the future, maybe she'd find out more about Robert Carmichael, like whether or not he was married. Not that she was interested. She didn't even know if she'd ever see him again.

"Are there any other black-owned businesses down there?"

"Just a small card shop."

"Well, that's why they sent that reporter. They probably don't want any black businesses down there. You better be careful and watch yourself."

"Mama, I don't get that feeling. Everyone on the Riverfront is pretty nice. I don't think race plays a part here. It's all about money. Since the area holds the future for Brunswick, I guess anything that goes on around there is under scrutiny."

"If you say so." Anna tilted her head, looking down her nose in disbelief.

"They don't want anything to stop the flow of money into the area. Or, at least, I think that's what it is."

Deirdre bit her lip as she recalled the events of the day. The break-in was a small incident, maybe too small for the *Constitution* to send a reporter to cover. Or was her mother right? Maybe an article on the break-in would cause people to stay away from the center, and her office. If the community center moved out and she didn't get the loan, then there would only be one black-owned business on the Riverfront.

"Well, look who finally woke up." Anna said, as she looked toward the kitchen entrance.

Deirdre turned in her chair and saw Mia rubbing her eyes. She snapped her last bean and wiped her hands off. "Hi baby, come here." With outstretched arms, she gestured for Mia to come to her.

The child shook her head and pointed behind her, still rubbing her eyes.

Deirdre looked up at the clock. Five-thirty, time for Mia's favorite cartoon, *Rugrats*. She turned and smiled at her mother.

Anna reached across the table and took the bowl of green beans from Deirdre. "It's amazing I tell you. How that child knows to wake up at five-thirty without an alarm clock, I'll never know. She won't miss that cartoon for anything."

She hated to admit it, but Deirdre enjoyed the show as much as Mia. Watching cartoons was one thing they did together that relaxed her. For a moment, she didn't have to try and solve someone's problems. She could rest her mind.

"Okay, honey, I'm on my way." She washed her hands at the sink. "Mama, did she eat lunch?"

Mia turned and disappeared from the entranceway.

"Of course she ate lunch. On the way back from Mrs. Druer's, I tried to stop at McDonald's. But that child won't eat it. All children love hamburgers, except for my grand-baby. She's from California, she doesn't eat red meat."

Deirdre laughed on her way out of the kitchen. "Mama, be thankful she's healthy and doesn't get sick or have colds as much as other children her age."

"That's the problem, she doesn't do anything like children her age."

Mia stood at the top of the basement stairs. Her grandparents had instructed her never to go down the stairs by herself, and she obeyed. Deirdre took her hand and together they descended the stairs. Once in the den, Deirdre took her father's easy chair and reclined it back as Mia positioned herself in her lap.

"Did you have a nice day today?" Deirdre asked as she gave Mia a soft kiss on her head.

Mia nodded her head, still not fully awake and ready to talk.

Deirdre turned on the television, then selected Mia's favorite show. At the sight of Tommy and Chuckie, Mia dropped her head back into her mother's breast and smiled.

Robert sat at his desk and stared at the computer screen. Earlier he'd turned in his piece on the Brunswick Counseling Agency break-in. Now he found it difficult to concentrate on his next piece. He read the article again, still not comfortable with it. He also hadn't been able to get Deirdre off his mind.

"Burning the midnight oil?"

Robert looked up at his coworker, Wayne, in the doorway. "Hey man, I want to make sure this story's perfect, you know what I mean?"

"I've been there. For me, those articles turn out to be some of my best pieces." Wayne leaned against the door frame with his hands in his pockets.

"Well, I don't know." Robert sighed. He didn't want to tell Wayne his thoughts were on Deirdre and not his work.

Without an invitation, Wayne walked into the small room and took a seat across from Robert's desk.

"Say, I heard you left the *Philadelphia Chronicle* to come here?"

It didn't take long before someone at the paper inquired about his past. "I sure did."

"Man, what made you leave that spot for Brunswick? I mean this isn't exactly the hottest place to be." Wayne crossed his legs as he made himself at home.

Robert reflected for a moment. He didn't know Wayne from Adam. Aside from himself, Wayne was the only other black male reporter at the paper. He covered sports, while Robert had the metro beat.

"Let's say I needed a change of scenery. I lost my wife a few years ago in a automobile accident. So, I moved back to be close to my family."

"Man, I'm sorry to hear that. It must have been hell," Wayne said in a sympathetic tone.

"Thank you, it was." Robert had gotten to the point where he could mention Karen's death without needing a drink afterward. It took him a year to pull himself out of the bottle, but he'd done it. He still considered himself bruised from the memories, and didn't like to talk about it much.

"I moved up here from Florida after college," Wayne said. "It's nice and peaceful, but I've been thinking about a position in Atlanta."

"Oh, you're ready for the big time, huh?"

"Why not? There's a lot more action."

Robert laughed. "You're looking for action in Brunswick?"

"I'm looking for women in Brunswick." He shared a laugh with Robert. "I like it here, but it's not big enough for me, so I might be moving on."

Robert pictured Deirdre standing in her office with that short skirt hugging her hips. She wasn't the same girl he remembered from high school, that's for sure. None of his old female high school friends looked that good. He could imagine Wayne's dilemma, there weren't many single women in Brunswick that looked like Deirdre. He hoped she wasn't married or dating.

"Have you been to Atlanta?" Wayne asked.

Robert looked up and saw the excitement in Wayne's eyes. "Yes, I have. A couple of times, but not recently."

"I've got two buddies who work there, and they've invited me up a couple of times. I hear there's a lot of eligible women there. Not that I'm ready to settle down at thirty, but nothing's wrong with looking."

Robert leaned back in his chair and propped his feet up on the corner of his desk. His sister, Shirley, would have called Wayne a goober. He'd heard her use the tag before on men with big ears. Wayne's ears weren't that large, it was more in the way he dressed. He seemed to like his pants considerably high-waisted. Robert could tell Wayne had a lot to learn.

"At your age I was married and had purchased my first home. Now at thirty-six, I'm single and just purchased my second home."

"Man, you move fast. How about marriage again? Would you ever do it?"

Robert hesitated before answering. He hadn't dated anyone seriously in quite a while. Though he had to admit, he enjoyed the married life.

"Yes, I would. I liked being married. I liked having someone to go home to."

Wayne nodded as if he had someone in mind. "It would be nice to have someone to go home to. A little lady to have dinner cooked and ready for me." He crossed his legs and waved a hand across the air. "But I'm not ready to lose my freedom."

"Freedom?" Robert laughed. "Man, you make it sound like women enslave you or something."

"They do. Somewhat anyway. Let's say I'm not ready to give up on bachelorhood yet."

"Well, I wouldn't mind a little enslavement as you put it." He pulled his feet down, and lost interest in their conversation.

Wayne got the hint, and stood to leave. "Hey, before I go, I heard you met that new counselor at the community center earlier."

"Yes, I did. What's up?"

"I haven't had a chance to meet her yet. What's she like?"

"What do you mean?" Robert asked, not sure what Wayne wanted to know.

"You know, is she single or married?"

Robert shook his head and slowly blinked his eyes. "I believe she's single. I don't think I saw a ring." Could Wayne have plans to meet her in the near future? Not that he cared or anything, he told himself.

"So what's going on down there?"

Robert adjusted his monitor. He looked up at the screen wanting to get back to his work. "Nothing really. I'm not even sure why Dean sent me down there for such a short piece."

"I guess with all the renovation going on, Dean wants to get the exclusive on everything. He said be sure to get all the details on anything that happens on the Riverfront, it sells papers."

Wayne slowly walked toward the door brushing at lint on his jacket.

"Then tomorrow's piece should make him happy," Robert commented.

"Well, don't spend all night hanging out in this place. I've noticed you like to put in the hours. Don't let me come along and find a cot in your office."

Robert leaned back in his seat laughing. "No way man."

Wayne said good-bye and left. Robert looked at his watch and for the first time realized it was past eleven and he'd come in after seven this morning. This wasn't the first evening he'd spent at work and it wouldn't be the last. He'd thrown himself into his work. After being at the paper a year, he hoped to move up the ranks as fast as possible. He didn't have time to play around.

His attention returned to the computer monitor and he read the article again. Something was still amiss.

The next day, the break-in was all but forgotten as Deirdre focused on her last client of the day. Her only elderly client, Geneva, lost her husband around the time Deirdre moved to town. She reminded Deirdre of her own grandmother. She had aged gracefully with long gray hair and soft, wrinkled skin.

Deirdre held Geneva's hand as they walked back to her office together. Geneva had cried all the way over. Deirdre's heart went out to her.

"Geneva, have a seat. Everything's going to be all right." Deirdre reassured her. She snatched a tissue from the box on her desk and handed it to her client.

"I don't know, I just don't know," Geneva spoke through her sobbing tears. She took off her glasses to wipe her eyes.

Deirdre took a seat in the chair next to Geneva. "Well, what's got you so upset today?"

Geneva dabbed at her eyes with the tissue and eased her hand from Deirdre's to open her purse. "I got this in the mail today." She handed over a white envelope.

Deirdre opened the letter and read the contents. Her husband's untimely death left Geneva with some notable debts. Creditors threatened to take her home. Angry as hell, Deirdre closed the letter and handed it back.

"They can't do that, can they? I mean, that house is all I have."

"No. They can't. And don't you worry, we'll stop them." Deirdre leafed through her Rolodex and stopped when she found the number she wanted. Picking up the phone, she quickly punched in the number.

"Thank you so much. I don't know what I'd do without you." Geneva's sobs turned into sniffles.

Most of the session was spent on the phone trying to solve Geneva's financial problems. She scheduled an appointment for the two of them to meet with creditors and work out a payment plan.

After the session, Geneva hugged and kissed Deirdre before she left. Emotionally drained and tired, Deirdre sat in a reception area chair to relax. She needed time to get Geneva's problems off her mind. After each session, she performed a clearing process in her mind. A few deep breaths and positive affirmations usually rejuvenated her for the next session.

"Well, they arrive in tears, then leave with smiles on their faces. You must be performing miracles behind those doors," Susan said as she smiled at Deirdre.

"No, I'm only listening. I really feel for Geneva. The minute we get one issue resolved, something else emerges."

"But you're there for her to help solve the problems. You didn't refer her to someone else for financial help. Once you even accompanied her to the auto repair shop." Susan laughed as she cleaned off her desk.

"Yeah, because she doesn't have anyone else to help her, so what am I supposed to do? I knew they were ripping her off and that burns me up." Deirdre hadn't noticed until now that Susan was more dressed up today than usual.

"So, looks like you've got a big date tonight?" Maybe it was with one of the policemen from the other day.

Susan grinned and batted her eyes. "In fact I do. I'm going to happy hour at Raven's."

Deirdre crossed her legs and leaned forward, giving Susan a raised brow stare. "Well, sounds like somebody's hobnobbing with the elite crowd."

Susan smiled a coy schoolgirl smile. "Honey, the men in that place are so fine. They all wear suits and drive expensive cars."

"Gonna catch you one, huh?"

"I think I already have." Susan opened her purse and pulled out her lipstick and a mirror. "I met this guy there a few weeks ago and we've been dating. Tonight we're kind of celebrating our anniversary." She applied more ruby-red color to her lips.

"An anniversary already?"

"Three months today. And since that's the longest I've dated a guy in years, I think it calls for a little celebration."

"A three-month anniversary; that's cute." Deirdre was ten years older than Susan, and couldn't imagine celebrating such a small anniversary. *Is that what young people do?* she asked herself.

"I didn't tell him about the celebration yet, but I will tonight. Deirdre, he's fine too. Like that reporter, Mr. Carmichael, who came in here yesterday. He's built, wears nice suits all the time, and spends too much money on me. I just love it." She laughed at herself and looked in the mirror again to powder her face.

"Susan, you're something else." Deirdre laughed. If her date even resembled Robert Carmichael, he was indeed fine. Deirdre hadn't stopped thinking about that man since he walked out of her office.

"Well, I'm out of here." Susan locked her desk, and stood to leave. She walked from behind her desk and stood in front of Deirdre. "Do you think my skirt is too short?"

Deirdre looked at her skirt. "If my legs were as shapely as yours, I'd show them off too. I think it's fine."

"What do you mean if your legs were shapely? There's nothing wrong with your legs."

Deirdre stood up and looked down. "Well, they're not Tina Turner's, that's for sure."

"I just wish I had your chest. Girl, I'd give anything to have cleavage like that. I wear those damn push-up bras, that don't push up enough for me." Susan looked down and touched her breasts pushing them up.

Both women laughed as Susan headed for the door. "You're not working late tonight are you?"

"No, I purposely schedule Geneva last because I'm usually drained after her. I'll be leaving right behind you."

"Okay, make sure you lock this door behind me. You don't want Mr. Creepy to walk in on you."

"Susan, I swear, you need to leave that poor man alone."

"I'm serious. He creeps around when you least expect him. The man's a pervert."

"Bye, girl. Enjoy your celebration." Deirdre laughed as she waved Susan out of the office.

"Okay, I'll see you tomorrow."

Deirdre locked the door behind Susan and watched her walk toward her car. She went back into her office to call Mia and let her know she was on her way home.

As she stood up to leave, she needed to use the rest room. She set her purse and satchel down, and walked out of her office down the narrow hall to the back door.

Turning the lock, she opened the door and stepped into the dimly lit kitchen of the community center. All the stainless steel in that massive room gave her the creeps. It reminded her of a high school trip to the local morgue, that left a lasting impression. She quickly walked through the kitchen, and into the hall where the rest rooms were located. Most of the children's parents had picked them up after work and headed home. She heard a few faint voices coming from the front office.

Inside the rest room Deirdre turned on the light switch and heard a loud pop. She jumped and nearly wet herself before she realized that one of the light bulbs had blown out. After a few deep breaths she calmed herself and used the rest room. On her way out, she noticed a run in her hose and cursed because she had on a brand-new pair.

The door swung open a little too easily and she was almost knocked off balance.

"Sorry."

She jumped at the sound of a man's voice. It's deep tone sent a chill through her. Who was coming into the womens' rest room? She looked up into the tired and battered face of a middle-aged white man. Alfred, the facility janitor, stared back at her.

"Alfred, you scared me to death," she said, as she placed a hand over her heart.

"I . . . I heard the light blow so . . . I came to change the bulb." He held the door open.

Deirdre always had to listen carefully when Alfred talked, because of his speech problem. "Yeah, it blew when I came in. I didn't see you out here when I went inside." It was odd for him to show up out of the blue.

"I heard it from the men's room." He pointed to the next door. "I . . . I was in there."

"Oh, okay. I'll leave you to change the light, thanks." She hadn't realized the walls were that thin between the rest rooms. She walked past him and back into the kitchen. Alfred had to be the most silent man she had ever encountered. He came and went as quiet as a mouse, without much conversation.

Back in her office, she locked the door and went to retrieve her belongings. She picked up the newspaper on her desk that she hadn't had time to read all morning. She turned to the Metro section and noticed Robert's article. On her way out of the office, she read it, turning off lights as she walked down the hall.

Engrossed in the article about the Brunswick Counseling Agency break-in, she managed to open the front door with one hand and turn off the light. The minute she stepped outside, someone grabbed her arm.

THREE

"Deirdre."

She jumped, dropping the newspaper and her purse. "Susan!"

"I'm sorry. I thought you were gone. Did I scare you?"

Deirdre pulled her purse back on her shoulder. "Yes."

Susan retrieved the newspaper. "I got halfway there, then remembered I forgot something." She handed the paper back to Deirdre. "Sorry about that."

Deirdre took the paper, thankful Susan hadn't noticed Robert's byline. "Thanks. I should have been watching where I was going. Especially, after what happened around here anyway."

"If you want my opinion, I think it's safe. Nobody's here but the river rats, if you know what I mean, and those bad kids next door."

"Let's hope that's all it is. Well, have a good time tonight. I'll see you tomorrow." Deirdre stuffed the paper under her arm and left once Susan walked back into the office.

Deirdre drove to Leroy's Garage with all four windows down trying to catch a breeze. She pulled into the first empty lane and got out. The twenty-minute drive with a broken air conditioner left her blouse sticking to her back.

She found Leroy inside ringing up a customer. When he finished, he noticed her.

"Hey Deirdre, what can I do for you today?"

"My air conditioner has gone out. Can you look at it for me?"

"Sure thing."

Smiling, he moved from behind the counter in his navy-blue overalls and bulb-toe boots, and followed her outside. Leroy, Jr., had the same stocky build as his father, who opened the garage more than twenty years ago. Deirdre remembered him from her childhood visits to the garage with her father.

"I read where somebody broke into your place yesterday. That's a shame."

She reached inside the car to pull the hood latch. "It's no big deal. Probably some kids."

He propped the hood up and pulled a rag out of his back pocket. "Yeah, maybe so." He bent over to check the engine.

Deirdre reached inside the car again and pulled out her newspaper. She read the short article on the break-in. It only mentioned that her office sat next to the community center, and said nothing of value was taken. At least Susan had kept her mouth shut about the notes.

"You're gonna have to leave her with me you know," Leroy interrupted her reading.

"For how long?"

"Oh, I should have it ready sometime tomorrow afternoon. I've got a few cars ahead of you."

"How much will it cost me?" She braced herself for the bad news.

He took his baseball cap off and scratched his head, as if it helped him think better. "Well, if your warranty's expired, it'll run you around three hundred dollars."

Why didn't I purchase that extended warranty they tried to sell me? To dip into her savings, meant a longer stay with her parents. She tapped the newspaper against her palm as she looked at him.

"The warranty's expired. I guess I better get somebody to come pick me up." A car horn blew behind her. She jumped forward before she glanced over her shoulder.

Robert leaned into the passenger's seat and looked out the window. "I'm sorry. I didn't want to hit you."

She gazed at him, then backed against her car as he rode

past and parked. Susan was right. Robert was an extremely handsome man.

"Want me to get started on it for you?" Leroy inquired.

Deirdre turned at the sound of his voice. "Yes, I'm sorry. I can get my mom to come pick me up. Just call me when it's ready tomorrow."

"Sure thing." He closed the hood.

Robert approached them jingling his keys in his hands.

"Mr. Carmichael, I've got that battery all ready for you."

"Thanks Leroy, I appreciate that."

He stopped when he reached Deirdre and took off his sunglasses. "Hello, Ms. Levine."

"Hello, Mr. Carmichael."

"Call me Robert. Mr. Carmichael is too formal." He extended his hand to hers.

"Then call me Deirdre." She shook his hand and trembled when his fingers extended to her wrist. She liked a man with large hands.

"Did you see my article?"

She shifted her weight from one foot to the other. "Yes, I did. Of course, I wish it hadn't made the papers at all, but at least it was short."

"Hey." Robert held up his hands. "I aim to please."

Deirdre fought to wipe the smile from her face. He was still a charmer. In high school he'd always had a way with the girls. He could make them laugh, cry, or long to be in his presence.

"Having a little car trouble?" he asked.

"My air conditioner went out."

"Bummer. It's too hot to be without air in the middle of July. I'm sure Leroy can fix it for you."

"I trust he can." She opened her car door and grabbed her satchel and purse. Enough small talk, she had to go home. Mia would be waiting for her. Besides, Robert's mere presence made her nervous. Even now as he followed her into the office.

"Leroy, may I use your phone?" She walked over to the phone.

"Sure help yourself. I'll be right with you, Mr. Carmichael."

"No problem, Leroy, take your time." Robert sat in the waiting area.

Deirdre got her mother on the phone, who agreed to pick her up in a few minutes. All she had to do was wait in the same room with Robert. After hanging up the phone, she walked over to the chair farthest from Robert and sat down. The local news blared from the table-top television.

"Do you need a ride somewhere?" Robert asked.

"No. My ride's on the way."

"Are you sure? It's no trouble."

"I'm positive. Thank you." Deirdre didn't know if she could stand to be so close to him. The excitement might be too much for her.

Leroy emerged from the back room. "Okay, Mr. Carmichael, here's your battery."

Deirdre tried to focus on the news, but found herself checking out Robert at the counter. Once again, he had on a well-tailored suit, and expensive shoes.

Before he walked out the door, he asked again, "Are you sure I can't offer you a ride?" He smiled at her.

She melted like vanilla ice cream on a hot sidewalk. "No," she croaked, then cleared her throat and tried again. "I'm positive, but thank you for asking."

"Okay, then take care."

"You too." She sat there and tried to look as professional as possible, while tapping her foot against the floor. Had he left yet? She peered out the window for his car. The tail end appeared first, then the rest of the car moved into full view as he backed out of his parking space. Her chair almost fell forward.

"You okay?" Leroy turned at the sound.

Deirdre laughed. "Yes, I'm fine."

Robert wasn't the same boy she dreamed about in high school. He'd grown into a sophisticated, handsome man.

* * *

The morning stop at his mother's house had taken longer than Robert expected. When he got to work, his voice mail was full. He turned on his computer, then checked his voice mail. He picked up a note that was on his desk. *Another break-in at Brunswick Counseling Agency, Get over there fast, Dean.*

"What time is it?" Robert asked himself and looked down at his watch. Nine fifteen. The time on the note was five after eight. He dropped everything and raced to the parking lot.

He doubted he'd be the first reporter on the scene. For such a small town, news traveled fast. Dean would expect him to get the exclusive, and maybe he would have if he hadn't stopped at him mother's earlier. If he were lucky, he still might beat another reporter there. The *Constitution* was across town from the Riverfront. He probably could walk it faster than driving through all the traffic lights.

As he approached the center, he could see a few people standing outside the door. "Damn. A little too late." He parked around the corner and joined the other reporters talking to Deirdre.

"Ms. Levine, can you tell us what happened this morning? Is this a reflection of business on the Riverfront?" The perky reporter shoved her tape recorder in Deirdre's face, ready for her response.

Deirdre felt sick to her stomach. Their questions made her head spin. Minutes after the police arrived, reporters were right behind them. She'd stepped outside to answer their questions as best she could. Where had these people come from? She didn't know Brunswick had so many papers.

"Yes, Ms. Levine, who do you think is responsible for this?" Another reporter shot questions at her while the group waited for answers.

Deirdre clasped her moist palms together preparing to respond, however, not wanting to. Why couldn't something more newsworthy have happened this morning? She asked herself.

"What happened here has no reflection on the renovation progress. We've had two minor break-ins, that's all."

Mr. Hamel, from the community center, stepped out of the door behind her and whispered in her ear. "Tell them the center has no involvement in this mess."

She took a deep breath and wished he'd go away. He reminded her of a bee buzzing in her ear. Even when she swatted at him, he wouldn't go away.

"Ms. Levine, do you feel these break-ins are connected to any of your clients?"

"No, I don't feel like the community center, nor my clients are involved in any way. I'm sure the police will catch this person soon, and everything will be resolved. I'm sorry but there's nothing more I can tell you."

"Were any important papers stolen?" The perky female reporter asked.

"I'm afraid . . ." Deirdre stopped mid-sentence when she noticed Robert approaching. *Oh no, he's come for his share of me too.*

"We heard client files have been stolen. Do you think someone is after one of your clients?" A reporter asked.

"As I was about to say, I'm afraid I can't discuss the details of the break-in."

"Ms. Levine, was any money stolen?"

"I'm sorry, that's all I have to say."

From the corner of her eye, Deirdre saw Robert step forward and stand next to Mr. Hamel. They exchanged words, but she wasn't close enough to hear them.

Mr. Hamel moved in front of Deirdre and took charge.

"Okay, folks she's said all she has to say this morning. You'll have to talk with the police if you want anything else. The community center will be open in a few minutes. I'll have to ask you to please leave."

Robert grabbed Deirdre by the arm. "Say, grab your purse and come with me."

"What?"

"Come on, grab your purse, let's go."

"I can't! Don't you realize what's happened here?"

"Yes. That's why I'm taking you to breakfast. I won't let you say no, so let's go before Mr. Hamel returns."

Deirdre watched Mr. Hamel escort the reporters out to the parking lot. He appeared to be loving every minute of it and since she could use a break, she went inside to retrieve her purse.

Once outside, Robert took her hand and whisked her to his car. He opened the door to his silver Galant and helped her inside.

Deirdre tried to relax, but couldn't. Here she was in the car with Robert Carmichael and she couldn't believe it. She glanced at his hands on the steering wheel and didn't see a wedding band. *He's not married.*

After driving several blocks, Robert broke the silence. "How are you feeling?" he asked, as he glanced over at her.

"Okay, I guess. Thanks for the help back there."

"No problem. You looked like you needed to be rescued."

"I did." She leaned her head back against the headrest. "Man, how I hate reporters, they're like leeches. Did you see that one from the college shoving her microphone in my . . ." She stopped and covered her mouth the moment she realized what she'd said.

Robert laughed. "Okay, we're leeches, and what else? Don't stop there."

"I'm sorry. Why don't I open my mouth and insert my foot. I didn't mean all reporters." She laughed at herself.

"Just some reporters are leeches?" he asked, with a smile on his face.

"Oh . . . you know what I mean. I hate their guerilla tactics. You saw how they kept pumping me for answers."

"I know what you mean. That's why I stepped in."

"Thank you, because I hate to deal with reporters." *Except for you.*

They pulled into the local Cracker Barrel restaurant for breakfast. Robert stepped out and walked around to open Deirdre's door. Once inside, they placed their orders and started off with moments of awkward silence.

Deirdre had calmed down from this morning, but now Robert's presence made her nervous again. She was given the opportunity to relive sixteen all over again. Her first date with Robert Carmichael. Her knees shook under the table.

"So," Robert clasped his hands together, "tell me what happened this morning?"

Deirdre looked across the table at Robert. *So that's what you wanted, your own private interview.* The nerve of him bringing her here under false pretense. She had to give it to him—he was smooth. Nonetheless, she wasn't about to tell him any more than she'd told the other reporters.

"You know what happened. We were robbed," she stated.

"Yeah, I know that much. Who do you think's responsible for it?"

The waitress brought their juice and a basket of assorted breads. The interruption gave Deirdre time to think about her answer.

"Some kids from the community center. And I'm sure they'll confess or the police will catch them soon." She reached for a muffin, and watched Robert nod his head as he drank his juice. His gaze stopped at her wrist.

Deirdre looked down at her small link design tattoo. It served as a constant reminder of her college years. Her "coming out" years as she liked to refer to them.

"Did that hurt?" He pointed toward her wrist.

"A little," she answered, and shrugged her shoulders.

"You don't strike me as the type of woman who would get a tattoo."

"Why not?" *What type of woman do you see me as?*

"I don't know, I remember how quiet and shy you were in high school."

"That was years ago. I try not to think about those days."

"Bad memories?"

Deirdre nodded and picked at her muffin. *He's not making me go there.* "I liked my college years better." She smiled up at

Robert with a renewed look. "I had a great time in college discovering who I was and thinking I could conquer the world."

Robert laughed. "Didn't we all think that? I wanted to have my own magazine. I envisioned something like *Vibe*. Then I wound up being a reporter."

"You don't like it?"

"Oh, I enjoy it. It just wasn't my original dream."

"I'm doing what I always wanted to do. My dream was to be able to help people, especially teenagers. I enjoy working with young people, although it's hard sometimes."

"I bet it is. I can tell you're good at it though. You've got patience. I could see that this morning."

"I'd better have. I've got a six-year-old daughter at home." She hesitated a moment. "Do you have any children?"

The waitress interrupted again with their breakfast. Robert leaned forward for a second and his tie dipped into his gravy.

The waitress responded immediately. "Uh, Sweetie, let me get that." She grabbed a napkin and dabbed at Robert's tie. "I'm so sorry. I should have turned your plate around the other way."

Robert stopped her before she ran her hand down his chest. "That's okay, I've got it." He took the napkin from her and finished cleaning his tie. "I needed to take this tie to the cleaners anyway. Thank you."

"You're welcome." She walked away smiling.

Deirdre enjoyed the flustered look on Robert's face when the waitress tried to help. He looked uncomfortable.

After the waitress left, Robert shook his head and smiled. "Okay, where were we? Oh yeah, you were asking me about children. I've never had the pleasure. How many children do you have?"

"Just one," she stated.

They lowered their heads, and he blessed the food.

After they started their meals, Robert struck up another conversation. "I heard it took some convincing to get the community center to hire a counselor. How's business?"

"Where did you hear that?" she asked with raised brows.

He shrugged. "I'm a reporter. I've done my homework."

"I see. What can I tell you that you don't already know?"

"Plenty."

She glanced at her watch, she needed to return before her first client showed up. She'd left things in Susan's hands.

"Well, aside from these minor incidents, everything's fine. It did take the board a while to put out the notice for a counselor. From what I've been told, Mr. Hamel was the holdup."

"I gathered he has a problem with the whole thing."

"Yeah, well, I'm not sure what his problem is."

"Do you counsel many of the children from the center?"

"Not yet. I'm there if they need me, but most of my young clients are referred from school counselors."

"Still it's good that the center provides affordable counseling." Robert gestured with his fork as he talked.

"Yes, and that's its objective." Deirdre pushed her plate to the side and talked with her hands. A nervous habit she hated and couldn't control.

"There are other counseling services in town, but the average working African-American can't afford their services. Not that we cater exclusively to African-Americans, but that's who most of my clients are. Besides, it's a great place for me to start making a name for myself."

"You must plan on living in Brunswick for awhile?"

"I think I'm home for good. That's not to say that I won't ever leave."

"I hope you won't be leaving anytime soon, we just met." Robert winked at Deirdre. He liked that she blushed when he did. Every time she moved her arm, he examined the tattoo on her wrist. A tattoo definitely made a statement. He was far too conservative for such a thing, but what about Deirdre? Was she the wild type? A risk taker? A woman who lived on the edge?

Deirdre stopped talking when the waitress returned to clear the table and leave the check.

Robert wanted to know more, but could tell from her agitated movements that she was ready to leave. He knew she had to get back to work and take care of business.

"Thank you so much for breakfast." She dabbed at her mouth with her napkin.

"You're quite welcome." Deirdre peaked his curiosity. "I hope we can do it again sometimes, of course, under better circumstances."

"Yeah, maybe so." She smiled as she tucked a strand of hair behind her ear.

A simple gesture, but one he found extremely sexy.

FOUR

On the ride back to Deirdre's office, she chatted amiably. The minute she stepped inside the office, she noticed how quiet it was. No more soft office music. Deirdre didn't see any police officers or community center staff milling around. Things were too quiet for her.

Susan jumped out of her seat and counted off her fingers. "Deirdre, the police are all finished in here. They're in the community center. Mr. Hamel wants to see you in his office. And, the locksmith will be here before five o'clock. Now, tell me how was your breakfast? That man is so fine."

Deirdre walked back to her office. "Susan, I've got about thirty minutes before Cathy shows up. Would you tell Mr. Hamel that I'll see him after this session? Right now I need to talk with the police."

"And they want to talk to you. I've listed all the stolen files. I guess we've got to re-create all those notes, huh?"

Deirdre sighed. "Yes, and I dread it. Do you know how much work that is? It'll take me a couple of weeks to pull the details from those sessions together." She took a seat behind her desk as Susan sat across from her.

"Well, I'll try to get them typed up as fast as I can. Too bad we don't copy them to diskettes."

"Well, we're going to start. Only as a backup of course. I still want hard copies to work from." She ran her hands through her hair and rested an elbow on the desk.

"I'll take the petty cash and purchase some diskettes next time I go for supplies."

"Thanks. Let's pray this doesn't happen again." Deirdre jumped to her feet. "I'd better go talk to the police."

Susan stopped inside the door as Deirdre walked through the back door into the community center.

Deirdre turned around. "Oh, and Susan?"

"Yeah?"

"Breakfast was great."

When Robert returned to work, he found another note on his desk. *Come see me when you return, Dean.* He balled the piece of paper up and shot a two-pointer in the trash on his way out.

He spoke to several coworkers along the hallway. The *Brunswick Constitution* wasn't a large paper. The two-story complex held approximately ten offices, and a large area where most of the reporters worked. Because the area was full when Robert showed up, his office was a small converted storage room. Wayne had called that area the bull pen.

Robert found Dean alone in his office amid a clutter of papers and folders. "Hey boss, did you want to see me?"

Dean looked up and dropped his pen. "Robert. Come on in and have a seat."

The editor-in-chief's office was the largest in the complex. Robert unbuttoned his suit coat, pushing it back for comfort. He removed several folders from a chair and set them on the corner of Dean's desk.

"So, what happened down on the Riverfront? Did we get the exclusive?" Dean grinned and leaned back in his chair. He tapped his fingers nervously on the arms of the chair.

Robert let out a sigh. "Not exactly."

"No?" Dean's expression changed from one of happy to troubled. He stopped rocking. "Why not?"

"I was the last reporter on the scene."

"Damnit, I thought you would be the only one there."

"What gave you that impression?"

"The call I got this morning." Dean leaned forward and glanced around the room. "Somebody called and said the agency got hit again, and if we wanted an exclusive, we'd better get a reporter over there fast. Of course, they didn't leave a name or phone number."

"Got any idea who it might have been?" His guess was the same person who left him a message the first time the agency was broken into.

"No, he covered the receiver."

"A somewhat muffled voice?" Robert asked, peering at Dean for confirmation.

"Yeah. Not completely because I could hear him, but the voice was altered."

Robert grinned and gave a slight nod of his head. "I guess I didn't get in early enough for him."

"What are you talking about?"

"The last time the Brunswick Counseling Agency was broken into I got a call from the same guy. I got there pretty fast, so I was the only reporter on the scene. This morning, I was delayed, and by the time I got there, it was too late." Robert sat back and crossed his legs. With his elbow on the armrest he played with his goatee. *What's going on down there?*

"You didn't show up fast enough, so he called another paper," Dean concluded.

"Exactly."

"So what have we got here? Someone on the inside who wants to make sure the break-in makes the papers?"

"That or something much worse." Robert and Dean stared at each other, both contemplating what to make of the calls.

Robert left Dean's office understanding he would keep an eye on the entire Riverfront area. It wasn't unusual for someone to call the paper to report a crime, however, anonymous calls usually spelled trouble.

Before he could make it back to his office, Robert bumped into Wayne.

"Hey, how goes it?" Wayne gave his usual greeting.

"Fine. What's been up?"

"I read your piece on the Brunswick Counseling Agency break-in yesterday. Good thing no one got hurt."

"Yeah, it is." Robert needed to start his latest article and didn't have time to shoot the breeze with Wayne. However, he hated to be rude toward him.

"I guess you covered the break-in this morning too?"

"Yeah. Me, and every other reporter in town."

"Oh well, so much for Dean's always wanting the exclusive, on any story," Wayne chuckled and shook his head.

"He'll get over it." Robert looked down at his pad. What would it take for Wayne to get the hint?

Wayne glanced around to see if anyone was looking, then stepped closer to Robert. In a whisper he said, "If you ever need any investigative work done, I know somebody."

Now, Wayne caught his attention. "Somebody local?" Robert knew every investigator in town, and there weren't that many.

"No. He's an outside man, and likes to keep a low profile. He doesn't do much work for reporters. I doubt that anyone around here has heard of him." Wayne patted Robert on the shoulder, then stepped back.

"Just keep that in mind. I gotta run, so I'll catch you later."

"Yeah, later." Robert strolled down the hall, then looked back over his shoulder. Wayne was one strange character. He shook his head and went into his office to call Officer Duncan.

Deirdre found Officer Duncan in the activity room of the center. He held court with several staff members. When she entered the room, he stopped and excused himself.

"Hello Deirdre."

"Hi. Susan said you were looking for me."

"Yes." He placed a hand on her shoulder, and guided her from the room. "Do you mind if we step outside a moment?"

"No." She followed his lead.

Once outside, she looked around her at the surroundings of the Riverfront area. When she lived in Brunswick as a child, the area consisted of warehouses and a few tired shops. What they were doing to the area now was great. She didn't want her office to blemish the renovation process.

Officer Duncan watched her and made a few observations himself. "It's amazing what they've done down here isn't it?"

"Yes, it is. I remember once I rode my bike down here and my mother spanked me good when she found out. All those abandoned, ragged buildings were a child's wonderland, and a parent's nightmare."

"Well, they've turned it into something great for the community as a whole. All these gift shops draw more of the tourist trade from St. Simon's and Jekyll Island." He turned around and smiled.

"All we have to do now is catch this thief before he moves onto another business."

"Do you really think he'll do that?" she asked.

"I have no idea. We haven't had any other reports of break-ins. Whoever came in your back door didn't break into the center. They were already inside, or someone let them in."

Deirdre stood with her hands clasped behind her back. Just as she thought, someone from the center. Probably an older child.

"I invited you out here because I wanted to ask you something. Who has a key to your office, other than your secretary?"

Deirdre turned and looked back at the two-way glass door. She couldn't see Susan inside, but figured she was there behind her desk. "No one, why?" Her gaze focused on Bill Duncan.

"What about your secretary?"

"What about her?"

"Could she have taken the files for some reason?"

Deirdre didn't even have to think about that question. "No

way. Susan's been with me for more than six months. She's a great employee. Besides, she has no reason to want those files."

Officer Duncan nodded his head. "How does Mr. Hamel get in if he needs to?"

"He never comes in without one of us present." Deirdre answered shaking her head.

"Who cleans your offices?"

"Alfred. He cleans all the offices."

"So he has a key?"

"I forgot about him. Yes, he does. On his belt he has keys to all the offices."

Officer Duncan took out a small pad. He looked over his notes. "He had an alibi, or so it appears."

Deirdre hadn't realized that the police had already questioned Alfred. If he had an alibi, then so much for Susan's theory of him being the thief.

A few minutes outside in the sweltering heat was enough for her. She wanted to go back inside.

Officer Duncan cleared his throat, and stared intensely at his pad. "Let me ask you something?"

"Yes." The tone of his voice concerned her.

"How well do you know Robert Carmichael?"

She shrugged, then crossed her arms. "You know, from Lincoln High, just like I know you. I hadn't seen him in years either, until he came by after the first break-in. Why?"

"Then you hadn't heard about his wife?"

"He's married?"

"No, his wife died in a car accident a few years ago."

"I'm sorry, but what does that have to do with this?" If there was a connection, she didn't get it.

"Because the Philadelphia police were never convinced he didn't have anything to do with it." He closed his pad and returned it to his pocket. "I always liked you Deirdre. I just wanted you to be aware of that, that's all."

Deirdre stood there dumbfounded. She bit her lower lip and thought about Robert. *Why is Bill trying to scare me?*

Officer Duncan said his good-bye and again told Deirdre to call if she remembered or saw anything that might help the case.

He sat in the motel room and peered out the window every five minutes. His patience had worn thin. It was already half past ten, and he had someplace to be.

The carpet gave way to his weight as he paced over the same spot again and again. He glanced at the annoying television, and wanted to pitch it out the window.

"If you want something done right, you have to do it yourself," he mumbled as he continued to pace and flick ashes from his cigarette onto the carpet. What did it matter? He looked down at the rusty, dirt-colored carpet.

Moving back toward the window, he pulled open the curtains. Two women looked in his direction as they passed. He released the curtain and waited for them to pass. Seconds later, he peered out the curtain again. Still, nobody.

"That's it! Nobody makes me wait like this." He dropped his cigarette on the floor and smothered it with his shoe. After snatching up the remote, he shut off the television, then went into the bathroom. He washed his hands twice before drying them.

The minute he walked back into the bedroom, the doorknob turned. He reached for his jacket. The door opened slowly.

"It's me." A young man stepped inside and closed the door behind him.

"What the hell took you so long?"

"I had some business to take care of first."

Both men walked over to the bed.

"Here you go." A large gray envelope landed on the bed. "I'll take my money now." The younger man held out his hand.

After examining the contents, the older man reached into his jacket pocket and pulled out a small envelope. He handed it to the younger man. "You know this is just the beginning. Stick around. You might get lucky."

"I already have."

After Deirdre met with the loan officers Friday morning, her spirits were high. The loan department wasn't aware of the break-ins and her paperwork would be processed on schedule.

She swung the office door open and found an empty reception area. Sheila, her first appointment, hadn't shown up yet. Susan walked in from the back room in a bright green suit, and a fresh hairdo.

"How did your meeting go?" she asked, resting her hands on her hips.

"Great! I don't think I'll have any problems securing money for a loan."

"So, you're really going to do it?" Susan asked.

"Of course I am. What's wrong? You don't think it's a good idea?" Susan stared at her with such intensity it made her uncomfortable.

Susan dropped her hands from her hips. "Oh, I'm not saying that. It's just that with all the trouble around here, I thought you might have changed your mind. I know I would have."

"I don't scare that easily."

Deirdre grabbed Sheila's folder off Susan's desk and went into her office. Thank God, the folder was intact.

Minutes later, Sheila had Deirdre's undivided attention. However, this morning Sheila seemed agitated and fidgeted in her seat a lot.

"So you see, I don't know how much longer I can keep my appointments. I want to keep coming, but I don't know." Sheila picked at her acrylic nails and nibbled at her lip.

"So, your husband's more concerned about my being black, than about your marital problems." Sheila wasn't her only white client, but the only one who had a problem with Deirdre's race.

"I don't think Brad realizes how fed up I am. He thinks since

I'm dependent on him for money, he can tell me how to live my life. I have a mind of my own, and I want to tell him that." She slumped in her seat.

"Then why don't you?" Deirdre asked, realizing they hadn't gotten any further since their first session four weeks ago. Sheila had such low self-esteem; it reminded Deirdre of herself years ago. If she could rebuild her self-esteem, then so could Sheila.

"I don't know. I would, but he's afraid I'll leave him like his last two wives. I don't want him to feel that way." Sheila opened her purse and pulled out a pack of cigarettes. "He's sensitive about being married again." She shook out a cigarette and returned the pack.

Deirdre watched the weekly ritual. Sheila fondled her cigarette as she talked, since smoking wasn't allowed in the office. The cigarette served more like a security blanket.

"Yet he won't come to therapy and talk about your unhappiness?" Deirdre clarified.

"He said he would if you weren't . . . you know . . . black. Also, he read about another break-in in this morning's paper. He said this time they stole files." She shifted in her seat.

Deirdre bit her lower lip. "What paper was that?" She asked in disbelief.

"I think the *Constitution*. He wouldn't let me see it."

Shocked, Deirdre forced herself to blink. She told the police she wanted that fact kept out of the paper. Her blood boiled as she wondered who printed that.

"I had to pretend to visit a friend to come here."

"Sheila, your file is safe right here on my desk." She pointed to the manila folder on her desk. The session had to be steered back to Sheila's issues.

"Yeah, well, what he read added to the fact that he doesn't want me coming here."

"Let's talk about that. Do you think keeping our sessions a secret is healthy for your marriage?"

The time left was spent discussing Sheila's marriage. Deirdre really wanted to get Sheila's husband into her office, so they could stop going around in circles.

At the end of the session, Sheila hugged Deirdre. "Thank you for listening to me spout on about my crazy marriage."

"That's what I'm here for." Deirdre returned the hug and led Sheila out of the room. "Now remember the things we discussed today. I want to hear next week that you've given some of them a try."

"Okay. I feel stronger already." She smiled before they began strolling down the hall.

They entered the reception area where Susan sat typing. She stopped when the women emerged.

"Bye, Susan. I'll see you next week."

"Bye, Sheila. You take care now."

Deirdre always walked her clients to the front door, and closed the door behind them. She stood there a minute and watched as Sheila walked out to a new Volvo.

"Now that woman can afford an expensive therapist out in the suburbs, so why do you suppose she comes all the way down here?" Susan asked, leaning back in her chair with her arms crossed.

Deirdre left the doorway and went over to Susan's desk. "Do you have this morning's paper?"

"No, why?"

"Sheila said her husband read about the break-in, and the paper mentioned the files."

Susan's hand covered her mouth. "Uh-oh . . . somebody printed it."

"Yes, and after I asked Bill Duncan not to let it out. She stunned me when she said it was in the *Constitution*." Deirdre couldn't wait to get her hands on the paper. She looked at her watch. Her next client was due in fifteen minutes.

"If you want, I can run next door and see if anybody over there has the morning paper?"

"Would you please? I've got to get ready for my next session." Deirdre said.

"Sure, oh, and there's Cathy's file on the desk." Susan pointed to the corner of her desk before she got up.

"Thank you." Deirdre picked up the file and returned to her office.

Susan hadn't returned before Cathy showed up, so Deirdre would have to read the newspaper after the session.

Later, she lead Cathy out of her office. Susan sat behind her desk typing. Deirdre noticed the newspaper on the corner of the desk.

"Bye, Cathy." Susan spun around toward the door.

Cathy turned and glanced at Susan. "Yeah, I'll catch you next week, maybe." With a dubious expression on her face, she shuffled to the door.

"You'll be here next week. Now remember to think positive." Deirdre patted Cathy on the back.

Deirdre turned from the door and shared a sigh with Susan. "She'll be okay."

"I hope so, I like her." Susan picked up the paper and held it out to Deirdre. "Here you go, section B, bottom of the page."

Deirdre took the paper and noticed Susan wasn't smiling. *Was it that bad?* She closed her door and hurriedly sat down. She didn't want Susan to watch her reaction as she read Robert's words.

FIVE

She flipped to the story. There it was, midway down the page. *Brunswick Counseling Agency Facing Troubles, by Robert Carmichael, Staff Writer.* Deirdre sighed and sat back to read the article. The more she read, the more she saw how much Robert got from their breakfast yesterday. It included information on her educational background, also a mention about her charitable work. The next thing she read stunned her. He reported that several case files were stolen.

"I don't believe this." She shook her head, and laughed. Snatching up the paper, she went to talk to Susan.

"Did you read this?" Deirdre asked as she marched into the room. She abruptly stopped when she saw Susan on the phone. "Oh, I'm sorry."

"Okay, bye." Susan hung up and spun her chair around. "No problem, we were finished."

Deirdre held the paper out and examined the article again. "I don't believe he wrote this. Who told him about the case files anyway? I never mentioned it to him." She dropped the paper to her side and stared at Susan.

"Not me." Susan shrugged innocently.

"He should have consulted me first. All he had to do was print a small article about the break-in. Just like he did last time." Deirdre walked around the reception area talking with her hands again. She smacked the paper with one hand and sent it flying across the room to land in a chair.

"Why do you think he did it?" Susan asked.

"That's what I'd like to know. He was such a gentleman at breakfast. So smooth. I should have known better, he's still a reporter." Deirdre flopped down into a chair next to the paper and folded it back up.

"Men, huh, can't live with them, can't live without them."

"Yeah, I guess." Deirdre halfway agreed with her.

"He may have been out of line by divulging that information, but you've got to admit that's one handsome man. He should be on somebody's pin-up calendar with that cute little goatee."

"Think about how he can destroy this office. People will read this article and say, 'I'm not going down there to see that woman.' Can't you see how he used me?" Deirdre asked.

"I guess so, but Lordy he's so fine." Susan crossed her arms over her chest and shook her head.

"I don't care how *fine* he is. I'm more interested in what he printed." She tucked the paper under her arm and stood up to return to her office.

"If what he printed bothers you so much, why don't you let him know?" Susan smiled and leaned back in her chair with her arms still crossed.

Deirdre thought about it for a few seconds. She looked down at her watch—lunchtime. "You know, I think I will. He didn't have to print that." She shook her head liking the idea more and more. "I don't appreciate this, and he's going to hear about it."

"You go, girl," Susan cheered her on.

Deirdre charged back into her office and pulled out the phone book. She found the number for *The Brunswick Constitution* and circled it. After a deep breath, she picked up the phone and dialed the number.

The operator answered.

"May I speak to Robert Carmichael?" She controlled the nervousness in her voice, but she couldn't help the butterflies dancing in her stomach. What would she say to him once he answered the phone? All she knew was that she had to do this right now, before she chickened out.

"Hello, Robert Carmichael."

His velvety-smooth voice reached through the phone lines. Deirdre's mind raced back to high school. Every fantasy she'd had always began with Robert Carmichael.

"Hello," he said again, more demanding this time.

"This is Deirdre Levine, I called about the story you printed."

"Hey, Deirdre, I'm glad you called. What did you think of the article?"

"I've got one question for you."

"What's that?" he asked in a cheerful voice.

"Why did you use me?"

"Why did I what?"

"Use me. Why did you pretend to be concerned about me?" *Did you think taking me to breakfast would give you permission to print anything you wanted in your article?*

Momentarily stunned, Robert stared across the room. How did he use her? She knew he was going to report on the break-in. He moved the receiver from one ear to the other, then cleared his throat.

"Maybe I missed something, but we did discuss me printing the article."

"I understood you were going to print a small article about the break-in, not mention the stolen files."

"I didn't mean to print anything that would upset you. I was just doing my job."

"Yes. Well, your job is bad for my business."

"The break-ins are bad for your business. I have no control over that." *Was he to blame for her troubles?*

"I know that. But, it took me six months to establish myself in this community, and it wasn't easy. Now you come along printing things like this. . ."

Robert had to cut her off. "Deirdre my article isn't the only one printed in this town about your break-in. I wouldn't get upset about it if I were you. Once the police catch the person, everything will die down." He hoped Deirdre wasn't mad at him.

"I wanted you to know that I didn't appreciate the sneaky way you got your information."

"But I didn't. . ." Before he could finish his sentence she hung up.

Stunned, he hung up and leaned back in his chair. He understood her being upset about the break-ins, but why did she have to turn her anger toward him? Every reporter knew about the files. All you had to do was ask the police. He'd stated the facts, and a little information on her that he'd gathered in his research. What would his chances be to ask her out now? Probably close to none, he told himself.

When the phone rang, he jumped and snatched up the receiver. "Robert Carmichael."

"Rob, it's me. Are you very busy?"

"No, ma'am, what's up?" Robert leaned forward and placed his elbows on the desk. His mother had called him at work once in the last few months.

"I need you to talk to Omar; he won't listen to me."

Robert detected the sadness in his mother's voice and knew his little brother had messed up again.

"Mama, don't worry, I'll talk with him. Where is he?"

"He didn't come home last night, I don't know where he's at. Robert, what's going to happen to that boy? He's so hardheaded."

"I'll find him."

"Baby I hope so. Then talk some sense into him."

"I'll try my best." Robert hung up the phone and thought he knew exactly where to find his younger brother.

Deirdre answered her fifth phone call of the day. Everyone seemed to have read the morning paper.

"Hey, Belinda, everything's fine."

"You didn't tell me you were having problems down there." Belinda and Deirdre were old friends in high school. After she moved back into town, she ran into Belinda at the mall and they'd become reacquainted.

Deirdre closed her eyes and shook her head. *Now he's started something.* "See, that's what everyone will think—I'm having problems. I wish he hadn't printed that stupid article. We had two small break-ins, nothing to warrant a half-page article."

"Two, is more than one too many, don't you think?"

Deirdre stroked her forehead to soothe the headache coming on. "I know it is. All this mess is driving me crazy. I wish the police would hurry up and capture those little punks."

"Well, I know I hadn't chatted with you in awhile. Then when I read this morning's paper, I had to call and make sure you're all right."

"Thanks girl. I'm fine. Maybe a little stressed, but I can handle it."

"We'll have to get together soon, and do something fun to take your mind off your troubles. When's the last time you went out with someone other than your six-year-old daughter?"

"I don't even remember." Deirdre thought about her breakfast with Robert, but that didn't count.

"Then I'm going to take it upon myself and see to it that you get out and have some fun. Maybe introduce you to a nice big chocolate bar."

"A what?"

"A man! Where have you been? I bet you haven't had a date since you've been here, have you?"

"No, and I'm not looking for a man right now."

"Deirdre, a man is what you need now. Someone to take your mind off things and help you relax. Girl, I've got to fix you up with somebody."

"Belinda, don't even think about it. When the time is right, I'll look for somebody."

"Who's to say when the time is right? When Mr. Right walks into your life, you have to make the time right. I'll just help set the stage a little. But, I'll let you get back to work for now. We'll do something soon."

"Okay, sure. Catch you later."

Deirdre hung up the phone, and reached for the next folder. Two more clients and her day would be over. She opened Geneva's file—it was empty.

* * *

The minute Deirdre entered her parents' living room she sensed tension in the air. Her mother opened the door in her robe, which shocked Deirdre. Five-o'clock in the evening and Anna hadn't dressed yet.

"Mama, are you feeling all right?"

"Yes, I'm fine." she answered, in a shortened tone of voice.

Deirdre shook her head and followed her mother through the living-room into the kitchen. Anna had to be upset, because she didn't look sick.

She hadn't said another word to Deirdre. Once in the kitchen, Anna picked up a cup from the counter and strolled out the back door. Deirdre dropped her purse and satchel in a kitchen chair and followed her mother outside to the screened-in back porch.

"Where's Daddy?"

"He's downstairs in the den teaching Mia to play marbles." Anna sat in a patio chair, crossed her legs and sipped from her cup of coffee.

A chill ran through Deirdre's body when her mother didn't look up. The last time she'd seen her in such a sour mood, she'd had a fight with Deirdre's father. Her mother wasn't her cheerful, feisty self. Deirdre walked back inside and went downstairs to look for her father.

The loud blare from the television met her at the bottom of the stairs. In the den, she found Mia and her father settled on the floor, their eyes focused on a group of marbles.

Mia's marble flew across the room, as she let out a loud giggle. "I won."

"Young lady, you're a little too good at this," Ralph declared as he picked up the marbles.

"So, who's winning?" Deirdre asked as she glided into the room.

"Mama, Mama." Mia jumped up from the floor, ran across the room and grabbed Deirdre at the knee. "I can beat Papa."

Deirdre looked across the room at her father. He glanced up

at her, then averted his eyes. In that one motion, he confirmed what she already knew. Her parents had argued, and she didn't want Mia to hear them yelling. While she was married to William, they never fought.

Mia yanked at her pants to get her attention. She looked down and stroked her daughter's hair. "That's good, honey. What are you playing?"

"Peaches, I'm trying to teach her what little I remember about marbles." Ralph called Deirdre by his nickname for her. He pushed himself up from the floor, moaning a bit in the process.

"Yeah, and I beat you, right Papa?" Mia giggled and pointed at her grandfather.

"Yes, you did." He looked up at Deirdre, then lowered his eyes to his granddaughter. "You're a fast learner little lady." He hobbled over to his easy chair and sat down.

Mia followed him with arms raised. He smiled as he picked her up.

Deirdre wanted to ask what he'd said this time to upset her mother. She walked over and sat on the couch across from his easy chair.

"So what have you guys been up to today?" He looked across the room at her, this time making eye contact. "Nothing much. Why do you ask?"

"Because mama still has her robe on, and she won't look at me." Deirdre leaned back in the chair and crossed her legs.

Her father helped Mia down from his lap, and gave her a light swat on the bottom. "Honey, run upstairs and check on your grandma for me."

Deirdre watched Mia skip out of the room with a smile on her face, as she whispered to herself. She grinned at her daughter, who was in a world of her own most of the time. Deirdre turned her attention back to her father, once Mia left.

"We read this morning's paper." He said.

She forgot about the article. The present situation worried her too much.

"What does the paper have to do with you and mama fighting?"

He straightened in his chair. "We didn't fight. We had a little discussion."

"About the article?" she asked suspiciously.

"Yes." He nodded. "You can't trust reporters, and you should know that. You need to handle this situation with silence. It'll all blow over soon, and people will forget."

"Daddy, I have to answer their questions. I'm responsible for that office. I didn't want to talk to them, believe me."

He leaned forward in his seat and placed his elbows on his thighs. "But Peaches, you shouldn't have told that reporter someone stole your files. He couldn't have printed it then. Once that gets out, people won't trust you. You know folks talk too much around here."

Deirdre stared at her father. He blamed her for the article. Everything was always her fault in his eyes.

"I didn't mention the files to him. He's a reporter, he did his research and found out on his own. Besides, I've already told him how much I didn't appreciate it."

Ralph sat back, and turned to the television. "Well, be careful who you talk to from now on." He frowned as he picked up the remote control and turned off the television.

Deirdre jumped up from her seat ready to grab Mia and storm out of her parents' house. Her father could be cold as ice sometimes. Before she left the room, he called out to her.

"Peaches."

"Yes." She stopped in the doorway, then turned around.

"I don't want you to get hurt, that's all." He looked up at her with a slight smile on his face.

He cared, but didn't know how to express it. She bit her lower lip and nodded her head. "Yeah, Daddy. I'll be careful."

Robert pulled his car in front of the dilapidated apartment building and killed the engine. He could dash in and out in a matter of seconds, he told himself. All he wanted to do was grab Omar and take him home.

An unshaven, tired looking man answered the door and blew small puffs of smoke in Robert's face. "Yeah man, what can I do for ya?"

Exactly what he needed, Robert thought, cigarette smoke up his nostrils. This rude guy stood a few inches shorter, and several pounds lighter than Robert.

"Is Omar here?" he asked.

The man narrowed his eyes and looked up at Robert as if he recognized him. "You Omar's brother?"

"Yeah, and I need to see him." Robert stood in the doorway, with no desire to go inside.

The man turned and looked behind him. "Hold on a sec. I'll check." He walked away and left the door ajar.

Robert moved over and looked out the cracked window in the hallway. Years of dirt caked the windows, making it impossible to see through. He pushed his suit coat back and stuffed his hands in his pockets. When he heard the door squeak, he turned around.

Omar ambled out with his head lowered and closed the door behind him. His warm-up suit hung from his thin, wiry body like he'd purchased it a few sizes too large. Only three-inches shorter than Robert, but sixteen years younger, he still resembled a high school student.

Robert wanted to see Omar's eyes. The last thing he needed was for his brother to start using drugs again.

"Hey, what's up?" Robert asked.

Omar averted his gaze and started down the stairs. "I guess Mama sent you after me?"

"Hold up." Robert reached out and grabbed him by the arm.

Omar raised his arm defensively and glared at Robert. "What man? She sent you after me, right?" He stopped and leaned against the wall.

His brother looked tired and sleepy, but Robert didn't think he was on drugs. "Yeah, she did. You didn't come home last night; she's worried sick about you." He walked past Omar and down the stairs.

Once in the car, Robert cornered him. "Man, why do you still hang out with these guys anyway?"

Omar turned away from him. "They're cool."

Robert shook his head as he started the car. "They're a bunch of deadbeats. And your association with them will keep you from getting anywhere in life."

Omar sneered at Robert. "They can't stop me from doing what I want to do. Have you forgotten, I'm a grown man? I decide what I want out of life."

"Omar, you're a twenty-year-old man with no job, who still lives with his mother. I think you've forgotten you're a grown man. What do you want to do anyway?"

Omar dropped his head back onto the head rest and let out a long loud sigh. "Why are you always on my case? Man, you're as bad as Mama. She won't let me breathe."

"Man, look, while you're under Mama's roof you need to respect her."

Omar raised his head and stared at him. "What do you mean, I need to respect her? I do respect her. You don't know what you're talking about."

"I know she called me to complain about you not coming home last night. Man, you know how she is. Just let her know you won't be in. That way she doesn't worry so much. She doesn't want you hanging in the street all night, then sleeping all day. She wants you to go to school and make something of yourself."

"Like you did, huh? You don't live there so how do you know what I do?" Omar almost broke his neck looking out the window at a woman as they passed her.

Robert watched him. "Hey, why haven't I seen you with Maria since I've been here?"

Omar laughed and shook his head. "I kicked her to the curb a long time ago. Don't worry about me. I gets all the honeys I want." He turned to face Robert. "But you my man, you're the one that probably needs a woman."

Robert had experienced one short-lived relationship since he had been back in town. Now, Deirdre came to mind. "We weren't talking about me."

"Yeah, right. We never are," Omar responded sarcastically, as he turned from the window.

SIX

Omar used his key to let them in the back door. They stepped into the large eat-in kitchen. The home was modest, and the kitchen was the center of activity. The boys had hung the wallpaper and helped their mother refinish all the cabinets.

Pearl walked into the room in a blue and white housedress, with her hands on her hips and a stern look on her oval face. Her sons towered over her five-feet-two-inch frame. She turned her head and caught Omar starting up the back stairs.

"Don't you have something to say?"

He stopped and took a deep breath. "Look, I'm sorry I stayed out so late. I figured I'd better crash over at a buddy's house."

"I only wanted to know that you were safe."

"Mama, I said I'm sorry. I need some sleep if it's okay with you." He gave them both a sarcastic look and waited for a nod of approval.

"Go on upstairs, boy." Pearl rolled her eyes as she waved him up the stairs.

Robert stood back and observed his brother's behavior. He wished he knew what bothered him. If only he could get Omar to talk to him.

Pearl shook her head. "What am I going to do with that boy?"

"First of all Mama, he's not a boy. He's a man, and you need to treat him like one. It's time he moved out." Robert declared. He knew his mother wouldn't agree.

"Where would he go? And how would he pay rent? What he

needs is a job. I've threatened to put him out twice, but he knows I won't do it."

Robert followed his mother into the kitchen. He grabbed a glass from the cabinet and poured himself some cold water. "You have to quit babying him and let him be a man. He'll be okay. Give him a deadline to find work and get out. I had his battery fixed, so he can get his car back on the road."

"Thanks. I just might put him out this time. You watch and see."

"Yeah." Robert drained his glass. His mother wasn't about to put Omar out. But somebody had to help him grow up. For the first time in awhile, Robert wished his father was still alive. His mother was too overprotective and treated his brother like a child. He watched her sit down to read her evening paper.

The sight of the paper made him think of Deirdre. He set his glass on the table, then pulled out a chair.

"Mama, did you read my article this morning?" he asked.

"Um-hmm. Honey I always read your articles." She looked up from the paper.

"What did you think of it?"

Pearl lowered her paper and looked at him. "I think it's terrible that someone broke into that place twice."

"I mean what did you think of the article? Did it make the agency sound incompetent in any way?"

Pearl turned down the corners of her mouth as she contemplated her response.

"Not that I could see. You reported on the situation, and everybody knows where that agency is. They're down on the Riverfront, right?"

"Yes, ma'am, in the renovated area."

"Years ago, some people might have been too afraid to go down there. It's always been such a dark and deserted area. But, that was a long time ago."

Robert stood, convinced that his article was all right. "Well, it's all lit up like a Christmas tree now." He deposited his glass in the sink, then went to kiss his mother on the cheek.

"Mama, I gotta run. I'll see you tomorrow."

"Okay, honey." Pearl stood and followed Robert to the door.

Deirdre sat at her computer thirty minutes into her session. She typed her response on her keyboard, then she hit enter. *Almost everyone has issues from their past that need to be dealt with. Have you entertained the thought of seeing a counselor?*

It took a few minutes for the response to appear.

I've only been able to discuss this with you here in cyberspace. Don't know if I'm ready to do face-to-face with anyone.

Deirdre had been talking with Keith for three sessions now, and he still hadn't opened up to her.

I'm not sure how much more help I can be unless you tell me what's really on your mind.

Deirdre could only be of so much help on her Internet chat sessions. Afraid to seek out therapy in person, most of her clients felt safer with a stranger. She used the Therapist Information Network on the Internet as a referral source, and weekly she ran into people in need of help with their problems. Therapists from all over the United States called and sent her e-mails to confirm the referrals.

Where should I begin? He asked.

Tell me about that first experience.

I've never told anyone this, but it was with my coach.

He was opening up. She looked at the paperweight style clock on her desk. She'd been online for close to an hour. His session was almost over.

"Mama, can I have some ice cream?" Mia asked, from her spot on the floor in Deirdre's office.

Deirdre continued her session with Keith as she looked over at Mia. She had entertained herself for most of the hour and Deirdre was proud of her.

"No honey, it's almost your bedtime."

"But, I'm not sleepy." She whined.

"Mia, we do this every night. Your bedtime is eight o'clock."

"I don't wanna go to bed. Can I stay up and watch cartoons?"

"Honey, we don't watch cartoons at this hour." Deirdre informed Keith it was time to wrap things up.

"Mama Anna lets me. I want to watch cartoons." She kicked her feet on the floor as she whined.

"Mia, stop it."

"Mama Anna lets me watch cartoons when you're not here," Mia pouted.

"You're about to go to bed." Deirdre made a mental note to speak with her mother about letting Mia watch the Cartoon Network late in the evenings.

"Why?"

"So you can get up early tomorrow."

"Why?"

"Honey, stop it." She turned to look at her daughter who had a devilish smile on her face.

Mia laughed and got up from the floor to stand by her mother at the computer. "What cha doing?"

"Counseling people on the computer."

"Can I help?" She leaned against the desk and her long plaits fell across Deirdre's papers.

Deirdre caressed Mia's wavy hair and kissed her on the cheek. "I'm sorry, honey, but you can't help Mama tonight. I'll tell you what, though. Tomorrow you can help me on the computer, okay?"

"Can I talk to people too?"

"You sure can."

Mia gave her one big smile as she leaned her head over onto the desk. Deirdre shook her head thinking Mia looked more like her Daddy when she smiled. Sometimes so much so, it gave her chills.

William was out of her life and she planned to keep it that way. Every Sunday, Mia called him for their father—daughter talk. Afterward, Deirdre had to listen to Mia cry. She wanted to see her Daddy. Unfortunately, he was thousands of miles away in California.

Minutes later, Deirdre ended her session and went to tuck her daughter in bed. She walked back into her mother's old sewing room, and her new office. It housed her computer and boxes of books and files. She picked up Mia's toys from around the room and stacked them away.

When she returned to the computer to start on her files, she noticed a message on the screen. Someone had sent her an instant message. Deirdre read the message typed in all capital letters—WATCH YOUR BACK.

SEVEN

Deirdre pranced into the office Monday morning ready to work. Over the weekend she'd re-created several of her case notes and had them ready for Susan to type. Three more and she would be all caught up. She wore a white linen suit and a pink silk shell. She didn't mind the wrinkles today; her mood was so chipper. The moment she opened the front door, she heard the soft sounds of music.

"Morning, Susan."

"Good morning, Deirdre. I found this for you when I came in." Susan held out an envelope to her.

Deirdre looked down at the envelope addressed to her. "Where did this come from?"

"I don't know." Susan shrugged her shoulders. "It was under the door."

Deirdre hesitated, staring at the envelope. If its contents served to change her mood, maybe she shouldn't open it. She shook off the strange feeling she had and opened the letter. Nothing would kill her good mood today.

She stood there and read the letter from Mr. Hamel. For a moment she was speechless. Had they decided to close her office? She hoped not.

"What is it? Is everything okay? You look a little funny," Susan's concerned voice broke Deirdre from her daze.

"Mr. Hamel has called a brief emergency meeting this morning at nine o'clock. He wants me there."

Susan let out a long sigh. "Oh man. Here we go. I bet Mr.

Hamel has told them all types of stories. How do they know you don't have a client at nine o'clock anyway?"

"Mr. Hamel knows we don't start before nine-twenty every morning. Why would he do that, unless he wants to fire me? That's another reason I want to work for myself. I won't have to be accountable to anybody but me." She looked down at the letter again.

"He wants to discuss the break-ins, but why call the board in on it? That's going too far."

"He has, and only because of two break-ins."

Deirdre looked up at the clock. Eight-thirty. She had time to think about what they might ask her, and how she would respond. She'd only met two board members before when she came in for her interview. She hoped all twelve didn't show today.

She folded the letter and replaced it in the envelope. The heavy load returned to her shoulders that she'd gotten rid of over the weekend. One more thing to worry about, she told herself.

"Well, let me go clear my head before nine o'clock."

Deirdre walked into her office with a new outlook on the day. What if the board decided to let her go? Or, what if they'd figured out who the thief was? She told herself not to think about it until she faced it. Calling this meeting didn't necessarily mean bad news was on the way. She had to look at it that way.

Thirty minutes later, Deirdre faced the eight board members who attended the meeting. Mr. Hamel had ushered everyone inside the conference room, and closed the door. Deirdre lightly tapped her fingernails against the table anticipating the worst. Everyone waited on Mr. Hamel to begin.

"Folks I want to thank you for coming on such short notice." Mr. Hamel cleared his throat. "I realize it's not easy for everyone to get off work, so I'll be brief. I'm sure you all read Friday morning's paper?"

Several board members nodded their heads. All eyes were on Deirdre. She hated to be the center of attention.

"Friday afternoon I received numerous phone calls from concerned parents. They aren't comfortable with their children in the center since these break-ins started. It's the little ones that I'm the most concerned about." Mr. Hamel declared.

"Mr. Hamel, are the police getting closer to arresting anyone?" asked Ms. Smith, a retired schoolteacher, and the chairperson of the board.

"Last I heard, they don't have any leads. They wanted me to question the children at the center and my staff. I can't imagine anyone from the center would break into Ms. Levine's office."

"Have you questioned the children?" Deirdre asked. She didn't believe he had even tried to talk with anyone.

"The children. Please. I've asked if they saw any strangers around the center, but I don't for one minute believe any of the children are responsible for this." He leaned back in his seat and laid his crossed arms on his stomach.

"Other than the summer camp programs, what other activities are held here after hours?" asked Mr. Turner, a bald, older gentleman who sat at the end of the table.

"Let's see, we have the evening basketball games, and the scout meetings," Mr. Hamel answered.

"Have you spoken with any of those children?" asked Ms. Smith. "Or, their team leaders?"

"Yes I have. No one has seen anything."

Deirdre sensed Mr. Hamel's resistance and it made her mad. Why was he so dead-set against her?

"Ms. Levine, we've all read the articles, but why don't you tell us what you think happened, and what should be done about it?" asked Ms. Smith.

After a long, hard sigh, Deirdre gathered her thoughts. "I really don't know. My gut instinct tells me that some young adults broke into the agency and took those files out of spite. A better lock on the back door might be the answer."

"You mean young adults from the center, don't you?" Mr. Hamel asked in a defensive tone.

Deirdre turned and looked him in the eye. "Yes, I do. Whoever broke into my office, was already in the community center. They didn't break in through the front door. They came in through the back door, which leads into your kitchen area."

"I still don't believe it was any of the children. Someone could have fixed the back door to the community center and gotten inside. It doesn't mean they work here, or have anything to do with the center for that matter."

The debate between the two of them escalated. Deirdre couldn't believe that he took no responsibility for what happened.

"Let me say something here that might help you both." Mr. Turner interjected. "Maybe we should discuss some sort of security for the center. Since this thief came in through the center, we're lucky they didn't steal more than her files."

"Yes, and that may make the parents feel more comfortable. I can understand their uneasiness. First there was that rapist on the loose a few years ago, and now this. I'd be afraid to send my children down here too," Ms. Smith agreed with the suggestion.

"Did they ever catch that rapist?" Mr. Turner asked everyone.

"I'm afraid not." Mr. Hamel leaned back in his seat.

"Well, Mr. Hamel, until the police catch someone, what do you propose we do?" Mr. Turner raised his hands in a gesture for help.

"I vote we close the agency." Mr. Hamel crossed his arms and waited for the board members to agree.

Deirdre jerked her head in his direction. She knew that's what the meeting was all about. "To close down because of two break-ins? Don't you think you're overreacting?" She prayed the board members would agree with her.

"Are we voting?" asked the young lady who represented Georgia Pacific.

"No," Ms. Smith responded. She cut her eyes at Mr. Hamel. "The board needs to discuss this alone, and decide what course of action to take. We have to remember that closing the office means putting two young women out of work. Plus, Ms. Levine would have to refer her clients to other counselors."

Deirdre liked to see Ms. Smith assert herself, and not let Mr.

Hamel have the final say. One look at Ms. Smith would tell anyone that she could take care of herself. She had a commanding
presence and a strong baritone voice.

"Mr. Hamel, we understand your concern for the children.
However, to close the agency down is a decision the majority of
the board would have to make."

Deirdre had to bite the side of her mouth to keep from grinning.
Mr. Hamel was about to explode, so she sat back and marveled
in the moment.

"I think we need to get a status report from the police before
we discuss this matter any further." Ms. Smith got the board's
approval on her suggestions and ended the meeting.

Deirdre returned to her office. She was glad the meeting hadn't
lasted too long. Susan and Cathy were engaged in a conversation
that she interrupted.

"Is everything okay?" Susan asked.

"Yes, it's fine." Deirdre couldn't tell her too much at the moment. "We'll talk later." She turned her attention to Cathy.

"Hey, lady, how are you doing?" Deirdre greeted Cathy.

"I'm here. That's about all I can say. Might be gone tomorrow,
but I'm here today." Cathy smiled as she stood and threw her
backpack over her shoulder.

Deirdre shook her head and laughed, she knew Cathy wasn't
going anywhere. She'd found a town she liked. "Then we better
get started and take advantage of your presence."

As they stood there, the phone rang. Susan answered it and
turned to Deirdre.

"Excuse me, can you take a phone call?"

"Who is it?" Deirdre asked annoyed. Susan knew she was
about to start her next session.

"It's Mr. Carmichael." Susan smiled with raised brows.

Deirdre looked up at the clock. It was already five minutes
into Cathy's session. Besides, she didn't want to talk to him.

"Tell him I'm in a session and unavailable." She turned to

Cathy, "Let's get started." With her right hand, she gestured toward her office and Cathy followed her direction.

"Okay." Susan returned to the phone call.

After Cathy's session, Deirdre made lunch plans with a colleague of hers. She needed advice on how to handle Mr. Hamel. He seemed obsessed with closing the office, and she couldn't afford to let him.

Before she left for lunch, Deirdre stopped and talked with Susan about the board meeting. She filled her in on most of the details.

"So, they want to close the office?"

"I don't know. They want to discuss it and get back with me. They might put a better lock on the community center. Someone mentioned security, but I don't think they want to invest that type of money since their lease is about to expire." Deirdre stood alongside Susan's desk.

"I can't believe they're taking this so seriously."

"Susan, stolen files is a serious issue. It's against the law, and who knows who has them. But, I believe a better lock is good enough."

"I hope so. I don't want to lose my job."

"Neither do I."

"Yeah, but you're a counselor, you can get another job. What about me? My whole family works for Georgia Pacific, and I don't want to work there."

"I don't think you'll have to worry about that. If they were going to let us go, I think they would have done so. Maybe we have a fighting chance." Deirdre shrugged her shoulders and motioned to leave for lunch.

Susan nodded with a half smile. "Well, enjoy your lunch."

"You too. I'll be back before my next session."

"Okay, see you in a little while."

Robert leafed through the paperwork of his next few assignments. He had to cover the Jazz in the Park concert, and an

Antique Fair on St. Simons Island. First, he had to make a call about some local puppies that were up for adoption. He stared at the papers until they all blended in his mind. Not one assignment that he could get excited about.

Before liquor detoured his career, he had a challenging position with exciting assignments. Now he had to wait out the grueling climb to the top again.

"Hey, how goes it?" Wayne knocked on the door.

Robert looked up from his papers.

"Everything's fine. How's sports?"

Wayne shrugged. "It's cool, you know. No high school sports right now. I enjoy that the most I guess."

"Yeah, well, it won't be long."

"I meant to ask you, how's everything on the Riverfront? With the break-ins and all. Has it settled down any?"

"Things are rather quiet right now. No construction mishaps or break-ins."

"How's Ms. Levine?"

"Fine."

"You know, she must not advertise. Until the break-ins, I didn't even know that center had a counseling office."

Robert frowned. "Neither did I."

"It's a wonder she even has enough business. But, this stuff happening now will let people know she's there. Not the best type of advertisement, but it's free."

Wayne triggered an idea that ran through Robert's head. Maybe, he'd come up with another way to see Deirdre again.

"Oh, she has clients. Every time I call over there she's with a client."

"She counsels young people from the community center a lot, huh?"

Robert shrugged. The only client he'd seen was the guy who walked in once when he was there. "She's a family therapist, so I think she sees everyone."

"Well, I wish her luck. There are enough looneys around here to keep her in business," Wayne chuckled.

"Sounds like you've never seen a counselor before."

"No need to. I live a fairly dull life."

Robert grabbed a folder from his desk and held it up. "Then you should be doing this story about the puppies for adoption instead of me. You might find it a little exciting." Both men laughed.

"I'll pass." Wayne waved good-bye before disappearing from the doorway.

Damon paced inside the tiny office like a caged cat.

"This is ridiculous. I don't need to be here. I don't understand how talking to you about my frustrations is going to change anything." He shook his head and rolled his eyes toward the ceiling. "I'm an aggressive man by nature, and I don't want to change that."

"Not even if it scares your fiancée?" Deirdre inquired.

He stopped and stared at Deirdre. She sat in a chair across from her desk. "I wouldn't hurt her and she knows it." Seconds later, he returned to pacing and slammed his fist into his palm.

"People just piss me off, that's all." He raised his tone. "And when I get pissed-off I speak my mind. I won't be pushed around. She wants me to hold my tongue and let people walk all over me. Well, I'm not about to let that happen. If my height and build intimidate them, good."

"So you want people to fear you?"

"I don't care if they do or not. That's what I'm saying. I'm me, and I don't care what other people think. I'm aggressive toward someone when I need to be. If I have to hurt somebody, I will."

"Damon, I don't think you mean that." Deirdre shifted in her seat when he moved behind her. Then she heard his voice thundering over her head.

"How in the hell do you know what I mean? You don't know anything about me." He sat on the edge of his seat, and faced Deirdre.

"I come in here every week and discuss my anger. But you see, I don't have a problem with it." He pointed at Deirdre. "You have a problem if you're supposed to change me, because I don't want to. Not for Rachel or anybody." He jumped up, threw the door open, and stormed out of the office.

Deirdre raced after him as far as the reception area, then let him go. She looked at Susan's startled expression.

"What's wrong with him?" Susan asked.

"I don't know. He's upset about something."

"Wow! He scared me banging the door like that. I almost jumped out of my seat. For a minute there, I thought I needed to call the police."

"He's okay. He just needs to cool off." For his treatment to be successful, Deirdre had to get him to open up about his father's absence. He'd bottled the anger up for so long he didn't know how to release it.

The minute she turned to go back into her office, Damon walked back in. She stopped.

"Look, I'm sorry. I had a bad morning. I didn't mean to take it out on you."

An apology from him was a step in the right direction.

"That's okay. I know this is hard for you. It's hard for a lot of people."

The telephone rang, and Susan answered it on the first ring. She put the caller on hold and held the receiver toward Deirdre.

"Who is it?"

"Mr. Carmichael again," Susan smirked.

Deirdre glanced at her watch, and shook her head. She didn't have time to talk. "Tell him I'm busy.

She addressed Damon. "You still have some time if you want to continue."

"Yeah." He walked past them back into her office.

Susan smiled and shrugged her shoulders at Deirdre. She returned to the phone and explained that Deirdre was in session.

Deirdre returned to her session, and pressed Damon further this time.

* * *

Robert hung up the phone disappointed that he hadn't caught Deirdre between sessions. Earlier, Wayne had given him a great idea. What the businesses on the Riverfront needed was more publicity. The minute Wayne left, Robert went to Dean's office and threw out the idea of profile pieces on the Riverfront businesses.

That angle hadn't been covered yet, so his boss liked it. He gave Robert permission to choose the businesses to profile. Each day of the week, Robert would profile a different business. Then for the weekend edition, he'd write a nice wrap-up piece.

Now, he had to sell Deirdre on the idea. If he couldn't reach her by phone, he'd have to pay her a visit. If he showed up one day after her last client, she wouldn't have any excuse for not seeing him.

EIGHT

Thursday evening at five o'clock, Robert pulled into the Brunswick Counseling Agency's parking lot. He saw Deirdre's car parked in the lot. He hoped all her clients had left for the day.

As he stepped out of his car, he buttoned his suit coat and prepared to give the pitch of his life. When he walked in, Susan looked startled to see him.

"Mr. Carmichael. It's good to see you again. Did you have an appointment with Deirdre?" She smiled.

"It's good to see you too. I don't have an appointment, but I thought I'd catch her before she left for the day. Could you let her know I'm here?" He took a seat against the wall.

"I sure will." Susan strolled into Deirdre's office, closing the door behind her.

Robert chuckled and shook his head. He'd give anything to be a fly on the wall in Deirdre's office. The last time he talked to her, she hung up on him.

Deirdre stared at Susan, alarmed by the way she closed the door and leaned against it. She had a huge grin on her face.

"What is it?" Deirdre asked.

"You're not going to believe who's out there."

"Susan, I don't feel like playing games. Who?"

"Mr. Carmichael, and he wants to see you. He's called every day, sometimes twice. He's a persistent little devil isn't he?"

"What does he want?" Deirdre's pulse quickened from sheer excitement.

"He didn't say. He just said he wanted to catch you before you left. Should I show him in?" Susan motioned toward the door.

Deirdre didn't have time to powder her face or anything. *What did he want with her?* She'd avoided all of his phone calls, but she couldn't avoid this visit.

"Okay, show him in."

Susan turned and opened the door.

"Oh Susan?"

"Yes." She pushed the door closed again.

"Were you leaving?"

"Yes, I was on my way out. That is, unless you want me to stick around?" she asked.

Deirdre shook her head. She shouldn't be afraid to be alone with that man. She'd ridden in his car, had breakfast with him and knew him from school.

"No, go ahead. I was just checking. I'm sure he won't be long."

"Okay."

Seconds later, Robert entered Deirdre's office. They shook hands and he took a seat across from her desk. Always so handsomely pulled together, he wore a navy pinstripe suit, crisp white shirt, and an expensive-looking tie.

"You're a pretty hard lady to catch." Robert said in a lighthearted tone.

Especially when I don't want to be caught. "I'm sorry. I haven't been able to return any of your calls. We've been so busy."

"That's good to hear. For a minute there, I thought you were still mad at me about my article."

She pointed her ink pen at Robert. "Let's not talk about that, I haven't quite gotten over it." She added a half smile to her answer.

"Then you'll have to let me make it up to you." He crossed his legs and grinned at Deirdre.

Caution bells went off in her head. *What's he up to?* "I believe the damage is already done."

"Okay, then let me put a bandage on it. I've got an idea that I think you'll like."

Deirdre played with her pen, clicking the cap repeatedly. She smelled a rat. A slick, smooth, well-dressed rat. The last time he helped her out, he did more damage than good. Or, was this another journalistic trick to get more information out of her?

"I can tell by the way you're looking at me, that you don't trust me. Hear me out though. I think you'll be glad you did." He uncrossed his legs and scooted his chair close enough to rest his forearm on her desk.

"Okay let's hear it," she said cautiously.

"I want to do a profile piece on you and the agency. Of course I'll clear it with the center. There won't be any mention of burglaries. I'm talking something positive here. We can make the community aware of your background, and let them know what good work you're doing in the community."

There had to be a catch. So far, it sounded like a win-win situation for her. "And what does this profile piece do for you?"

"I get the satisfaction of seeing a smile on your face, instead of a frown."

Hogwash. His reason didn't sound good enough. "Let me get this straight. You're doing this for me?"

"For you and several other businesses on the Riverfront. But, I'd like to start with your agency. That is, if you like the idea."

And she did. She liked it so much, she couldn't believe it was his idea. This was exactly what she needed to put the burglaries out of people's minds.

She smiled. "I like the idea. Who wouldn't, it's free publicity. And you promise you won't mention the break-ins?"

Robert held up both hands. "You have my word. It's not about that. It's about you, and the good work you're doing."

She could publicize her Web site as well, which should mean more business for her, and more money in the long run. After a few seconds of consideration, she decided.

"Okay, I'll do it." This time she'd use him and his paper. A free article in the newspaper was better than a paid advertisement anywhere else.

"Great." Robert sat back and rubbed his palms together. "Now, how about dinner tomorrow night?" His eyes revealed his eagerness.

"Dinner?" My how the subject had changed.

"Yes. I know your days are full seeing clients. A dinner interview at the restaurant of your choice, won't disturb your schedule, or mine."

Deirdre didn't say anything. A dinner-date with Robert. No, an interview with Robert. She didn't have an Internet counseling session scheduled for Friday night. And it wouldn't be a problem getting her mother to watch Mia.

"Okay, we can have the interview tomorrow night at the Allegro Garden Room."

Robert nodded his head. "That sounds good. What time should I pick you up?"

"Don't bother, I'll meet you there at seven o'clock." She didn't want him to get the impression she thought this was a date. She wanted to keep things strictly professional.

"Okay, then I'll see you tomorrow night at seven." Robert thanked her for her time and left.

Friday night, Deirdre stood in front of her mother's cheval mirror and examined herself. Green wasn't her color, so she took off the green suit. She changed into her favorite red crepe suit. Red was her color, and she looked good in it. A pair of dangling pearl earrings gave her the business touch she wanted.

Now she looked as professional as she had at work this morning. She turned from the mirror to see her mother standing in the doorway.

"Don't you look nice tonight."

"Thanks, Mama."

"Got a date?"

"No ma'am. I'm meeting Robert Carmichael at the Allegro Garden Room for a business interview."

"Business huh. Isn't that your favorite outfit?"

"It's my power suit. You know, good for business dinners and such."

"Uh huh. I guess the navy pants outfit you had on earlier just wouldn't do? That short red skirt says business better anyway." She smiled and winked at Deirdre.

Both women shared a laugh as Deirdre turned back toward the mirror. "Mama, I know it's business, but I can still try to look nice."

Anna walked over to adjust Deirdre's collar. "Well, honey, I'm just glad to see you're going out. You spend all day at work, then all evening with Mia. A little male companionship will do you good." She stood back with crossed arms admiring her daughter.

"I'm not interested in him that way. All I want is some free publicity. That's the only reason I agreed to this meeting. I need to be more visible in the community, so I can make a name for myself."

The chime of the doorbell sounded throughout the house.

"I'll get that, it's probably Sister Louise from church. She's supposed to bring over those robes for me to hem." Anna went to answer the door.

Deirdre walked down the hall, and peeked into Mia's room to say good night. She found Mia glued to the new television her grandmother had bought her. Deirdre kissed her forehead, then left the room. She grabbed her purse, then descended the stairs.

At the bottom of the stairs she turned into the living-room, and got a shock.

"Yes ma'am, I hope she won't mind."

Robert Carmichael! What was he doing here? He was supposed to meet her at the restaurant. As she entered the room, Robert stood and smiled. She followed his gaze from her feet to her eyes. Was she overdressed?

"What are you doing here?" She asked sharply.

"I hope you don't mind, but I remembered where your parents' house was and thought I'd ride by. When I saw your car parked in the driveway, I figured you hadn't left yet. So, I asked myself, *Why not save her a little gas and pick her up?*"

"Great," Deirdre replied, gritting her teeth.

At the restaurant, they had a nice, comfortable booth with an oceanview. A little too romantic for a business date, Deirdre thought. After placing their orders, Robert asked questions about the agency.

"Why don't you tell me about the type of clients you handle? Then, anything else you want. This is just as much for you as it is for me," he said nonchalantly.

"My area of study is general family therapy. So, my clients range from single men and women to couples to young adults. I even have a few elderly clients. I also have a Web site where I counsel over the Internet."

"You're kidding?"

"No, I'm not."

"I didn't know you could do that, how does it work?"

"Clients send E-mails to schedule appointments. I set up a chat room, and they meet me there. Then I have clients who prefer e-mail-only sessions."

"That's remarkable. You're an incredible woman."

Deirdre watched the way he smiled and wanted to retrieve her notes from her purse. She hadn't wanted to chance getting nervous, and forgetting all the important things she had to say.

"It's not that big of a deal. I usually schedule sessions between Friday and Sunday."

"Do any of those people come into your office?"

"No, most of them are from out of state. If I know of someone, I refer them to counselors in their area."

"The magic of the Internet. It never ceases to amaze me."

"Be sure to put that in your article, along with my Internet address." She pulled a business card from her purse and handed it to him. Then she smiled, and sipped her wine.

Robert laughed and took the card. He stuck it in his jacket pocket. "That's right, let me know everything you want printed. I don't want to make a mistake like last time, and print something you don't want mentioned."

She smiled, but didn't mention the last article. She hadn't heard anything from the police about her files. Even if she had, she wouldn't mention it to him, for fear he'd print it.

Robert poured her a second glass of white Zinfandel. This dinner was better than their breakfast. He was getting to know her. And he wanted to see that big smile of hers again.

"Well, before you know it, you'll have your own radio or television show. Live from Brunswick, *The Deirdre Levine Show.*"

She laughed. "You must be kidding. I'm not a famous counselor. I help real folk, people like you and me. People who need a little support coping with the realities of life. But, you know, a radio show doesn't sound half bad." She contemplated, while biting her bottom lip.

"Hey, it's something to think about."

"It sure is. I bet you're loaded with all sorts of ideas." She sat back and relaxed into the soft leather seat. Two glasses of wine were her limit.

"Baby, I'm loaded with more than ideas." He snapped his finger. "Which reminds me. I've got a little something for you. Sit tight. I'll be right back."

Deirdre nodded as Robert left the table. What on earth could he have for her? She didn't like surprises, especially from someone she didn't know too well. She took advantage of his absence and pulled out her compact to powder her face. The minute she glanced into the mirror, Robert returned to the table.

"Don't worry, you look great." He gave her an enticing smile and sat down.

"Well, you weren't supposed to catch me." Embarrassed, she stuffed the compact into her purse.

Robert reached across the table and handed Deirdre a large gold envelope. "Look at that."

She took the envelope, apprehensive about the contents. "What's this?"

"Open it. Trust me, you'll be surprised." He crossed his arms and laid his elbows on the table.

She slowly opened the envelope. "I hope it's a good surprise."

When she peeked inside, she saw a picture. She glanced up at Robert's huge smile. She grabbed the edges and pulled the picture out. The first thing she noticed was a bunch of nappy-headed teenagers. After pulling the entire $8\frac{1}{2}$ x 11 black-and-white photo from the envelope, she wanted to die.

"Oh my God!"

Robert's smile broadened. He seemed proud of the photograph. "Remember that day?"

Deirdre stared at the teenagers. Everyone had big smiles except Deirdre, who looked like she was in pain. She resembled an outcast from some horror movie. She wore all black before it was a fashion statement.

"Where did you get this?" She asked, shoving it back into the envelope. The picture made her feel naked, exposed and ashamed. She never wanted to see it again. Was he trying to embarrass her?

Robert picked up the envelope and pulled it back out. "I found it in my mother's attic. It must have been some field trip we took together."

"We went to the museum. I remember it." Deirdre played with her food. She'd lost her appetite.

"Don't we look pathetic? Look at my hair. Man, I must have had the largest afro in the school in those days." He laid the picture and envelope on the table.

"Now that's the Deirdre I remember. Quiet as a mouse. You've changed a lot since then."

"I hope so. If you don't mind, can we talk about something else? And could you put that away. I'm not too fond of those days."

"Sure, I'm sorry." He picked it up and put it back in the envelope.

"It's okay." This was why she couldn't spend too much time with him. He reminded her of the reasons she'd dreaded moving back to Brunswick.

Robert didn't think she looked so bad back then. He hadn't meant to, but somehow he'd upset her again. Man, he was batting a thousand with this woman.

He took the envelope and sat it in an empty chair next to him. He then reached across the table and took her hand in his.

"I didn't mean to stir up any bad memories. I thought maybe we'd get a kick out of the picture, that's all."

"Well, you didn't know, so let's drop it."

"Done." Robert let go of her hand and tried a different approach.

"Tell me what you did after you left Brunswick. Like, what led to this tattoo." When she looked down at her wrist, he knew he'd found a safe subject.

Deirdre traced her finger along the link design on her wrist. "The day my mother saw this, she freaked out. She thought I was ruining my life."

Robert recaptured her hand. He ran his index finger along her tattoo. She watched the slow, seductive way he traced the design. When she looked up, their gazes locked. He kept rubbing his finger over her tattoo.

"What does this symbolize to you?" he asked.

"Freedom."

He leaned back surprised. "Freedom from what? If you don't mind me asking."

"Everything. Depression, failed relationship attempts, you name it. I got this at a time in my life when things were going right for a change. I joined a social group and met people who accepted me, and I began dating."

"Why didn't you get his name tattooed on you instead?" Robert asked, grinning.

She laughed. "Really now, it wasn't about him. It was more about me."

"You didn't date in high school?"

"No, never." She tried to concentrate while he massaged her hand. She wanted to pull away from him, and keep it there at the same time.

"I can't believe that. Didn't you go to the prom?"

She shook her head. "Are you kidding? I wasn't about to waltz in there by myself. I spent prom night watching a movie with my mother. It wasn't so bad."

Robert shook his head. "Some guy really missed out, didn't he?"

"Yeah, I guess he did." She pulled her hand away and pretended to search for something in her purse. One minute she felt totally relaxed with him, the next extremely awkward.

"So how about after college? What did you do?" he asked.

"To sum it up, I got married, had a baby, got divorced, then moved back to Brunswick," she concluded.

"Whew," Robert said, pretending to wipe sweat from his brow. "You've been busy. And after all that, now you have to deal with break-ins."

"Not to mention your articles," she chuckled as she shot back at him.

"You're pretty sharp you know that?" He winked at her and grinned.

"I'm a small-town counselor now, trying to keep my practice going."

"You won't have any problems with that. You wait and see, this mess will blow over and you'll have all the clients you want."

"So you think the police will catch the thieves and my problems will be all over with?" She waved her fork around in a circle.

"I don't have much faith in the Brunswick police, but Bill seems to like you. He just might catch somebody for once."

Deirdre laughed. "For once. What does that mean?"

Robert shook his head and stared at her. "Nothing. Forget I even said it."

NINE

Sunday morning Deirdre woke up with Robert on her mind. She'd enjoyed the dinner interview, but it was time to get back to reality. Robert was attracted to her last night and she didn't want to read too much into it. After all, he was a reporter trying to get a story. She figured he'd do whatever he could to get her to relax and talk. And it worked. She couldn't believe she'd told him so much about herself.

After church, Deirdre and Mia went to Neptune Park. Mia ran straight for the swings and waved at Deirdre. "Mama, come on."

Deirdre shielded her eyes from the sun with one hand and carried a picnic basket in the other. She set the basket on a picnic table before joining Mia on the swings. Now that church had let out, a crowd formed in the park.

"Mama, can we go see Daddy?" Mia asked as Deirdre pushed her on the swing.

Deirdre dreaded this question.

"Not right now honey. Mommy can't get off from work, and California is a long way from Brunswick."

"Then can Daddy come see me?"

Deirdre noticed Mia's carefree little body begin to tense in the swing. She hoped she wouldn't start to cry in public.

"I don't know, honey. You'll have to ask him next time you talk to him." Deirdre knew full well William wasn't about to visit Brunswick. When they lived in California, he spent more time at work than he did at home. They weren't successful in making the marriage work.

Mia became quiet, and that meant she was about to cry for her Daddy. Not that they had spent much time together in California, however, absence did make the heart grow fonder. Besides, she was daddy's little girl. Deirdre stopped the swing, and helped Mia out.

"You want an orange?"

Mia shook her head. As they headed to the picnic table, Deirdre heard someone call her name.

"Deirdre," a female voice came from the other side of the swing set.

She turned around and saw Belinda and her son, Niles, approaching. Niles and Mia were the same age. He let go of Belinda's hand and ran to Mia.

"Hey, girl. What's up?" Belinda greeted Deirdre with a hug.

"Nothing much. I see you've got your main man with you today." Deirdre returned the hug and sat down on the picnic bench.

Mia and Niles ran to the swing sets together.

Belinda smiled at the children as they left. "Yeah, that's my little buddy. I saw his Daddy, Melvin, yesterday." Belinda cut her eyes at Deirdre with a smirk on her face.

"No kidding. Where?"

"In Savannah. Me and Kenneth ran into him with his new wife."

"What did you say to him?" Deirdre asked.

"We just spoke, like strangers. I don't have much to say to that man. His wife's lucky I'm a lady, or I would have decked her right outside that restaurant."

Deirdre laughed, knowing Belinda would not have done that. "So when do I get to meet Kenneth?"

"Funny you should ask that. I've had you on my mind a lot lately. Do you remember our discussion about you needing a little R&R?"

"Yeah . . . and?" What was Belinda up to? She prayed it wasn't a blind date, something Belinda had been trying to persuade her to do.

"Well, I'm having a pool party next weekend. Kenneth's cooking on the grill and we've invited a few friends. So, don't make any other plans for Saturday. You can even bring Mia, my cousin has volunteered to watch the children."

"That sounds like fun, but a pool party. Girl, you know I need to lose weight. Do I have to wear a bathing suit?"

Belinda leaned away from the bench and placed both hands on her hips. "Yes you do. That's what makes it a pool party. Honey, Melvin built that pool before our divorce, and I'm going to use it."

Deirdre looked down at herself. "I suppose I can still squeeze into my bathing suit."

"If not, then go buy a new one. Trust me, you'll have a good time."

"Yes ma'am, if you say so."

"Hey," Belinda reached over and hit Deirdre in the arm playfully. "I forgot to congratulate you on that spread in this morning's paper."

Deirdre jumped with excitement. "It was in this morning's paper?"

"Yes ma'am. Front page of the local news section."

"Was it flattering, or did he take another shot at me?"

"Here," Belinda reached over and pulled the newspaper from her bag, "read it for yourself." She handed Deirdre the paper.

Deirdre quickly turned to the local news section. There it was. *This Week in Brunswick, Spotlight on the Brunswick Counseling Agency.* Deirdre read the article to herself and smiled all the way though. Robert did what he said he would. He painted a positive picture of her office.

"Of course, all the beginning is about the renovation, but the part on you is good, isn't it?" Belinda asked.

Deirdre nodded and smiled. "It's better than good. He's mentioned my Web site, and that I'm taking new appointments." She folded the paper back up and handed it to Belinda.

"Well, wait until Mr. Hamel see's that. That's positive exposure for the community center, too. Maybe you can even get a raise out of this."

"Belinda, Mr. Hamel is out to get me. He'd fire me before he okayed any raise. He fights to keep my office as separate from his center as possible."

"Oh, he's not out to get you. He's just looking out for the best interest of the kids there."

"No, he wants to ruin my career in this town. I wouldn't be surprised if he broke into my office."

"Girl, stop talking crazy, you know he's not that smart. He would have never thought of that."

"He's smart enough, and he's got the board behind him."

"What do you mean?" Belinda asked puzzled.

"He called an emergency meeting to discuss what happened. Now they're trying to decide whether to close the office or invest in better security."

"Really? What do you think will happen?"

Deirdre pointed to the paper. "Maybe after the members read this, they'll give it a little more thought, and leave the office alone. After all what are we talking, two break-ins."

"What are you going to do if they don't?"

"I don't know. It sure will hurt my plans of opening my own office anytime soon. Let's hope they do, or I'll have to devise a plan B."

Susan spent the weekend with Gus, at the Park Suite Hotel in Jacksonville, Florida. They had a wonderful time swimming and lounging around the resort-like hotel. In Jacksonville, no one had to know Gus was married. As soon as his divorce was final, he'd promised Susan they would be married.

Sunday evening as she packed her overnight bag to return home, Gus strutted up behind her and put his arms around her waist. "Did you have a nice weekend?"

Susan smiled, and rested her head back onto his chest. "You know I did. I love our weekends together."

He gazed down into her eyes. "Me too." He kissed around her neck and moved until he stood in front of her. "Reach inside my shirt pocket."

Susan's face lit up. Gus was always surprising her with little gifts. He said he liked his woman to have the finer things in life. That's why he dressed her in the latest fashions.

She put her hand into his pocket and pulled out a gold bracelet. "Oh, Gus, this is beautiful."

"Just like you, baby." He pulled her closer and gave her a long kiss.

She put her new bracelet on and held out her wrist. "I can't wait to show Deirdre my new bracelet."

Gus pulled away from her, lit a cigarette, and blew circles of smoke into the air. "You like working for her, don't you?"

Susan turned to him and smiled. "Yes, I do. Deirdre's cool. You couldn't ask for a better boss."

"She just moved here didn't she?"

"Yes, but she's from Brunswick. Born and raised."

Gus walked over and looked out the window. "What's she going to do once the community center moves out of that building?"

"How did you know about that?"

"Some friends of mine want to purchase property down on the Riverfront. They told me about the property coming up for sale. I was just wondering."

"She wants to purchase it, if she doesn't change her mind."

"Why would she do that?"

"I told you about the break-ins. Some of her files were stolen, and that's a serious matter."

"So a couple of people's dirty laundry got aired. I'm sure she won't let that stop her, will she?"

"Gus, nothing can stop her from purchasing that building."

He took a few more drags from his cigarette and blew the smoke into the air. He put his cigarette out in an ashtray on a side table. A few smooth strides and he stood next to Susan.

"Let's not leave yet."

Susan smiled. "You're wicked, you know that?"

"And you love it, am I right?" He gave her a seductive wink and ran his tongue across his lips before embracing her.

Susan pushed her overnight bag off the bed to make room for their bodies.

A week later, Deirdre attended Belinda's pool party. She'd found a white mesh cover to go over her snug one-piece bathing suit. Belinda had assured her it wouldn't be a huge party.

Deirdre got out of the car and followed the music around the side of the house into the backyard. Several people were mingling about and dancing. She searched the crowd of unfamiliar faces for Belinda. Two empty chairs and a table sat at the end of the pool. She made a beeline for one.

She took a seat and dropped her tote bag beside her. All she had to do was relax, and enjoy the hypnotic melodies of jazz music that filled the air.

A few minutes later, she heard a man's voice beside her. "Deirdre, is that you?"

She had put on her sunglasses. When she tilted her head up, she saw Mr. Turner, a member of the Brunswick Community Center board of directors. She hadn't expected to see him here. For some reason, she wanted to cover her body with a coat.

"Mr. Turner, how are you?"

He sat in the chair next to her. "Call me Jonathan." He extended his hand and shook hers.

"Okay. Jonathan, I didn't know you knew Belinda?"

"Actually, I met her today. Kenneth introduced us, and I've known him for years."

Deirdre sat there, not sure what to say next. She didn't want to discuss work, and have him tell her they were about to close the agency. If he didn't mention work, neither would she.

"I believe this is the first time I've seen you outside of the center." He scooted his chair closer to her.

She nodded and smiled. "I'm afraid I work a lot and don't get out much for parties like this."

He crossed his legs. "Hey, I'm glad these guys decided to have this little shindig. Maybe I'll get to know you better." He winked at her as he sipped his drink.

Is he flirting with me? Shocked, Deirdre kept smiling. She was young enough to be his daughter. Unable to bring herself to say anything, she continued nodding. She didn't want to be bothered with Jonathan.

"Would you like something to drink?"

She seized the opportunity to get rid of him. "Yes, I'd love a soda."

He stood and left his drink on the table.

After he walked away, Deirdre opened her bag and took out a towel. When he returned, she'd be ready to join the others in the pool.

"Hey, girl. I see you made it." Belinda walked over with a pitcher in her hand. She sat in the seat Jonathan had vacated.

"Where's Mia? I said you could bring her."

"I know, but my mother wanted to take her to the zoo today. So. I'm here alone, determined to relax some."

"Good. You look great. I've got some people I want you to meet in a few. I like your suit. And you were worried about it."

"It is snug." Deirdre tugged on her suit.

"No it's not. Now, help yourself to a drink or some food. Everything is right over there." Belinda pointed to a long table on the other side of the pool.

"Jonathan's already gone to get me a drink. And I'm not hungry at all."

"Jonathan?"

"Jonathan Turner. He's on the board of directors for the community center, and he said he knows Kenneth."

"Oh, I met him tonight. A real ladies' man." She laughed.

"That's him," Deirdre confirmed, as she rolled her eyes heavenward.

Belinda slapped her hand against her leg and laughed. "Girl, don't tell me that old dude is flirting with you? He's got a thing for younger women. He's worked his way around the pool."

"Why did he stop at me? As far as I'm concerned he can keep moving. I'm not into older men. Girl, that man wants to get to know me better." Deirdre rolled her eyes at Belinda who wiped the tears from her eyes as she laughed.

"Well, you haven't had a date yet have you?" Belinda asked through her laughter.

"And I won't if he's my only choice." Deirdre looked up and saw Jonathan walking toward them with her drink.

"Here he comes. Belinda do something, help me," she pleaded.

When Jonathan reached the table, Belinda got up. "Jonathan, I see you know my friend, Deirdre."

He smiled as he handed Deirdre her drink. "Yes. You know I'm on the board down at the community center. We're real happy to have Deirdre down there." He took a few gulps from his can of beer.

"Yes, she was just telling me about that." Belinda smiled as Jonathan took his seat across the table from Deirdre.

"And who do we have here?" A tall handsome dark-skinned brother sporting a full beard joined them.

Belinda put her arm around his waist.

"Kenneth this is my good friend, Deirdre."

They shook hands. "Deirdre, it's nice to meet you. I've heard so much about you."

"All good I hope?"

"Nothing but." He turned and kissed Belinda on the tip of her nose.

"Okay you guys. Time to replenish the food." Belinda managed to get Kenneth to take Jonathan inside and help him with the food. Deirdre got up after both men left.

"Okay, that's it. I guess I better join the crowd in the pool before he comes back. Belinda, find someone else to introduce him to." She took off her cover and walked to the edge of the pool.

Belinda followed. "I'll try, but it looks like he's got his mind set on you."

Deirdre entered the pool and looked back at Belinda. "Then I'll stay in here until I shrivel up."

Belinda walked away shaking her head.

Deirdre pushed off the side of the pool and relaxed her body as the cool water washed over her. All the tension left her as she worked her arms and legs in the water. She looked toward her seat and didn't see Jonathan. No one had taken her seat, so she decided to get out for a few minutes.

When she reached the edge of the pool, she grabbed the hand-rail and pulled herself out of the water. With both hands, she brushed her hair back off her face and looked into the face of Robert Carmichael holding out her towel.

"You're a good swimmer."

She froze the minute she saw him, then snatched the towel from him and wrapped it around her body.

"Thank you," she mumbled.

Robert wore a pair of trunks and a T-shirt. He'd startled her and she didn't know what to do. She hadn't meant to snatch the towel from him, but she was uncomfortable exposing her body to him.

He smiled as she passed him, then grabbed her bag from the yard chair. "I hadn't expected to see you here." He followed her and sat in the chair across from her.

"I didn't expect to see you either. I'm sorry, but you startled me when I stepped out of the pool." She pulled another towel from her bag and dried her hair.

He leaned back and watched her. "That's okay. I seem to have that effect on women."

She frowned at him, not too sure what he meant by that. Why did he have to be here to ruin her relaxation? Maybe she should return to the pool.

"Are you here alone?" he asked scanning the guests.

He glanced at the drinks on the table, and she remembered

Jonathan. She hoped he'd found another victim. "Yes, I am." She reached into her bag and pulled out a headband.

Robert grabbed the glasses from the table, and moved them to a tray on the other side of him. "You don't mind if I join you do you?"

She wanted to scream out, *Yes*. Then she saw Jonathan and Kenneth stroll along the side of the pool.

"No. I don't mind at all." If she kept Robert here until Jonathan left, everything would be okay.

Robert also saw them approaching. He turned to Deirdre. "I noticed Jonathan with you earlier. If you want, I can leave."

"No. Don't go. He's on the board of directors for the community center, that's all." She hoped she didn't sound too desperate.

He stood as the men approached. "Hey fellas, what's up?" They shook hands and engaged in a brief conversation.

As the men talked with their backs to her, Deirdre slipped the towel off and put her cover back on. She excused herself and went over to have something to eat and chat with a few women she now recognized.

She returned with a small plate of fruit. Kenneth rose from her seat and excused himself.

"Before I go, let me refresh your drinks."

"Nothing for me, I've had too many already," Jonathan confessed.

"How about you Robert? Would you like something?"

"No thanks. I don't drink. Belinda told me that path leads down to the beach." Robert pointed behind him toward a path cut into the bushes. "Deirdre and I were about to walk down to the beach. Are you ready?" He turned and smiled at her.

Taken off guard, Deirdre almost choked on a grape. She stared at Robert.

"Yes, I'm ready whenever you are."

"Okay, we'll catch you guys later," Robert said.

"Deirdre, it was nice talking with you." Jonathan tilted his head at her.

"It was nice talking with you, too, Jonathan."

Robert picked up Deirdre's bag and pulled it on his shoulder. He gestured toward the path for her to take the lead. "Let's take a walk."

She popped another grape into her mouth, then set the saucer on the table. They strolled down the path. "Are you sure you'd rather go for a walk with me, instead of sitting around with those guys?"

"I had a problem a few years ago with alcohol." Robert glanced at Deirdre. "I can be around people who drink, but I don't need to have one myself. Liquor almost destroyed my life, and I'm not going to let it happen again."

"So, you're a recovering alcoholic?" she asked.

Robert raised his hand. "Yes, ma'am." He glanced at her again. "That doesn't bother you, does it?"

She shrugged, and shook her head. "Why would it bother me?"

"I don't know. Some people get a little uptight when I tell them. I guess they think I'll slip back into a bottle."

They strolled through the clearing onto the beach. The breeze met them as they approached.

"At least you recognized it was destroying your life, and you did something about it. That takes strength."

"Yeah, I guess so."

As they strolled along in silence, Deirdre gazed out at the ocean. How romantic it would be to walk along the beach with the man of her dreams. The only reason she was on the beach with Robert was to get away from Jonathan—not exactly a romantic stroll.

"So how are things at work?" he asked breaking the silence.

"Everything's fine. I'm sorry I didn't get around to calling to thank you for such a nice profile piece. But, I appreciate it." She reminded herself that Robert was a reporter and she couldn't say too much around him.

"I'm glad you liked it. Don't be surprised if a lot of your old friends call for advice after reading that piece. Readers love those local girl done good stories. The fact that you moved all the way to California to get your education, then returned to Brunswick to work is newsworthy."

"Almost anything around here is newsworthy isn't it?"

Robert held her bag in his hands behind his back as they continued down the beach.

"Hey, it's not that bad."

"Maybe not. I guess I'm a little bitter about things. But, I want to thank you for dinner last week, and for doing the profile."

"I'm just glad you didn't curse me out, and hang up on me this time," he laughed.

"I didn't curse you out." Deirdre stopped and put her hands on her hips.

"No, but I think you wanted to."

They shared a good laugh. Robert held his hand up to his ear as if it were the receiver and mimicked Deirdre's voice. She reached out and playfully pushed him closer to the water's edge. He ran a little farther down the beach, then turned and waited for her to catch up. When she did, he held out his hand.

"Miss Deirdre, I'd like to introduce myself. I'm Robert Carmichael. You might remember me from high school," he said with a southern drawl.

She smiled and shook his hand. "Yes, Mr. Carmichael, I remember you. What can I do for you?"

"For starters, you can say you'll let me take you to a movie, and maybe dinner. Then after that, we can have some stimulating conversation." Robert's expression was serious.

She stared at him, unable to utter a word. She closed her eyes not sure if he'd still be there when she opened them. Was this a dream, or had he asked her out on a real date?

He observed the blank expression on her face and was afraid she'd say no. He stepped closer and leaned in to kiss her on the lips.

Her heart beat so fast she hoped she wouldn't have a heart attack. He rubbed his nose close to hers. A soft kiss brushed her parted lips. The shore began to spin as she closed her eyes. His kiss was brief and soft. She opened her eyes to gaze deep into his coal-black eyes, and noticed he had long beautiful lashes.

He became a blur again as he moved closer for a second kiss. This time he dropped her bag and pulled her closer from the waist. His hand slid up her arm. Deirdre returned the kiss, but held her arms down to her side. Robert's hand moved from her arm to her shoulder, then to her neck.

Deirdre flinched as if he'd touched her with a hot poker. She pushed his hand aside, and backed away.

"Don't touch me," she said, barely above a whisper.

TEN

Robert raised his hand. "I'm sorry. I was way out of line." He reached down and picked up her bag.

Deirdre crossed her arms, then ran her hands up and down her arms. "I've just got this thing about my neck. It's silly really." She managed a chuckle.

"It wasn't the kiss," she tried to explain.

"You don't have to explain. I couldn't resist myself." She looked enticing in her bathing suit. The cover she had on didn't hide much. He saw the curves of her body through the holes in the mesh. She had shapely legs and a healthy body. Everything he liked.

"Should we head back?" He held his hand out for her to join him.

"Yes, I guess we'd better. I'll have to leave soon."

They walked back up the beach in silence. He wanted to say something, but changed his mind. When he looked at her, she was miles away staring out into the ocean.

She walked alongside him, afraid to say anything. She couldn't explain why she freaked out when he touched her. Ever since she could remember, she'd had a phobia about her neck. However, she had to admit that she'd wanted him to kiss her.

When they reached the path that lead to Belinda's house, she heard a rustling sound in the trees. When she looked and didn't see anything, she dismissed it. She took another fleeting look at the ocean.

"You know, I must have a thing for water."

Robert followed her gaze. "Why do you say that?"

"Well, I left Brunswick and moved to California. My first apartment was a few blocks from the beach. And now, I return home, back to the ocean. I've never lived anywhere that wasn't close to water."

"Yeah, I know what you mean. I missed the ocean when I was in Philly." He took a deep breath, then exhaled slowly. "The water is so calming. I sit back and watch the waves to relax sometimes."

"So do I."

"Hey, party poopers." Belinda yelled from behind them.

They turned around just as she took their picture. Too late to protest.

"No Belinda, don't." Deirdre held out her hands, then moved behind Robert.

Belinda lowered her camera. "Oh, come on you two, pose for me. I've taken pictures of everyone else. Put your arm around her Robert, come on."

He turned and smiled at Deirdre. "I don't think she's going to let us get out of it."

Deirdre wanted to dig a hole and crawl inside. "I don't like taking pictures. I always come out looking awful."

"I've got a cure for that." He dropped her bag and grabbed her by the waist, positioning her in front of him. "Here, stand sideways. It's an old trick a cameraman taught me. Not that you need it, you look great." He wrapped his arms around her and smiled in Belinda's direction.

"That's it. Now give me a smile you two."

"Pretend you're having a great time," Robert whispered in her ear.

Deirdre smiled into the camera. "But, I am having a great time," she whispered back.

A few clicks and Belinda was finished. "See that wasn't so bad, was it?"

* * *

The following week, Deirdre returned to work with Robert on her mind. Every evening she read his article in the newspaper. She had this perfect vision of him standing by the pool in his trunks. She admired his strong hairy legs and broad shoulders. When he'd put his arms around her, she wanted to close her eyes and lean back into his embrace. She'd wanted to pretend they were lovers. Maybe good things do come to those who wait.

"Deirdre, did you borrow the petty cash last week?" Susan asked as she walked into Deirdre's office holding a small cigar box.

"No. Why?"

"All of its gone. There's a receipt here for every purchase I made. But, the rest of the money's gone." She set the box on the desk and looked at Deirdre.

"How much?" Deirdre asked, picking up the receipts in the box.

"A little more than fifty dollars I think." Susan sat on the edge of the seat across from Deirdre's desk.

After examining the receipts, Deirdre put them back into the box and leaned back. Susan handled the office expenses. The community center provided a small amount of petty cash that she kept locked away for supplies.

"When was the last time you went into the box?"

"I purchased some stamps last week. It was there then." Susan shrugged her shoulders. "I leave the cabinet unlocked during the day. But I'm always in there."

"Have there been times when you had to leave the room?"

"Briefly, maybe." Susan nervously shifted in her seat. "I hope you don't think I took it."

"I'm not accusing you. Have you had anybody in the office whom you think might have?"

Susan shook her head. "No. I guess we better report this to Mr. Hamel."

Deirdre massaged her forehead. "I hate to do that. You know how he feels about this office. Another incident and he'll ask me to leave for sure." She had to do something.

"What about when it's time to turn in the receipts for more cash? We have to report it."

"No we don't. I'll put the money back. This time lock it in a file cabinet in the hallway."

"Deirdre, you shouldn't have to do that."

"Yes, I do."

"You mean the center won't replace this money?"

"Susan, I don't even want to ask them for it. But from now on let's keep everything locked up. Even while we're here."

"Okay, will do." Susan picked up the box as the phone rang. "I'll get it." She left Deirdre's office and returned to the reception area.

Deirdre dropped her head and rested her crossed arms on the desk. She'd have to dip into her savings again. Who would steal their petty cash? Could Susan have taken the money and lied to her? She had to trust that she didn't.

"Are you okay?" Susan asked, standing in the doorway.

Deirdre raised her heavy head. "Yes, I'm okay. I just can't believe this, that's all."

"Ah, Robert Carmichael's on the phone, and Geneva just walked in."

Deirdre sat up straight in her chair. It was time to put on a professional face and deal with her day. "Tell Geneva I'll be right with her. I'll take the call first."

"Okay." Susan left and closed the door behind her.

Deirdre took a deep breath before picking up the receiver. "Hello, Robert."

"Hey lady, how are you?" he asked cheerfully.

"I'm fine and you?" The energy and excitement returned to her body at the sound if his voice.

"I'm great. Susan told me you were between clients, so I'll make this brief. What are you doing Friday night?"

"Ah. . ." she stalled as she grabbed her DayTimer to make sure she didn't have an Internet session scheduled. "I don't have anything scheduled."

"Good. So we can catch a movie and dinner Friday night like we discussed last Saturday?"

She hesitated. Was she ready to date? Even if it was Robert Carmichael. "I don't remember us discussing it actually."

"Oh, that's right. We were about to discuss it, and you were about to say yes, before I interrupted you."

"Oh I was?" Deirdre asked playfully.

"Yes ma'am. I distinctly noticed your lips move to form the word *yes*."

He was definitely a charmer. She couldn't say no.

"What movie do you want to see?" she asked.

"Whatever. You pick the movie, and I'll pick the restaurant. How does that sound?"

She was so attracted to this man it didn't make sense. If he said let's go to the moon, she'd probably go.

"I suppose I can find a good movie for Friday evening."

"Great. You've got to relax sometimes. After you check the movie guide, let me know what time to pick you up."

"That's okay, I can meet you there after work."

"Deirdre, you tried that last time remember? I'm sorry, but you're talking to a real southern gentleman. I'll pick you up if you don't mind."

God, would she make it until Friday night? The anticipation would kill her. "No, I don't mind. Give me your number and I'll call to let you know what time the movie starts."

"Great." Robert gave her his home number.

Deirdre hung the phone up feeling like a sixteen-year-old about to go on her first date. This was the date she never had in school with Robert Carmichael. She made a note in her daily planner to check the movie schedules once she got home, then she wrote Robert's numbers in her address book.

A few soft knocks on the door interrupted her thoughts. Looking up, she remembered Geneva. She hurried to the door.

Susan stood on the other side. "I noticed you had hung up the phone. Are you ready for your next client?"

"Yes. Show her in."

Geneva slogged in with a dismal expression on her face. She set her purse in one chair and herself in the other. They had handled all her financial issues, now what brought on this sad look?

"Geneva, are you feeling all right?"

She sighed and crossed her arms. "I'm fine. Just haven't been getting much sleep lately. Someone keeps calling in the middle of the night hanging up. I wish I knew who it was."

"Have you contacted the phone company?"

"I called them today. I've got to go sign some paperwork before they'll do anything."

The vision of a file folder flashed through Deirdre's mind. Luckily there were no phone numbers in the files. "How often is this happening?"

"Darn near every night. I tell you, no sooner do I fall asleep, does that darn phone ring. I answer it and they hang up."

"They don't say anything?"

"One night I thought I heard a man say he was Walter. It scared me to death for a minute there. But, ain't no way Walter's calling me on the phone from the grave." Geneva rolled her eyes toward the ceiling and gave a slight chuckle.

Deirdre laughed with her, a nervous laugh. Someone had Geneva's file and had found her phone number. She was sure of that. Deirdre's heart sank from fear.

After leaving numerous messages, Deirdre finally reached Officer Bill Duncan the next morning.

"Deirdre, what can I do for you?"

"I'm afraid I've got some bad news. Yesterday, one of my clients complained about not getting enough sleep."

"And how is that a problem?"

"I'm not finished. Someone calls her house in the middle of the night and hangs up. One night she heard them say her dead husband's name."

Silence came from the other end and Deirdre hoped Bill was thinking about what this could mean to the case.

"How do you know the calls have anything to do with your office?"

"I don't. But, I think it's worth looking into. One of the files stolen was hers." He didn't seem excited.

"Deirdre, it could be a jealous boyfriend, or someone who didn't like her husband. Did you ask her if she has any enemies?"

"Bill, Geneva is a senior citizen. She doesn't have a jealous boyfriend somewhere, and I doubt that she has enemies."

"You're talking about Geneva Shaw?" he asked.

"Yes."

"Yeah, well, I see what you mean. It's not likely that she's done anything to provoke anyone."

"She called the phone company, but I wanted to let you know. Maybe this will lead to who's stolen my files."

"I'll give her a call. Thanks, Deirdre."

Susan walked in when Deirdre hung up. "What did he say?"

"He's going to look into it."

"When I read that in your case note, I couldn't believe it. What is this world coming to. Nice little ladies like Geneva receiving prank calls." Susan stood in the doorway with her arms crossed, shaking her head.

"And in Brunswick, can you imagine it? This is the type of stuff that happened in California."

"Girl, we've moved up to the big time in crime. First those unsolved rape cases years ago, then the car-jackings. But, those were some guys passing through ripping off tourists. Don't mess with the tourist dollars. They found those men quick."

"Well, after we find out who made those calls, that should be the end of this little mystery," Deirdre concluded.

"Let's hope so. But what if it doesn't." Susan asked with raised brows.

Deirdre bit her lip in frustration. "Then I'll turn into a detective myself and try to figure this out. I don't have any choice, my future depends on it."

After Susan left for the day, Deirdre went through the back door into the community center. She walked down the hall to the rest room. She heard someone humming as she walked inside.

"You're here rather late aren't you Joyce?" she asked the community center secretary.

"Hi, Ms. Levine. I usually leave at four, but Mr. Hamel came in with some papers he needed typed up before tomorrow. And you know how he is when he wants something."

"Yes, I do." Deirdre thought about what a horrible boss he must be.

"Joyce, let me ask you something? You come in pretty early don't you?"

"Yeah. I'm here at seven o'clock."

"In the last couple of months have you seen anybody around my office? You know, someone who didn't look like they belonged there."

She shook her head. "I'm sorry, but the police asked me the same thing. All I've seen are the children coming in and out of here. And Alfred, when he shows up."

Deirdre figured she'd say as much. "Does anyone other than Alfred have a key to my office?"

Joyce tapped a finger against her bottom lip. "Let's see. Oh, Mr. Hamel. He has keys to all the locks around here. Or rather, he keeps them in a lockbox that only he has the keys to."

"Thanks, Joyce."

"You're welcome." She reached for the door to leave. "Have a nice evening."

"You, too," Deirdre added as she thought about Joyce's response.

He walked to the front of his car where the headlights shone into the forest. Leaning over, he checked his watch for the time. Twelve-fifteen in the morning—the bum was late again. He lit another cigarette before he sat on the hood of the car.

A few minutes later, he saw a light making its way down the

dirt road. He jumped from the car and crushed his cigarette into the ground.

A black Ford Mustang pulled next to his car. Gus turned off the engine and got out.

"You're late again."

"Sorry, man. I ran into a little trouble." Gus walked over and stood next to him.

"Nothing that concerns me I hope?" he asked forcefully.

"No man, I've got everything under control. She held me up that's all." He nodded his head staring at his friend, then glanced around the woods.

"She doesn't know about this, does she?"

Gus gave his friend a startled look. "No way. I wouldn't do that. What do you take me for? Some kind of fool?"

"Look, if I find out you're talking—

Gus cut him off. "Man, who am I going to talk to, huh? Tell me that. I know what the deal is." Gus adjusted his jacket nervously.

The older man pulled out another cigarette and lit it. He threw his head back when he inhaled the aroma, then blew the smoke out slowly.

"Hey, you got my money? I gotta run, you know. I've got a few deliveries to make tonight." Gus looked him up and down.

After eyeing Gus for a few seconds, he reached into the backseat of his car. He pulled out a white envelope and handed it to him. When Gus reached for it, he pulled it back.

"What's up?" Gus shrugged and tugged on his Kangol cap.

"Make it clean, I hate sloppy work."

Gus smiled, then snatched the envelope. "You know me. Have you ever known me to do a sloppy job?" He opened the envelope to count the money.

He grabbed Gus by the collar, then pulled him close enough to whisper in his ear. "Don't mess with me, unless you want to be found floating in the ocean." He pushed him back against his car.

With fear in his eyes, Gus stepped back and smoothed out his shirt. "I got the money, and I got the directions. You don't have anything to worry about."

"Good. Now get to work."

He stood there and watched the Mustang pull away. Some men would do anything for money.

ELEVEN

Deirdre dashed around her bedroom, trying on every outfit she owned. She chose an ankle-length, indigo, jersey dress with a side slit, instead of jeans. She didn't have to dress up for the movies, however, she wanted to look her best.

She held the dress in front of her, and looked in the mirror. "Watch out Robert Carmichael, you're about to be knocked off your feet."

There was a soft tap on the bedroom door.

"Come in."

Her sixteen-year-old baby-sitter, Vita walked in. She often stepped in when Anna couldn't watch Mia.

"Ms. Levine, your date's here."

"What? I didn't hear the doorbell."

"We're out on the front porch. He just pulled up, and he's cute, too."

Deirdre laughed. "Yes, he is nice-looking." She turned back to the mirror still holding the dress. "I better get dressed. Tell him I'll be right down."

"Yes, ma'am."

A few minutes later, she came downstairs to an empty house, then heard voices outside.

"I'm these many." Mia held up six fingers.

"You're six. Wow, such a big girl. I would have guessed you were sixteen at the most. You look so good for six."

Mia giggled and buried her head into Vita's chest. The two of them sat on the front porch swing. Deirdre watched through the screen door, while no one had noticed her.

"How old are you?" Mia asked Robert.

"Mia." Vita hit her gently on the arm. "You don't ask adults things like that."

"That's okay." He replied, and started to tell his age.

"No, it's not okay." Deirdre stepped out the door. She walked over to the swing and gave Mia a kiss on the forehead.

"Honey, what did Mommy tell you about asking adults their ages?"

"I don't know." Mia played bashful and buried her face into Vita's chest again.

"You remember." Deirdre ran her hand along Mia's hair. "You girls be good and go inside now. I won't be late."

"Okay, Ms. Levine. Come on, Mia." Vita helped Mia out of the swing and held her hand as they went back inside.

"Bye." Mia waved at Robert.

"Bye, Mia. It was nice meeting you, and you, too, Vita."

They giggled and ran inside.

"That's a bright little lady you've got there."

"Yeah, she's my pride and joy. Even though she can ask too many questions."

"That's fine. It means she's inquisitive and has a desire to know things. I'm sure she'll grow up and be as smart as her mother." Robert leaned against a column on the front porch.

Deirdre blushed. "Thank you."

He pulled away, ready to leave, when Deirdre walked toward him.

"By the way, you look great," he said.

She glanced down at her dress. Bingo. "Thanks, I'm glad you like it."

"So, what are we going to see?"

"I thought we'd catch, *He Got Game,* the new Spike Lee movie that starts in—" she glanced at her watch. "About forty minutes."

"Good, we've got plenty of time."

They walked to Robert's car. He held the door open for her.

Deirdre adjusted her dress nervously as she sat down. In a million years she never would have dreamed this possible.

Robert got in and closed the door. The radio came on when he started the car.

"I hope Mia and Vita didn't ask you too many questions before I came down." Deirdre asked.

"No, they were fine. Your daughter's cute. I like little girls." He pulled away from the curve.

"You do?" She inquired.

"My ex and I never had children. We talked about it, but she was never ready."

"Children are a lot of work, but I couldn't imagine life without Mia." She didn't want to talk about herself too much. Whenever they met, she was always the subject of conversation. Tonight, she'd let him do most of the talking.

"Do you want more children?" Robert asked.

Deirdre hesitated before answering. At thirty-five she wasn't too old to have another child. "Maybe. I'm not sure. I love children. But, I don't see myself getting married again."

Robert glanced at her and shook his head.

"Are you sorry you never had children?" she asked.

"Kind of. I think I'd make a good father."

As they rode along, Robert changed the radio station, but the music wasn't any better. He picked up a cassette and popped it into the tape player. The music of George Benson's "Breezin" took over.

"That's better, huh?" he asked.

"Much." Deirdre agreed. "George Benson is nice and smooth."

"You must be a jazz fan?"

There he goes, asking more questions about her. *How can I turn this around?*

"I like all types of music. Is George Benson one of your favorites?" she asked.

"Yes he is. I really like jazz," he answered.

"And what else does Robert Carmichael like?" she asked.

"Let's see, I like sports. I'm afraid I watch more than I participate these days. I played basketball on a small league when I was in college."

"Where did you go to school?" she asked.

"Penn State. I played on a league for a local liquor store, believe it or not." He chuckled.

"Were you any good?"

Robert glanced at her. "Are you kidding? Of course I was. I started to try out for the school team, but with my studies and all I would have never had time to play." His expression was serious.

Deirdre didn't know whether to laugh or not. When he gave her a raised brow look, she knew he was joking. "Yeah, right. Too bad. You could have played for the NBA."

"That's true. But, I had a journalistic calling. And you know how it is, you have to answer to your calling."

"Oh, most definitely." She shook her head and they started laughing.

When they got inside the movie theater, Deirdre couldn't believe how crowded it was. Robert grabbed her hand and they made their way to the counter for popcorn. She had to bite her lip to keep from smiling. A high school fantasy of hers included going to the movies with Robert and they would sit in the back of the theater and neck. Something she never did as a teenager.

When they entered the screening room, Robert chose a seat near the back of the theater. Deirdre stopped and looked at him.

"What's wrong? You don't like this seat?"

She smiled and nodded. "This is fine."

Deirdre ate her popcorn and tried not to think about her fantasy while they watched the movie. Robert was such a perfect gentleman, that she had no reason to think he might not be.

"I'm glad you chose a Spike Lee film," Robert whispered.

His breath against her ear made her shudder. He'd only been that close once. "Why's that?" she asked.

"It's a little something I learned in Philly. When the numbers are good on opening weekend, Hollywood takes notice. And, black filmmakers' chances will be good at securing money for another film."

"I didn't know that."

"It's true."

After they left the theater, Robert drove over to St. Simons to his restaurant of choice, Chelsea's. Deirdre had never eaten there, although she'd heard of the popular tourist spot.

They agreed to eat outside. The waiter lead them to a small white table set aglow with candlelight. How romantic this is, she thought.

Robert pulled Deirdre's chair out for her. She looked so beautiful in her dress tonight. He liked it better than her business suits. She resembled a twenty-year-old, instead of the mother of a six year old daughter. He had to make sure tonight's date lead to others.

"This is a very nice restaurant," she commented.

"It's my favorite," he said. "This might not be the most exquisite restaurant on the island, however, it's one with the best food."

"And that's the most important thing," she said, picking up her menu.

"You got it."

As the night progressed, the conversation turned back to the movie.

"I can understand how that kid felt in the picture. When I was thirteen, I wanted to be a professional basketball player, too. I think most black boys dreamed of being a Michael Jordan or a Dr. J. I was out in the backyard playing basketball every day. What were you doing?"

Deirdre reflected for a moment sipping her tea. "Well, when I was young, I dreamed of being a movie star. But, I don't really remember my early teens."

"No kidding?"

"Weird, huh? I can remember me and my sister, Barbara, fighting most of the time. Then a few events in high school, but nothing else."

Robert shrugged. "I remember a lot about my childhood. Like the time me and Omar set our model cars on fire, and accidentally burned the garage down."

They laughed.

"But those were supposed to be the best years of our lives. You don't remember being devilish like that?" he asked, trying to jar her memory.

"No. I never burned my dolls. But, I do remember one that if you pulled her hair it grew."

"Yeah, my sister had one of those."

"I pulled my doll's hair all the way the first day I got her. I couldn't get her to work anymore after that." She frowned.

Robert didn't like the look on Deirdre's face. Seemed like she didn't like talking about her childhood as much as she didn't like talking about high school. He changed the subject. He wanted to see her smile again.

"I'd like to know something," he asked.

"What?"

"What does Deirdre like to do when she's not at work or taking care of her daughter?"

The waiter brought out their catfish nuggets, giving her time to think.

"I collect dolls."

"What kind of dolls?" Robert asked, as he watched the delicate way she dipped her nuggets in the sauce and ate them. He could sit there and watch her lick her fingers all night. If she kept it up, he'd be more aroused than he already was.

"Black dolls. I have a collection of more than twenty dolls so far."

"Really? What made you want to collect dolls?"

"I saw this doll from The Order of NZingah Doll Collection, and she was faceless. I guess that intrigued me, because it was up to me to put a face on the doll."

"So, you bought a doll that you had to paint a face on?"

"Not really. You don't paint a face on, you use your imagination. I made her who I wanted her to be. The dolls are named after Anne NZinga. She was an African queen who helped save her people from enslavement in the 1600s."

"That's amazing. Do all of your dolls represent something to you?"

"Yes, they do. I found the woman who makes The Order of NZingah Dolls in Atlanta, and ordered a few more from her. They're a special part of my collection. I've got other dolls that I've picked up here and there over the last several years."

"I can't say that I collect anything other than bills." Robert ate a few nuggets and drank his tea as the restaurant filled up around them.

Robert scooted his chair closer to hers when a couple took the table next to him. He didn't mind this opportunity to get next to her. His knee touched hers and he shifted in his seat.

"I'm sorry," he said when he bumped her knee.

"That's okay." A quiver ran from her knee up her thigh, and then up her spine. He moved close enough for her to catch a whiff of the robust scent of his cologne. And unfortunately, close enough for him to notice how nervous she was sitting next to him.

He reached out and ran his finger along her tattoo. "I still can't get over this. I don't know that I could ever do something so brave."

When he touched her, her body came alive. He stirred up emotions in her that she'd never felt with William.

"Yes you could. After you get over the initial shock, it's okay." The intimacy of the sitting and the romantic candles on the table all worked together in this little seduction scene. What else had he planned for the night?

"You know, I just thought of something I collect," Robert added.

"What's that?" she asked.

"Music, especially jazz. I like everything from Branford Marsalis, to the innovative sounds of Quincy Jones. I guess you can call my music a collection." Robert leaned toward Deirdre and placed his arm on the back of her chair.

"Got a big collection?" *Oh God, what a loaded question.* She prayed he didn't read too much into that question.

"I've got a pretty big collection, yeah. Would you like to see it sometime?" Robert stroked his goatee and gave her a grin.

Embarrassed beyond belief, she didn't want him to think she meant anything other than music. She heard herself stumble over her words as she tried to answer him.

"Oh, yeah, uh—I—I'd like that."

The waiter escorted another couple pass them, and a man stopped in front of their table.

"Good evening."

Deirdre and Robert looked up. Jonathan Turner stared down at them. Deirdre grew embarrassed.

Robert stood and extended his hand. "Jonathan, good to see you again. How's everything?"

"Fine, fine." Jonathan shook Robert's hand, never taking his eyes off Deirdre.

"Hello, Mr. Turner." She addressed him.

"Now, call me Jonathan, Deirdre. We're a bit closer than that." He gave her half a grin as his date called him.

Deirdre turned to see a young woman. *He likes them young,* she remembered Belinda saying.

"You kids enjoy your dinner." He tipped his hat and walked away.

Robert sat back down and cleared his throat. "Think that's his daughter?"

Deirdre laughed. "Are you kidding? He should be ashamed of himself. She's almost a child."

"He looked a bit miffed with you."

"No he didn't." She rolled her eyes at him laughingly.

"Yes he did. And you should have felt the way he gripped my hand."

"I am not the least bit interested in that man. Nor have I ever been for that matter."

"I don't know, he probably feels like I stole you from him at the party last weekend."

"Stole me! I didn't go to the party with him, and I had no intentions of leaving with him. He's on the board at the community center, and that's how I know him."

"Sure. That's what he meant when he said, you're a bit closer than that," Robert teased.

She laughed along with him. "He did give me a funny look, didn't he?"

"He sure did. I think he had his eye on you Ms. Levine."

"Well, my eyes weren't on him." *They were on you!*

As they walked out to the car, Robert told Deirdre about his next assignment, which would take him to Florida.

"I thought you covered local news?"

"I do. Occasionally though, I have to travel for some information. I'll be gone for about a week." When they reached the car, he opened the door for her, then stopped her from getting inside.

"Deirdre, I want to thank you for tonight. I had a great time, and I hate to see the night end."

"I had a wonderful time myself. I enjoyed the movie, the dinner, and the conversation."

He took Deirdre's hand in his and kissed her knuckles. Her knees weakened. "Are you trying to make me blush?"

"Have I?"

"Yes."

"Good." He helped her into the car and closed the door.

She could have screamed while she was in the car alone. She was so excited. Instead, she settled for a few deep breaths. *This guy is smooth.*

Robert jumped in, started the car, and took off.

"You know I really do hate to see this night end. I'd like to take you to Harbor Lights for some dancing."

"That sounds nice, but I've got a little lady waiting for me at home. I hate to leave her for too long."

"I understand. Maybe next time we'll go dancing."

"It's a date."

They rode along the highway in silence for a few minutes until Robert said, "Deirdre, I never asked if you were seeing anyone."

Deirdre laughed to herself. This was the first date she'd been on since dating her ex-husband. However, she wasn't about to tell him that.

"At the moment, no."

"Then maybe when I get back we can see each other more often. That is, if you're interested."

Deirdre looked at Robert, speechless. Everything was moving in the right direction, and it scared her.

"You're not saying anything, and that's a bad sign." He glanced over at her as he pulled in front of her parents' house.

She snapped out of her dream state. "I'm sorry. I don't know what I was thinking. Sure, when you get back we can get together. Kind of get to know each other all over again." She smiled at him before he turned and got out of the car.

Robert opened her car door and helped her out. He held her hand as they walked up to the front door.

The curtain in the front window moved, which meant Vita had let Mia wait up. The door swung open as they stepped onto the front porch. Mia's tiny body appeared in the doorway.

"Hi, Mama."

Deirdre gave Mia a stern look. "Young lady what are you doing up?"

"Ms. Levine she wouldn't go to bed. I read to her and even laid down with her, but she kept getting up." Vita stood behind Mia and shrugged.

"Okay little lady, go upstairs and wait for me."

"Bye." Mia pouted her lips and gave Robert a sad wave goodbye.

"Bye, Mia. I hope to see you again."

Vita closed the door. Mia peeked through the curtain.

"Thanks for tonight, Robert."

"You're welcome. Why don't you go ahead and plan something for when I get back."

"You sure you don't want to wait?"

"No way, and let Jonathan steal you while I'm gone."

Deirdre balled up her fist, and hit him playfully on the arm. "Stop it. I'm not interested in him."

Robert laughed as he moved closer to Deirdre. "I hope not, because I want you interested in me."

"I am," she said, barely above a whisper. This time when Robert put his arms around Deirdre's waist, she moved closer to him. He kissed her softly on the lips several times, before tilting his head and moving in even closer.

His tongue danced with hers as they explored the newness of each other. Her heart raced and her body temperature rose as she wrapped her arms around his neck. The sweet taste of his mouth and the heat of his body rendered her lost in love. It was happening all over again. She was falling in love with Robert, the man, this time. Deirdre lost herself completely in his embrace, enjoying the kiss she'd been waiting for all her life.

Then she heard the faint sound of a child's giggle. She stopped herself and pulled away.

"What's wrong?" Robert asked.

Deirdre pointed at the two smiling faces pressed against the window. Mia and Vita.

"I see we have an audience." He grabbed Deirdre's hand, and they took a bow.

TWELVE

Robert put his suitcase in the trunk and drove by his mother's house before heading to the airport. When he pulled up, Omar was in the driveway with the hood up on his car.

"What's wrong now?" Robert asked, as he tapped on the hood.

Omar reached inside the car and turned down the radio. "Nothing. I'm just looking her over." He held the dipstick in a rag.

Robert nodded. "So, now you can look for a job, right?"

Omar replaced the dipstick and shook his head. "Is that why you came by here? To make sure I go look for work?"

"No, but I hate to think I got you that battery for nothing. If I knew you weren't going to look for a job, I wouldn't have gotten it."

Omar raised from the hood and released the catch that held it. It slammed shut. Robert stepped back and stared at him.

"Don't worry. I'm going to look for a job, first thing in the morning."

"Got any leads?"

He laughed. "Yeah, I hear they're hiring dishwashers at McDonald's," he joked.

Robert took a piece of paper from his pocket and handed it to Omar. "Here, take this."

"What's that?"

"Take it. I made a few phone calls. Go see these people; they'll be expecting you. And wear a suit."

Omar read the list of names and companies. He shoved the paper in his pocket. "Yeah, I'll check them out."

"Make sure you do, because I'm not fixing another thing on that car. You can fix it yourself from now on."

"I didn't ask you to fix the battery."

"I know you didn't. Mama did." Robert looked toward the house. "Is she home?"

"Nope, she's at church. Probably praying for me," he said with a chuckle.

"I wouldn't doubt it. Man you need to get your act together. What's up with you anyway?" Robert asked.

Omar lowered his head and tossed the rag over on a table. "I'm scared man."

"Scared of what?" Robert saw the sincerity in Omar's eyes. He was coming clean with him.

"I don't know. Myself, responsibilities, you name it."

"Omar looking for work's not going to kill you. There's nothing to be scared of."

"That's easy for you to say. You've always bounced back from anything. I'm not you, man."

"You don't have to be me. Just be yourself and do things at your own pace. But, you can't keep living off mama forever." Robert had sensed Omar was in pain, and he wanted to help him.

"I know, Bernice keeps telling me the same thing. You guys don't have to worry about me, I'm getting myself together."

"How's Bernice doing by the way?" Robert hadn't seen his sister in a long time. He hoped she'd been working on Omar from her end.

"She's fine. She keeps trying to get me to go work at Hercules."

"Why don't you?" he asked, glancing at his watch. He couldn't miss his flight.

Omar shook his head. "That's not for me."

"Look man I gotta run, use those names I gave you, and tell Mama I'll see her in about a week."

"Yeah, okay."

After Robert pulled off, Omar walked into the kitchen and pulled out the piece of paper Robert gave him. He stared at the names on the paper before balling it up and throwing it in the trash.

Wednesday afternoon Deirdre sat in her office reading a letter from the board of directors. The board members came to an agreement to leave the counseling office open for now. She wasn't sure, but she hoped the profile article in the paper had helped persuade them a bit. Robert made her office look like a beacon of success in the community. For once, she was pleased with what he'd written.

Lately, she'd been pleased about everything. She and Robert had talked on the phone twice and she couldn't wait for him to return. The buzz about her break-ins had settled down. Her life was running smooth again.

The phone rang and she let Susan answer it. Her next client was already five minutes late. She hoped the call wasn't a cancellation. Susan knocked on her door.

"Yes?"

The door opened. "Deirdre, it's Belinda."

"Oh, thanks." She picked up the phone. "Hey girl, what's up?"

"I was on my way over for lunch if you don't have other plans?"

"I sure don't. My next client is late, but even if she shows up I'll be free by twelve."

"Okay, I'll see you then. I've got a surprise for you."

Deirdre didn't like surprises. "What is it?" she asked.

"I can't tell you, that's why it's a surprise."

"Belinda, don't you dare try to introduce me to anybody. I mean it."

"Are you kidding, after the way you and Robert hit it off at my party. I wouldn't dream of introducing you to anyone else."

Deirdre smiled at the thought of Robert. What was he doing right now? she wondered. "He's called me twice since he's been out of town."

"Huh, sounds good."

"I still can't believe it's happening. Can you imagine it, Robert Carmichael interested in me?"

"Yes I can. Deirdre you held that man up on a pedestal back in school. He was no different from the other guys there. Believe me, he puts his pants on one leg at a time, like every one else."

"Oh, I know that. You'll never understand what I mean."

"Well, you can explain it to me over lunch. I'll see you at twelve."

"Okay, see you later."

The next phone call was Deirdre's client canceling her appointment because of car trouble. Deirdre read the morning paper instead, while Susan left for an early lunch to meet her new boyfriend.

At exactly twelve o'clock, there was a knock on the front door. Deirdre went to open the door for Belinda.

"You're right on time."

"Of course I am. You ready?"

"Sure, let me grab my purse." She walked back to her office, got her purse, then turned off the light. When she walked back into the reception area, Belinda held up a picture.

"Surprise." She gave it to Deirdre.

Deirdre looked down at it to see her and Robert smiling. They looked like a happy couple. She remembered taking the picture at Belinda's party.

"You like?" Belinda asked when Deirdre didn't say anything.

"It's good isn't it?" Deirdre asked.

"You're damned straight it's good. I took that picture honey." She moved next to Deirdre to see. "I especially like how he turned you sideways into his arms. Girl, you guys look good together. You better not let that man go."

Deirdre looked up at Belinda in surprise. "Let him go! He's not mine. We've gone on one date, and talked on the phone a few times."

"Well, when he comes back, move it to the next stage. Let the man know how much you want him."

"I can't do that."

"Why not? If you don't, I'm sure somebody else will. You know after you left the party several women tried to push up on him. Especially Felisha, with that fake hair all down her back."

Deirdre didn't know what to say. Felisha was a beautiful woman with a great body. Besides, Robert wasn't hers, and she wasn't even sure if she wanted to be involved with somebody right now.

"He's a free man. He can do whatever he likes." Deirdre shrugged.

"Sure, but wouldn't you like for that 'whatever' to be you? Think about that the next time he calls and you're talking to him."

"I'm not going to do that." Deirdre shoved the picture into her purse.

"Don't, I'm sure Felisha would."

Deirdre opened the door and looked back at Belinda. "Get out." They laughed as they left for lunch.

Robert lay in his Florida hotel room thinking about Deirdre. He couldn't get her out of his mind. He hadn't planned to return to Brunswick until Saturday, but he thought about surprising her and returning Friday. Every evening he picked up the phone to call her. A couple times he followed through with the calls. The other times, he'd hang up before dialing all the numbers.

He hadn't felt this way about any woman since his ex-wife. He wanted to take Deirdre places and hold her in his arms. Since dinner Friday night, he'd managed a couple phone calls that only made him want her more.

He picked up the phone to hear her voice one more time. When he looked at the clock on the nightstand, he changed his mind. It wasn't proper to call a woman who lived with her parents at one o'clock in the morning. He rolled over on his back and stared at the ceiling.

* * *

Bright and early the next morning, a dark car sat behind the counseling agency with a clear view of the parking lot. The man inside sat slumped in his seat, flipping through the pages of a file folder. He looked at his watch, then up at the sky. It had begun to rain, and he loved the rain. He put the folder down and opened a small bag he'd carefully prepared this morning. Inside he found a pair of latex gloves and pulled them on. His hands gripped the steering wheel when he saw a small blue car pull into the parking lot.

"Right on time."

Sheila Mitchell pulled up and sat in her car a few minutes. She was still upset with her husband after their fight hours earlier. Brad had demanded that she avoid Deirdre's office after she admitted to frequent visits. He'd raised his voice and slapped her across the face. After she threatened to call the police on him, he apologized. Now, she was late for her appointment. She decided to live her own life despite what Brad said.

After opening the car door, she popped her umbrella into the air. What a rainy, nasty day. When she got to the front door, it was locked. She pressed her hand and face to the glass and tried to see inside. The glass door was a two-way mirror that she barely saw through. The reception desk looked empty. After knocking several times, she figured Deirdre couldn't hear her from her office. She'd run next door to the community center.

In the rain she could hear the sound of a door flapping. When she stepped away from the front door, the sound got louder. The back door was open?

Great. She walked toward the back of the building, and looked down at her wet shoes. She stepped over the puddles alongside the building, and followed the noise. Once inside, she could knock on Deirdre's back door and she would hear that.

The door swung open and she lowered her umbrella to step inside. She placed her umbrella on the mat just inside the room. Shaking off excess water, she pulled the door shut. Everything was dark and quiet. She didn't see anyone in the kitchen area. Only a large stainless-steel room.

"Hello," she called out to whoever had left the door open. Nobody appeared to be around. She hit the light switch on the wall next to her, but it wasn't working.

Feeling extremely uncomfortable back there, she saw the door to Deirdre's office and took off for it.

A man stepped out of the shadows in front of her.

Sheila jumped, looked at his hands and saw the gloves. When she looked at his face, he leered at her.

Deirdre looked down at her watch; she was already fifteen minutes late for work. She hoped Sheila hadn't given up on her. She discovered a flat tire, and had to awaken her father to fix it.

He came back inside shaking the water from his jacket. "I'll take that tire over to Leroy's and get you another one."

"Do you think he can fix it?" Deirdre asked eagerly. She didn't want to have to purchase a new tire.

Fred scratched at his head, then looked at her. "Well Peaches, I don't think Leroy can fix that tire."

"Why not?"

He walked over to the stove and poured himself a cup of coffee. "That tire was punctured."

"What? You're kidding." She walked over and looked out the window at her car. Her father walked over and stood next to her.

"I'm afraid not. There's a hole the size of a quarter on the side of that rear tire."

Deirdre left for work with a funny feeling in the pit of her stomach. Who poked a hole in her tire? She didn't know if it was a random act of violence, or if it had something to do with the office break-ins. She drove according to the weather and her spare tire, which made her arrival at the office even later. Now, she wished Susan hadn't taken a vacation day today.

The minute she pulled into the parking lot, she saw two police cars and an ambulance. *Oh no, what's happened now?* Deirdre jumped out of the car and walked toward the back door to the

An important message from the ARABESQUE Editor

Dear Arabesque Reader,

Because you've chosen to read one of our Arabesque romance novels, we'd like to say "thank you"! And, as a special way to thank you, we've selected four more of the books you love so well to send you absolutely **FREE**!

Please enjoy them with our compliments, and thank you for continuing to enjoy Arabesque...the soul of romance.

Karen R. Thomas

Karen Thomas
Senior Editor,
Arabesque Romance Novels

3 QUICK STEPS
TO RECEIVE YOUR FREE "THANK YOU" GIFT
FROM THE EDITOR

Send back this card and you'll receive 4 Arabesque novels—absolutely free! These books have a combined cover price of $20.00 or more, but they are yours to keep absolutely free.

There's no catch. You're under no obligation to buy anything. We charge nothing for the books—ZERO—for your 4 free books (except $1.50 for shipping and handling). And you don't have to make any minimum number of purchases—not even one!

We hope that after receiving your free books you'll want to remain an Arabesque subscriber. But the choice is yours to continue or cancel, anytime at all! So why not take us up on our invitation to receive your free gift, with no risk of any kind. You'll be glad you did!

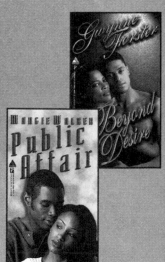

community center. Several center workers stood around with their umbrellas.

"What happened?" Deirdre asked one of the workers.

When he turned around and recognized Deirdre he moved out of her way. "You need to get in there. It's one of your clients."

"What!" She let down her umbrella and stepped through the door. An officer tried to stop her until she told him who she was.

Immediately, Mr. Hamel came up to her. "Deirdre, she's in the rest room. This is the type of thing I was afraid of." He lowered his head as she passed him.

The door to the women's rest room opened. Deirdre ignored Mr. Hamel and went to see who was in there.

"I'm sorry miss. You can't go in there." A police woman put out her arm to stop Deirdre.

"I'm Deirdre Levine, the counselor here. I believe my client is in there."

"Okay." The officer moved her hand and let Deirdre inside.

She saw Sheila sitting on the floor with a blanket wrapped around her body. Visibly shaken, she smoked a cigarette. She looked up as Deirdre walked into the room.

Deirdre's heart broke as she squatted down on the floor next to Sheila. She began to cry and buried her face into Deirdre's chest. The two women held each other and cried until the police-woman walked back into the room.

"Are you okay?" Deirdre asked as she examined Sheila's face. The skin around her left eye had begun to swell and her bottom lip was already fat.

"I'll live." Sheila managed a smile before taking a few more puffs from her cigarette.

"Sheila what happened?"

Her smile turned to a frown. "Well, the front door was locked and it was raining . . ." She stopped for a few deep breaths before continuing.

"I heard the back door swinging in the wind, so I tried to come in the back way. But, when I came in here, this man jumped out

at me. My God, I've never been so scared in all my life Deirdre."
She choked back the tears and continued.

"He grabbed me and pulled me in here. I tried to scream. I
scratched and kicked at him, but it didn't matter. The more I
fought, the more he hit me. Then he raped me." She started to
cry again and couldn't finish.

"I'm so sorry." Guilt consumed Deirdre.

"It's not your fault. I never should have come in the back door
anyhow."

"Did you see him?"

"He had on a mask and gloves. But, I could tell he was black.
He was big. And I think he was young, around twenty-five or
so."

"What makes you think he was young?" Deirdre asked.

"He had a gold tooth like I see the young kids with. And he
had on a raincoat, but he never took it off."

"A raincoat?"

"Yes."

The policewoman walked up and asked Sheila to come with
her. Deirdre promised her she would come down to the police
station when she finished talking to the police.

After Sheila and the policewoman left, Officer Bill Duncan
found Deirdre and asked to have a few words with her.

"Sure, let's go into my office."

He followed her through the kitchen to the back door of her
office. She turned the doorknob, and it was already unlocked.
They went into her office and sat in the chairs across from her
desk.

"I'm surprised the door was unlocked."

"Mr. Hamel may have unlocked it for one of my men." Officer
Duncan shrugged off the fact that the door was opened. Her
office was a part of the center.

"I still can't believe this happened. Who would do that to her?"
Deirdre sat with her arms crossed, shaken and upset at seeing
one of her client's beaten and raped here at her office.

"I don't know. She couldn't give us much of a description, but

I've got a few men working on it. I'll have an officer check out your offices if you don't mind. We examined the front door and it's locked, and hasn't been tampered with. I don't suppose whoever it was got into your office, but we'll just make sure."

"Thank you."

"I know you can't tell me what she was seeing you for, but do you know who or why someone would want to hurt her?"

Deirdre shook her head. "No I don't. Her husband doesn't like her coming here. But, that has nothing to do with this." She wanted to cry again, she felt so bad for Sheila.

"I need to get down to the police station. Sheila needs me." Deirdre stood up.

"Okay, we've about wrapped things up in the back and I'll be heading down to the station also. If you notice anything or think of anything that can help us out, don't hesitate to call." He walked to the door.

"I won't." Deirdre followed him out.

Something a board member mentioned came to mind. "Bill, do you think this is the same guy that committed those rapes here a few years ago?"

"Who told you about that?"

"Someone on the board. They said he was never caught."

"I doubt it. We've had a few rapes in the last five years. They were probably committed by somebody passing through town."

"Oh, well I hope they catch this one."

After Officer Duncan left, Deirdre returned to her desk and flipped open her Rolodex to call and cancel her next few appointments. She had to make the calls before she left for the police station.

She saw a shiny object on the floor and bent down to pick it up. It was a necklace. When she held it up in the air, she recognized it immediately.

She threw the necklace on her desk and dropped the phone.

It was the necklace her grandmother had given her for her tenth birthday. The necklace she'd lost years ago in school. Why was it reappearing after almost 20 years?

THIRTEEN

A frightening sensation moved through Deirdre's body as she saw a vision of a young girl being dragged through the woods. A man held his arm around her neck as she kicked and screamed. She tried to scream louder, but the man put his hand over her mouth almost cutting off her breath. He pulled her deeper into the woods.

The vision left Deirdre gasping for breath. She wore a navy-blue pea coat and a pair of jeans. The coat looked familiar to Deirdre. Something bad had happened to whoever she had the visions of. She looked down at the necklace again.

"Knock, knock," Robert said, as he knocked on the door frame.

Deirdre almost jumped out of her skin at the sound of a man's voice, and knuckles against wood. Gasping she jumped back from her chair holding her hand over her chest.

"Hey." Robert ran over to her side and grabbed her by the arm. "Deirdre, are you okay?" He held a hand on her back and motioned for her to sit down.

She took a couple of deep breaths before speaking. "Yeah, I'm fine," she said between ragged gasps for breath. "You scared me."

Robert kneeled, moving his hand from her arm to her hand. "I'm sorry. I didn't mean to scare you, that's why I knocked." He reached for the beeping phone receiver and replaced it on its base.

Deirdre grabbed a piece of paper from her desk and fanned

herself with it in an attempt to slow her heavy breathing. Looking at Robert, she realized it was Friday and he wasn't even supposed to be in town.

"What are you doing here?"

He stood up and walked around to sit in a chair across from her desk. "I came back early. I wanted to see you."

Any other time she would have been happy and excited to see him. However, this morning she was in a state of shock and wasn't ready for him.

"How did you get in?"

"The door was open." He pointed out toward the hallway.

"No it wasn't. The front doors locked." She had a funny feeling in her stomach.

"Not the front door, the back. When I pulled up, I saw Bill Duncan out back, so I went to see what was going on. He told me one of your clients was assaulted. I'm sorry."

So that explains it. Deirdre felt better. "Yeah, so am I." *And I'm sorry you had to see it. Now I'm sure it'll be in the paper.* Deirdre didn't want to ask him if he was about to print this, because she knew he would. It was his job.

"Is she going to be all right?" he asked in a concerned tone.

"I hope so. I need to go down to the police station now and check on her."

"Where's Susan?"

"She's on vacation today. I was about to call and cancel a few of my appointments when you walked in. But, something distracted me." She looked down at the necklace again. This time she picked it up.

"What's that?" Robert asked.

She held the necklace in the palm of her hand, then made a fist. "It's a necklace I found." She reached across the desk for her purse and put the necklace inside.

"Robert, I've got to make these calls so I can get out of here."

He stood up. "Okay look. I'm going to be outside. When you finish, come on out and I'll take you down to the police station. You look a little shaken, and I don't think you should be driving.

"Okay, thanks."

After Robert left the room, Deirdre called all her clients and canceled their appointments for the day. She wasn't emotionally able to help anyone today. She threw her head back and took a deep breath. Before she saw Sheila, she had to get herself together.

How did that necklace get into her office? The minute she saw it, she recognized it. The chain had dulled over the years, but the blue pear-shaped stone looked the same. Someone had gotten into her office between yesterday evening when she left for work, and this morning.

Something Bill Duncan said a while back, rang in her ear the moment she saw Robert. He always showed up when they had trouble. Now, here he was, when he was supposed to be out of town. Why had he come to her office this morning even if he did come back early? She grabbed her purse and decided to ask him on the way to the police station.

Robert and Deirdre talked as he drove. The police station wasn't far from the Riverfront.

"Deirdre, I'm sorry I scared you earlier, but I tried to surprise you by coming back early. Instead, I got surprised."

"Well, under normal circumstances, it would have been a great surprise. It's just that I'm worried about Sheila. Her husband is going to go crazy." Deirdre rested her elbow on the armrest and massaged her forehead.

"It's not her fault, why would he be so upset?"

"You don't understand. He doesn't want her coming to my office."

"Why not?"

She looked at Robert. That was confidential information she couldn't share. "I don't know." She laid her head back on the headrest. "I can't believe this is happening. Am I going crazy, or is someone out to get me? I don't understand it."

"Maybe this had nothing to do with you. It could be a coincidence that it happened at the center."

She laughed. "Yeah right. It's a coincidence that he dragged

her through the same door the thief came through. I don't think
so."

They pulled into the police station parking lot. Robert turned
off the motor and placed his arm on the seat facing Deirdre.
"Want me to go inside with you?"

"If you want to," she said.

He looked up at the station and turned around in his seat. "I'll
wait out here. I've got a few calls to make, anyway. But, when
you get finished, I'll be here waiting for you."

"Okay." Deirdre got out of the car and glanced back at Robert.
He pulled out his cellular phone, then a pad out of his jacket
pocket.

There he goes, calling the paper to let them know about the
assault. He had to make sure he got that in the paper. The mere
thought of him doing that made her mad. She didn't want him
to wait for her. She didn't want to get into the car with him again.

When Deirdre entered the police station, she didn't see Sheila,
so she went straight to the front desk.

"May I help you?" the front desk officer asked.

"Yes. I'm looking for Sheila Mitchell. She came in not too
long ago."

"Let's see. Sheila Mitchell." A middle-aged officer looked
over a list on his desk. "No Sheila Mitchell." He didn't seem
concerned that the name wasn't there.

"But, she just came in. She was assaulted at the Brunswick
Community Center this morning."

"Oh, that lady. Yeah well, her husband picked her up a few
minutes ago."

"He what?"

"He came and got her. You can speak to Officer Leigh if you
want. She brought her in."

"Yes, may I speak to her?"

"Sure, hold on." He picked up the phone and made a phone
call.

Deirdre looked around the station. This was her first time in the Brunswick police station, but the room gave her that déjà vu feeling. It was quiet, like she pictured a small-town police station would be.

"Okay, miss."

She turned around eager to talk to someone about Sheila.

"Go down the hall here and make a left. It'll be the first door on your right." He pointed in the direction.

"Thank you." She found Officer Leigh's name on the door and knocked.

"Come in."

Deirdre went inside and remembered Officer Leigh from the center this morning.

"Ms. Levine, we had a hard time getting Mrs. Mitchell to give us information. She called her husband the minute we got here. Once he showed up, she didn't want to talk anymore. We have a few details. I had to insist that he take her to the hospital for an examination. He wanted to take her home."

"Really?" Deirdre was shocked. Sheila's husband was upset; but could he be so upset he wouldn't want his wife checked out? The more she learned about that man the more she disliked him.

"Did you get a description of the man?" Deirdre asked.

"Partially. The description she gave is so generic, it could be any black male in Brunswick. All she saw was his eyes and mouth through the mask. Nothing really to go on."

"That's too bad."

"Yes it is. We understand it was kind of dark. All she could really remember was the way he laughed at her. She said it made her skin crawl."

Deirdre left the police station confused and concerned. She wished she'd been there for Sheila, instead of her husband. From their conversations, he didn't appear to be such a pleasant man. Deirdre hoped she was all right.

She walked back out to the parking lot and found Robert leaning against his car waiting for her. Reporters, she hated them. Why did he have to be a reporter? No matter what was going on, he always had to get his story. If she didn't have to go back to her car, she wouldn't ride back with him.

As she approached the car, he turned and smiled at her. "That was quick, is she okay?"

"She's gone."

"Gone. Where to?"

"Her husband picked her up." She opened the car door and got inside. Robert did the same.

"I thought you said she was hurt pretty bad?" he asked with a puzzled expression.

"She was. I don't understand it either, but her husband came and got her. The police insisted that he take her to a hospital. So, I guess that's where they've gone."

"Did she give a good description of the guy?"

Deirdre didn't like him asking all those questions. She hoped he wasn't trying to use her again. He was smooth, but she wouldn't be had a second time.

"I'm sorry, but you'll have to get your information another way. I'm not going to give you all the details for this article. You've used me once, and I won't let you do it again."

Robert started the car and turned on the air conditioner. He glanced at Deirdre as he pulled out of the police station. "What gave you that idea? I asked because I know how concerned you are about your client."

"Sure you are. Is that why you were on the phone calling in your report? I bet this story will be in the morning paper with all the information I've given you so far." Upset, she crossed her arms and looked out the window. How could he take advantage of such a tragedy?

Robert pulled his car over out of traffic and put it in park. He reached over and touched Deirdre on the arm. She pulled away from him still looking out the window.

"I know you think reporters are leeches, but I haven't called anyone to turn in a story. When you got out of the car, I called my service to check my messages, that's all. When I got off the plane this morning, I grabbed my car and came straight to your office. Believe it or not, I couldn't wait to see you."

Deirdre's eyes lowered to her lap. Maybe she was being too hard on him. After all, she had missed him.

"Now don't tell me you're mad at me?" He reached out and tucked a loose strand of hair behind her ear. "Are you?"

She cut her eyes up at him. "I'm not mad at you. This has just got me shaken up a bit that's all. And I hadn't expected to see you today. So, when you walked in, it reminded me of the break-ins." Deirdre was on the verge of tears. She fought to hold them back.

Robert slid his arm along the back of her seat and massaged her shoulders. He unfastened his seat belt and leaned over to kiss her on the cheek. "My only concern was you."

She took a deep breath and looked up at him. "Why did you really come back early?"

"I told you, to see you. A couple of phone calls weren't enough. I took a six-thirty flight this morning."

"And you came straight to my office?"

"Yes I did. Now, have I been cleared of any wrongdoings?" He smiled at Deirdre and raised his brows waiting for an answer.

She nodded. "I guess so. I don't mean to be so rude." She looked down and played with the ring on her finger. "But, you understand. After last time I have to be a little more cautious, and right now I'm a bundle of nerves."

Robert leaned back in his seat and refastened his seatbelt. "I know exactly what you need." He started the car and pulled back out into traffic.

"What?" Deirdre asked sitting up in her seat.

"You'll see." Robert turned and winked at her.

He missed the turn that would have led back to her office.

"I don't know where we're going, but I really do need to get back to my office."

"Why?"

"I need to check on Sheila. I've got to at least call her house and try to talk to her."

"You said her husband was taking her to the hospital, right?"

"I hope so."

"Well, that should take a while. In the meantime, we need to take care of Deirdre. There's no hurry. You've canceled your appointments for the day. Trust me, I've got something that will relax you. And you'll have plenty of time to call Sheila before the day's over."

Robert pulled into a new subdivision full of beautifully manicured homes. Deirdre would love to have one of these homes as soon as she got her money straight.

She couldn't get her mind off the necklace she'd found. She looked at Robert. Could he have put it there?

"Where are you taking me?" she asked.

"Somewhere so you can relax and pull yourself together."

"I'm okay now. I really need to get back to work," she said anxiously.

He pulled into the driveway of a farmhouse-styled home. He clicked the remote over the visor, and the garage door opened.

"Don't worry, this is my house and we won't stay long." He pulled into the garage and turned off the motor.

Deirdre unfastened her seat belt and opened the door to get out. Robert reached for her hand to help her out of the car. He closed the door, then went to retrieve his luggage from the trunk.

"Come on in and make yourself at home."

She followed him into the house. They entered a vaulted area with shelves and books galore. She didn't know Robert was such an avid reader.

"Wow, look at all these books. I didn't know you read so much."

"They were my wife's." He kept walking into the kitchen.

Deirdre bit her lower lip not sure how to respond. He never talked about his deceased wife.

She walked into a country-style kitchen that was nice and simple. His dining table set on an antique-looking area rug. The table had a maple finish with black metal-base chairs. There was a nice floral centerpiece in the middle and a baker's rack sitting against the wall. And she loved the hardwood floor.

"Your kitchen is nice," Deirdre complemented before sitting down.

Robert set his briefcase on the table while he took off his sports coat. He threw it across the back of a chair. "Thanks. I don't cook much, so it kind of stays like this. Looks somewhat unlived in, I know."

He walked over and turned the stove on, then filled the teakettle with water. "I hope you like tea."

"Yes, I do." He had on a short-sleeve shirt and Deirdre checked out his arms. Where was the home gym, because this guy definitely worked out.

"Great." When he returned to the kitchen table, he picked up his suitcase. "I'll be right back."

"Okay." A few seconds later, she heard Robert run up the stairs.

Deirdre leaned back into one of the fanback chairs, but didn't find it too comfortable. The chair she'd sat in had her facing the window. She decided she didn't want her back to the hallway, so she got up. Her intention was to change chairs, but she found herself walking into his empty dining room. The huge naked bay windows served as a great light source. His house was unusually cold.

She walked straight into the living room. "So this is where he spends all his time," she said aloud.

The first thing she noticed was the entertainment center with its built-in wide-screen television. "How nice," she said, as she walked up and examined the contents of the shelves. He had rows and rows of CDs. His music collection. He was correct, his collection was big.

Directly behind her was a nice big, black leather couch and two chairs. Unlike the kitchen, this room looked more lived in. He'd left a tray of dishes on the cocktail table and papers were all over the couch. At least the glass on the end table was on a coaster.

"I guess you can tell where I like to eat." Robert walked into the room and picked up the tray. He carried it into the kitchen and returned.

"Like most men. In front of the television," Deirdre said when he returned.

"Yeah. Do you want to see the rest of the house?"

Slightly embarrassed, she said, "Sorry, I got a little cooped up in there."

"No problem. Come on I'll show you the upstairs." He walked out into the foyer.

Deirdre watched him and wondered what she was getting herself into. She shook it off, and told herself this was the same Robert she'd been talking to for the last few days. Throughout the week she'd often wished he were there, and now here he was.

"Come on, your tea will be ready in a minute."

She crossed her arms to cut the chill of the room, then followed him upstairs to the second floor.

"I turned the air down. Sorry it's so cold. I forgot to lower the thermostat before I left town."

"That's okay."

At the top of the stairs Robert walked down the hall and stood back as Deirdre peeked into both rooms. "These are spare bedrooms." One was a guest bedroom, but the other was full of boxes.

"What's this room for?"

"It's my junk room. I've got lots of old things I'm not sure what to do with. I'm somewhat of a pack rat." He shrugged, then turned in the opposite direction and she followed him.

"This is my home office." He pointed to a small open area.

She saw a computer. "Are you on the Internet?"

"Yes I am."

She liked his office. "That's nice. I'm surprised you didn't turn a bedroom into an office instead of this open area."

"I don't like the closed-in feeling of an office. The Realtor called this the reading area. I saw perfect office space."

"And here we have the master bedroom." Robert walked into his bedroom.

Deirdre stared at the computer thinking of the strange message she'd gotten one night. When she turned around Robert had walked into his bedroom. She stood in the doorway and looked in, but didn't want to go inside.

"Yes, this is really nice." One look at his king-size bed made Deirdre want to run from this room. His bedroom was too intimate of a place for her right now.

"Do you think that tea's ready?"

"I'm sure it is, come on." They left the bedroom and went back downstairs into the kitchen.

"Okay, I want you to let this steep a few minutes, then sip it slowly." Robert dipped a tea bag into the mug he filled with hot water. He walked over to the kitchen table and set it in front of Deirdre.

"What kind of tea is this?"

"It's an herb tea. Trust me, it'll help you relax. I used to drink it all the time."

Deirdre blew on her tea to cool it off. She took a few sips and felt the hot liquid run down her chest. She couldn't believe that she was sitting in Robert's kitchen in the middle of the day.

"You know, every time something dramatic happens at work, you're there."

"Lucky me." He shrugged.

"And the last time I was stressed out, you came to my rescue and carried me to breakfast. Or, I thought that's what you were doing. What do you want, the inside story on Sheila and who I think raped her?"

Robert got up and grabbed a soda from the refrigerator. "You know Deirdre, I did that because I was concerned about you." He returned to the table. "And this morning, you should have seen your face when I walked into your office. You looked like you'd seen a ghost."

She had. Deirdre sipped more of her tea. "You startled me, that's all."

"Well you looked more than startled to me." He stood up and reached out for Deirdre's hand. "Come on, bring your tea."

She looked up at him. "Where to?"

"The living room. The chairs are more comfortable in there."

She stood up and took his hand, balancing her mug in the other hand. He held her mug as she sat down on the couch, then he sat right next to her. Her body tensed as she reached for her mug.

Robert grabbed the remote control off the coffee table and turned the television on. He flipped through several stations until he found something he thought Deirdre might want to watch.

He wasn't sure why he'd brought her to his house other than the fact that he wanted to be close to her. The minute he walked into the kitchen, he thought of the tea. Luckily, he still had some in the cabinet. For the last several days he'd thought of nothing but Deirdre. But when he saw her today he didn't like the way she looked. When he walked into her office and heard the phone beeping and the terrified expression on her face, he thought someone had hurt her.

She'd been acting strange all morning. He hadn't kissed her once, and he had the feeling she didn't feel comfortable around him. He wanted to know what had happened since he talked to her last.

"So did you miss me while I was gone?" He broke the silence between them.

Deirdre nodded. "Yes I did."

"You don't act like it. I'm offended." He pretended to pout.

"Robert I'm sorry. This morning just threw me off. I was upset, and then you walked in. I was really glad to see you, but also so concerned about Sheila." She set her mug on the coffee table. The hot liquid had helped to make her feel more relaxed. "I didn't mean to make it seem like I wasn't glad to see you."

"That's good to hear. Especially after all I went through to get back here early." Robert wrapped his arm around Deirdre's shoulders and pulled her closer to him.

All she could think about was the last time he kissed her. Every time he called, she relived that kiss all over again. Deirdre willingly moved closer to Robert, and rested her body against his.

He leaned over and planted a small kiss on the top of her head. She looked up into his eyes and watched them move closer as he planted another soft kiss on her forehead.

"I broke my neck getting back here to do just this." He kissed the tip of her nose.

"And I'm glad you did." Her stomach tingled and her body quivered at his touch. She initiated the next kiss. Her body craved him and she couldn't control it.

His lips found hers, his tongue found hers and her heart began to race. Deirdre found her arm wrapped around his body and couldn't control the thirst she had for him. Her jacket slid over her shoulders and she helped him by wiggling her arms out. Once her jacket was off, she was free to put her other arm around him. They embraced and held each other close.

Robert pulled back, and ran his hands up and down Deirdre's arms. "You still cold?"

"Not anymore."

"Then maybe I should turn the air conditioner back up. I'm on fire." His lips met hers again and their tongues danced as he caressed her body. He managed to get up on one knee and put his hands behind her back. He lowered her onto the couch.

Deirdre let her body relax into Robert's hold, and felt his hands on her back. His lips never left hers, and she kept her arms around his body. As he lowered her onto the couch, his hands moved up to her neck.

His hand sliding around her neck woke ever nerve in her body. She pulled her lips away from his and turned her head. In one swift motion she pushed him away and kicked her feet out from under her simultaneously.

"No!" she cried out.

FOURTEEN

"Girl, I know he thinks I'm crazy, but I couldn't help it. The minute he touched my neck, I wanted to scream. I had this flash of some man standing over me trying to hurt me."

"What did he do?" Belinda asked.

"It wasn't clear. He just stood over me."

"No, I mean Robert. What did he do?"

"Oh, he raised up and apologized. I felt so bad. It wasn't his fault, but I didn't know how to explain it to him. All I could say was that I have this weird thing about my neck, and I don't like to be touched there."

Deirdre and Belinda had taken their children to the park for a swim. They watched the children play while Deirdre told Belinda about her first visit to Robert's house.

"Are you sure he wasn't trying to get more than a kiss?" Belinda asked skeptically.

Deirdre shook her head and kept her eyes on Mia in a wading pool. "No way. All he did was kiss me, and I freaked out. And that wasn't the first time. I did the same thing at your pool party."

"Well, maybe it had something to do with your client being attacked that same day. He never should have tried to kiss you under the circumstances anyway."

"That's what he said. He apologized a zillion times. But I still felt like a fool. Girl, I wanted that kiss maybe more than he did."

"How's your client?"

"I haven't talked to her yet. When I called, her husband said she was asleep. He didn't want her to talk to me, and told me to forget about her returning to my office."

"That's too bad." Belinda responded, and shook her head.

"Yeah, but I feel like I need to speak to her. I need to make sure she gets help after this. Being raped is a very traumatic experience. She needs to talk to somebody whether it's me are not."

"The police should steer her to the rape crisis center, shouldn't they?"

"Yes, but her husband is such a trip. He might not let her go." Deirdre walked over to the edge of the wading pool. She ran her hand along the water looking at her reflection. *What's wrong with me?*

"So much for my fantasies about Robert Carmichael," she said unhappily.

Belinda walked over and stood next to her. "Quit beating yourself up about it. I'm sure he didn't think anything of it. He probably thought you didn't want him to rush you into anything." She squatted next to Deirdre.

"Sounds like you've got the beginning of a great relationship, as long as he doesn't touch your neck." They stood as the children ran toward them.

That night Deirdre tossed and turned in bed. She heard the faint sounds of a little girl crying. Her soft whimpers muffled by a body. Someone was on top of this little girl hurting her. Deirdre looked down at the children laying on the cold ground. Her body floated above them across the sky. She couldn't see their faces. And she couldn't do anything to help. Her outstretched arms struggled to reach out and help the child.

The child's bloody face turned toward Deirdre.

She jumped up on one elbow gasping for breath. The cries she heard as she lay in the dark bedroom were coming from her. She'd been crying in her sleep again. Her eyes scanned the room quickly to confirm she was alone. She sat up and looked over at the bedside clock. Three o'clock in the morning, and she'd never get back to sleep.

She laid back down and closed her eyes, trying to go back to sleep. She had to get up for church in the morning. Why did she keep dreaming about those children? She had dreamed about the same children when she found her necklace.

Sunday morning Deirdre started to ask her mother about the necklace, but changed her mind. In all these years her mother hadn't once mentioned her losing the necklace. Until she had a better feel for how it got there, she decided to keep her mouth shut.

Robert stopped at the mall on his lunch break to pick up his shoes. He'd wanted to run by Deirdre's office and take her to lunch, but decided against it. He wasn't quite sure she'd want to see him after Friday morning.

Every time he tried to get close to her, she pushed him away. Under normal circumstances, he figured she would have been excited to see him. However, the drama of the morning cast a shadow over his return. He never should have kissed her, but he couldn't help himself. He couldn't wait to get back and be with her. And he had hoped the feeling was mutual.

Walking out of the mall, Robert ran into Officer Bill Duncan and another officer.

"Well, if it isn't our friend, Mr. Carmichael," Bill said, and smirked.

"Hello, gentlemen, how are you this afternoon?" Robert asked.

"Fine, fine. You know we were just discussing the Brunswick Counseling Agency, and your name came up."

"Is that so?" Robert narrowed his eyes at Bill.

"Yeah, there's just one thing that bothers me, and maybe you can help me with it."

"What's that?" Robert knew Bill couldn't speak and leave him be.

"The other morning at the counseling center, you just happened to show up again. How do you suppose that happened?" He pulled down his sunglasses and looked at Robert over the rim.

"I told you, I'd just gotten back in town and wanted to see Deirdre. Do we have to go over this again?" he asked frustrated.

"Yeah, that's what you said."

Robert wanted to take this man's nightstick and shove it down his throat. This petty hatred between them had to stop. "Bill, what do you really want to ask me? Go ahead, get it off your chest?"

Officer Duncan pushed his glasses back up his nose. "Seems like I read somewhere about a woman dying in a car accident before you moved here."

The other officer cut in. "Come on Bill, everybody knows that was an accident," he said, in an unsympathetic tone.

"Yeah, but it's mighty funny Robert managed to walk away and his wife was thrown head first . . ."

Robert lunged at Bill, and not caring if he was a police officer or not. He was furious.

"Hey, man. Don't do nothing crazy." The other officer grabbed Robert and stopped him from making a terrible mistake.

Robert's fist missed Bill's chin by a few inches. Bill never flinched.

He sucked his teeth, and glanced past Robert at other people leaving the mall. The look he gave Robert said, stay out of my way.

"You're not a suspect—yet! But one more stunt like that, and your name goes at the top of my list."

Robert laughed and shook his head. "Man, this is ridiculous and you know it. I'm a reporter. I've been over there doing my job, the same as you."

"Yeah, looks like more than your job to me."

"Bill, I know you and I don't see eye-to-eye on everything, but I resent these questions. If you think I had something to do with any of this, charge me. If not, leave me the hell alone and let me do my job." Bill's accusations could blow up and cause Robert his job. His career would be over.

"Just be careful not to get in the way of my investigation," Bill said, as he walked passed Robert into the mall. The other officer followed him.

Robert could have put his fist through a wall at that moment. What could have given Bill the idea that Robert had anything to do with any of this?

From the day he mentioned sloppy police work in one of his articles, Bill had given him a hard time. Now, it seemed as if Bill didn't like to see him with Deirdre as well. Maybe Bill had feelings for her. Robert knew he'd have to keep his eye on Bill from now on. There was no way he'd let them pin any of this on him.

On his ride back to work he almost ran a red light. He slammed on the brakes and missed another car by a few inches. The driver yelled something out the window at him, but Robert had his air conditioner on and never heard him. He shook his head and tried to clear his thoughts and concentrate on making it back to work.

Deirdre was in her office Monday morning when Susan came in. At the sound of the door unlocking, Deirdre prepared herself for all Susan's questions.

Susan quietly walked into Deirdre's office. "Good morning Deirdre. What are you doing here so early?"

"Morning Susan. I came in early to check the recorder and get a jump-start on the day. I guess you heard what happened?"

Susan dropped into the seat across from Deirdre's desk. "Yes, I started to call you over the weekend. The paper didn't mention who the woman was—who was she?"

"Sheila."

"Oh no. I'm so sorry that happened. Did you talk to her?"

"For a little while. After she went down to the police station I never saw her again. Her husband picked her up, and you know how he feels about me."

"So you haven't heard from her all weekend?"

"No. I can only assume that she's holding up. I've tried to call, but her husband won't let me talk to her."

"Deirdre, that is so sad. Boy, I take one day off and all hell breaks loose. If I'd been here, maybe this wouldn't have happened."

"Don't do that. I've beat myself up enough about it. I had a flat tire Friday morning, which delayed me from getting in on time."

"Isn't that weird?"

"Actually, my father said someone punctured my tire." Deirdre added.

"Did you tell the police?"

Deirdre bit her lip and thought about the coincidence of her flat again. "No, I hadn't thought about it until now. But you know, that is weird. Maybe I should mention it to Officer Bill."

"Yes, I think you should. Maybe somebody didn't want you to come in early that morning. Maybe they wanted Sheila."

"But how did they know that you weren't going to be here? You just decided to take a vacation day the day before."

Susan crossed her arms and pondered the thought. "That's right. They couldn't have known I wouldn't be here." She shrugged, then added, "So maybe it was a coincidence. But, I'd still tell the police."

"I think I will."

Knock, knock, knock. A soft knock at the back door got their attention. Susan stood up and looked at Deirdre. "I guess I should get that?" she said in a nervous tone.

"It's probably just Alfred. You know he's the only one who comes in through that door."

"Yeah, you're right. What am I worried about?" She laughed off her nervous feelings and went to open the door.

"Morning. I came to get your trash." Alfred held out a large white garbage bag.

"Sure, come on." Susan stood aside and let him in. She returned to Deirdre's office while Alfred went into the front office.

"It's him. He came to dump the trash." Susan sat back down.

"He usually does that after hours." Deirdre frowned, and thought maybe he came for something else.

Alfred knocked on her door. "Excuse me, but I came to get your trash."

Deirdre pulled her trash can from under her desk. "Hi Alfred. Why are you collecting trash this morning, don't you usually do that after hours?"

"Yes ma'am. I was on vacation all last week. One of the guys next door collected it for me, but he didn't work Friday. So, I figured I'd better get it before it builds up. Mr. Hamel doesn't like trash to build up." He dumped Deirdre's trash into his larger bag and gave it back to her.

"You're serious about your trash aren't you Alfred?" Susan asked laughing.

Alfred turned and smiled at her. "I'm serious about my job." Before he walked out of the office, he looked back at Deirdre. "I'm sorry to hear about your client. We're going to change the lock on the back door. Looks like somebody lost their keys, or had some made."

"Thanks Alfred, that's good to know." She listened as he walked down the hallway and closed the door behind him. Susan had a smug look on her face.

"I don't trust that man. He might be the rapist for all we know. He wasn't here. Did they check him out?"

"I don't think he could have done it."

"Why not?"

"The man who raped Sheila was black."

Susan had crossed her legs and rocked her top leg at a speed that made her look nervous. "Maybe he had nothing to do with raping her, but I bet he's the one who broke in here." She jumped up from her seat and straightened out her suit coat.

"Well, we'll have to wait and see what the police find out on that."

Knock, knock, knock. Now someone knocked at the front door. "I guess it's time to get started." Susan left the office to answer the front door.

"Where is Deirdre?" Mr. Hamel bolted his way inside the office, right past Susan.

"She's in her office. I'm sure she's available to see you," she said as he ignored her.

The minute Deirdre heard his voice, her stomach fluttered. She didn't want to start her morning this way, but she knew he'd show up eventually.

"Ms. Levine, can I have a word with you?" Mr. Hamel stood in the doorway.

Deirdre stood up and motioned to a chair across from her desk. "Sure, come on in and close the door."

He closed the door and took a seat across from her desk. She watched as he squeezed his big behind into one of her chairs. He shifted in his seat and crossed his ankle over his knee.

"First, I want to reiterate how sorry I am about what happened to your client."

"Thank you." *But what,* Deirdre thought. There was always a but. He didn't come in here to tell her he was sorry.

"But, this is the type of thing I was afraid of. I don't know what's going on, but we've got to do something about it. First the break-ins, now a rape; who knows what's next. Until this person is caught we seriously need to consider closing this office."

"Mr. Hamel I understand your feelings, believe me I do. However, I still don't think we should close the office. If anything, the police need to beef up their investigation. You can't cut off all my other clients because of this."

"Ms. Levine, I think you keep forgetting that your office is connected to a community center. This place is a haven for children of all ages. Children with concerned and worried parents. These children have to be our first concern."

"Yes, I understand that. And to some extent I agree with you. But, this is not like something out of the movies, where a serial killer is stalking and killing my clients. I've had two break-ins, which probably had nothing to do with my clients. This rape may be an isolated case."

"Ms. Levine, I don't quite care how you see it. I'm the one who has to answer to these parents, not you."

"I know that, and I understand how difficult this has made things. But . . ."

He jumped in and cut her off. "You know, I never liked the idea of having a counseling office so close to the children. I suggested we lease the space to a real-estate broker who had big plans for this area. And now I don't mind saying, I wish the board had listened to me."

Deirdre wanted to pull out her hair. If she heard him say that one more time, she might consider committing murder. "Yes, Mr. Hamel, everybody knows how you feel about my office. I'll tell you what. Give me a week or so to talk with the police, before you make any decisions."

"What do you need to talk to the police for?"

"I want to see what leads they have, and if they're close to catching someone." She stood up and walked around her desk to the door. "If they don't have any leads maybe we'd better close the office. Can I let you know what they say in about a week?"

He uncrossed his leg and stood up. "I suppose that's fair. Of course, we'll have to discuss this at our next board meeting. But, I think it looks better if we all come to an agreement on closing the office, instead of us asking you."

"I agree." She wanted him up and out of her office as fast as he could wobble his fat butt through the door. Right now she would agree to anything to see him disappear.

"So we'll talk again in about a week or so," he confirmed.

"Yes, I'll get back with you. Thank you for stopping by." Deirdre closed the door behind him. She returned to her desk and sat down. Furious, she slammed her fist down on the desk. What had she ever done to that man to make him hate her so? He was probably glad about this latest disaster. And, it wouldn't surprise her to find out he was behind the whole thing.

She sat back and thought about everything for a few minutes. How could someone rape Sheila in the rest room with community staff members at work? No one heard her scream or call out for help?

Deirdre worked all day long, thinking about the necklace, and how it got into her office. Either the man who raped Sheila put it there, or it was someone who worked for the center and had the key to her office. When she got ready to leave at the end of the day she had an uneasy feeling. She promised herself to call Officer Duncan and let him know about the tire, and the necklace. Maybe it did have something to do with the break-ins and the rape.

She let Susan leave before her. On her way out of her office she placed a small piece of tissue paper in her office door as she closed it. If someone was sneaking in after hours, she wanted to know. Tomorrow when she opened that door, the piece of paper should fall to the floor.

FIFTEEN

Deirdre came in early the next morning so she could be the first one into her office. When she opened the door she watched for the tissue paper to fall, and it did. Confident no one had been in her office, she went inside.

It was so early, she thought she'd try to call Sheila again. Maybe her husband would be gone to work. She hadn't been able to catch her yet.

The phone rang five times before Deirdre started to hang up. Suddenly, she heard a man's voice.

"Hello."

Oh no, Sheila's husband was home. "Hello, Mr. Mitchell, this is Deirdre Levine again. I was hoping I could talk to Sheila for a minute."

"She's asleep," he said harshly.

Deirdre sighed. "Okay. Well, when she wakes will you tell her I called."

"Yeah, I'll let her know, but I told you she's not coming back down there."

"Mr. Mitchell I understand. I just want to talk to her for a minute, and make sure she's all right."

"Of course she's not all right. She was raped! She'll never be all right." The phone went dead.

Deirdre held the receiver back and stared at it. That man was impossible. He made her feel so guilty, yet there wasn't anything she could do. She couldn't talk to Sheila, or refer her to someone else.

She hung up the phone and told herself to get on with her day.

* * *

Robert finally got up the nerve to call Deirdre. He hoped everything was okay, because he wanted to see her again. She had the whole weekend to decide if she wanted to see him.

When she came to the phone, her voice sounded like music to his ears.

"Hello."

"Hey baby. How you doing?"

"I'm better. Things are still crazy, but I'm holding up."

"How was your day?" he asked cheerfully.

"Don't ask."

"That bad, huh?"

"Let's just say I may be looking for a new job soon."

"Want to talk about it?" He looked at his watch and wondered if she'd think eight o'clock was too late to see him.

"Actually, I could use somebody to talk to right now."

"Want me to come pick you up?"

"Let me put Mia to bed, and I'll be ready."

Robert couldn't believe his ears. "Okay, I'm on my way over. We can have a nightcap." He wanted to get over there before she changed her mind.

Twenty minutes later, Deirdre opened the front door and let Robert in. He looked equally as good in his casual wear as he did in a suit.

"I'm not too early am I?" he asked eagerly.

"No. I just put Mia to bed, let me grab my purse." She ran upstairs.

Her mother met her at the top of the stairs.

"Going out with Robert again?" Anna asked.

"Yes. We're going to run out for a nightcap. I promise I won't be long. Mia's in the bed and she shouldn't cause you any trouble." Deirdre walked into the bedroom with her mother in tow.

"Oh, she's no trouble. And take your time. You don't have to rush back on me and Daddy's account. We'll be going to bed pretty soon anyway. You've got your key."

Deirdre kissed her mother on the cheek as she left the bedroom. "Thanks Mama. I really need to get out for a bit tonight. I need to talk things over with someone, you know?"

"I know, honey." When Deirdre walked off, Anna reached out and grabbed her arm.

"Yeah?" She stopped.

"Honey, be careful. I know how you feel about him. And I know how long you've felt that way."

Deirdre had no idea her mother was aware of her crush on Robert. "How did you know?"

"When you mentioned his name, I remembered you talking about him in high school. Just watch yourself."

Deirdre shook her head. However her mother knew about him, she bet her sister, Barbara told her. All Deirdre remembered doing was writing about him in her diary. She never mentioned her crush to anyone at the time.

They shared a smile.

"I'll be fine Mama."

When Deirdre returned to the living room, Anna was right behind her. They entered the foyer where Robert stood.

"Hello Mrs. Stanley," Robert greeted her mother.

"Hello Robert, nice to see you again."

"You, too."

"Well, I won't be too late tonight Mama." Robert held the door open for Deirdre.

"Oh, I'm not worried. You're a big girl."

Deirdre turned and smiled at her mother. She did know how Deirdre felt about Robert.

Robert opened the car door for Deirdre and helped her inside. When he got into the car, she had a huge smile on her face that she couldn't wipe off.

He smiled back and asked, "What you smiling about?"

"Oh, nothing." How could she tell him what was running through her mind.

He shook his head and pulled off.

"I'm really glad you called when you did," she confessed.

"Yeah, me, too. I thought we'd go to Applebee's and have a drink. Is that okay with you?"

"Sure, that's fine. I need to unwind a little."

When they pulled into Applebee's parking lot, it was full.

"Wow, where did all these cars come from? They must be having something in town tonight." Deirdre hadn't seen Applebee's lot full since she'd been in town.

Robert snapped his fingers. "Damn, that's right. The music festival is going on this week." He glanced at his watch. "It's probably still going on. Do you want to go to try and catch the last act?" He asked as he rode through the lot and headed back out.

"Not really." Deirdre laid her head back on the headrest. "All I want to do is have a drink and chill." She looked at Robert. "You know what I mean."

Robert had to remind himself to breathe. She looked so seductive laying back looking at him. He smelled her floral perfume tickling his nostrils. She smelled and looked wonderful.

"Robert?" Deirdre called out when he didn't answer her.

He blinked to clear his thoughts. "I'm sorry, I just had an idea."

"What?"

"Let's stop and get something to drink, then ride by my house. I can put on a little jazz music and we can make our own atmosphere. How about it?" After her last visit to his house, he didn't think she'd say yes.

She raised her head. "That sounds nice. But I can't stay too long, I've got to get up early tomorrow."

"Great. My place is better than Applebee's anyway." He pulled out of the restaurant lot, and headed to the nearest liquor store for a bottle of wine.

Once inside the house, he poured each of them a glass of wine and they moved into the living room. Robert put on a Branford Marsalis CD and sat next to Deirdre on the couch.

"Robert can I ask you something?" Deirdre set her glass of wine on the cocktail table.

"Yes, anything," he responded eagerly.

"You're not playing reporter tonight are you?"

He sighed and sat back on the couch. "Deirdre, I just want to be here for you. My professional association with you ended that day on the beach when I kissed you. It's personal now. You don't have to worry about anything you say to me being printed."

"Thank you." She smiled.

"I know you're going through a rough time. Maybe I can do something to help, who knows."

She picked up her wineglass, but he stopped her from drinking.

"Hold on, let's have a toast." He picked up his glass.

"To what?" she asked, holding up her glass.

They touched glasses. "To renewed friendship, and a new beginning."

She repeated his words and they toasted. Could this be the beginning of a new relationship? The thought was too much for her to believe.

After a few sips of wine, she set her glass down again. "You know, I don't know what's going to happen next. It seems like once a week I get a little surprise at work. Anything else, and I know they're going to shut the office down."

"Has it gotten that bad?"

She looked up. "Yes. And I know Bill Duncan is doing his best to solve the case."

"Huh." Robert snorted and took a few sips of wine. "I wouldn't put too much faith in him if I were you."

"Why not?"

He wasn't too sure how close Bill and Deirdre were. She grew up with Bill in the neighborhood just as he had, but they seemed to get along.

"You know Bill and I aren't exactly best friends," he declared.

"I gathered that much," she said.

"I don't trust his police work. We've bumped heads a few

times over the last year. I've printed some things he didn't agree with."

"I know that feeling," she commented, grinning.

"Hey, it wasn't the same thing as the experience I had with you, believe me." He chuckled. "Anyway, I think he drags his feet a lot. Sometimes, I think he doesn't put as much effort into catching local criminals as he does in making sure tourists have good directions."

"You're kidding?" she asked laughing.

"No, I'm not. And, I'm not saying the whole Brunswick police force is like that, just Bill Duncan."

"I thought Bill was a good cop?"

"Bill's okay, He appears to do a good job, but I don't trust him."

"Well I hope he doesn't drop the ball on Sheila's case. I hope they catch that guy."

"Me, too. Have you talked to her?"

"No. Her husband won't let me speak to her. I have no idea how she's doing. And I feel terrible about the whole thing, like it's my fault." The words were almost caught in her throat, but managed to get out.

"You shouldn't blame yourself. It's not your fault."

"But I can't help it, I do. If I hadn't had a flat tire that morning I would have been there. This never would have happened to her. My office would have been open." The first tear rolled down Deirdre's left cheek. She didn't want to cry, but she felt so bad.

He moved closer and put his arm around her. "Deirdre if you'd been open, maybe he would have come into your office when you were alone."

She had rested her head against Robert's shoulder, but raised it at his statement. "Do you think that's what his plan was?"

"No, I don't. I think Sheila was in the wrong place at the right time. His target probably would have been whomever came along at that very moment. I don't mean to scare you, I just don't want you to blame yourself."

"I know, but whenever something like this happens you try to be strong for your client. Not being able to talk to her, or see her is what I can't stand. I want to help her." Another tear rolled down her cheek.

This time, Robert wiped the tear away with the back of his hand. "Do you want me to try and talk with her husband?"

"Trust me, her husband won't let you get close to her. If he's not very fond of her black counselor, he especially won't like the black reporter who comes calling."

"Oh, it's like that."

"I'm afraid so. But I couldn't let you do that anyway. Thanks for offering. I'm so tired of all this. I can't take much more." She sniffled and tried to hold back the tears.

Robert began to rock her slowly to the music, offering little words of encouragement. "Don't worry, I'll help you get through it."

Her body relaxed as he caressed her shoulders with his large hands. She closed her eyes and got lost in one of her school-aged fantasies. She could hear Robert whispering in her ear.

"Deirdre I can't stand to see you hurting like this. I want to help you in whatever way I can. Just let me know what you need me to do."

She managed to shake her head, as he kissed her on the top of her head. Her heart beat sped up and her palms began to sweat. She wanted to reach for her glass of wine, so she'd have something to do with her hands.

Instead, Robert reached out and took her hand in his. He affectionately laced his fingers with hers and pulled her hand to his mouth. The heat of his breath against the back of her hand sent chills down her spine and a tingle ran through her body.

She looked up into his eyes and saw the warmth and affection there. Her eyes lowered to his lips. His nice full lips that she longed to taste again. What stopped her from kissing him at this very moment?

As she thought about kissing him, Robert let go of her hand and put both arms around her. He pulled her body close to his and stroked her back.

"Deirdre, I haven't met a woman in years who makes me feel the way you do. We've got to start spending more time together." He held her back from him and gazed into her eyes.

Deirdre wanted to know if she was in another one of her dreams. She reached up and touched Robert's cheek with her hand. It was real. She could smell him, and she liked the musty smell of the outdoors on him. Before she woke from this dream, and it became nothing more than a memory, she wanted to kiss him.

With her hand on Robert's cheek still, she reached up and touched those luscious kissable lips of his. He graciously met her halfway, and pulled her into the most hypnotic sensual kiss she'd ever experienced. Every nerve in her body stood on edge. Her senses were experiencing the Fourth of July.

Robert caressed her shoulders, careful not to venture further to her neck. He slid the strap of her sundress down and kissed where the strap had been. Her shoulders were soft to his touch. With every stroke of his hand, his body screamed for her. He wanted to undress her and take her into his bedroom. Thoughts of being with her consumed his body so, he found it hard to breathe. The knot in his stomach grew more painful by the minute.

His desire to feel her skin next to his was so strong he found himself leaning backward on the couch, pulling her down on top of him. She followed his every move. With one strap hanging down her shoulder, she looked as if her desire for him was as strong as his for her. He lowered the strap on her other shoulder.

"Baby, you are so beautiful. I can hardly control myself around you."

She answered him with another kiss. This one more hot and passionate than the one before. Completely lost in the moment, she felt his hands run through her hair then stroke her head. His hands explored every curve of her body through her dress. She hungered to feel those big hands against her skin.

She felt the zipper on her dress slowly being lowered. His hands connected with her bare back setting her soul on fire. With her hands pressed against his chest, she raised to slide her arms out of the dress.

Before she could get one arm out, the horrifying image of a little girl being brutally raped flashed before her. She could see the girl's blood-filled face and hear her terrifying screams. Her skirt had been ripped off and lay in the grass. She reached for it as a boy bigger than her forced himself on her.

"Oh, God no!" She pressed her hands into Robert's chest and pushed herself up. "Don't hurt me!" Pain shot through her body and she tried to scream.

Her first blow landed on Robert's cheek. He grabbed her by the wrist to keep her from slapping him again. She made a 360-degree change. Suddenly, she didn't want him to touch her. She fought him has if he were forcing himself on her.

"Hey, Deirdre calm down, it's me, Robert, baby." He gripped her hands tighter and held them down. She continued to jump and lunge at him. When he looked into her eyes, they were filled with tears on the verge of spilling over.

"Deirdre, it's me!" He yelled louder, and shook her this time. Her movement slowed enough for him to let go of her hands and pull her into his embrace. He held her tight for fear she'd start to fight him again. *God, what was she going through?*

She sobbed as tears flowed all over his shirt. He held her shaking body in his arms. He asked himself over and over, "what did I do?" Something was terribly wrong, but he didn't think it had anything to do with him.

Once she stopped shaking so much, he pushed her up and looked up into her eyes. "Baby, I'm so sorry. Deirdre, what's wrong?"

Through glassy eyes she said, "He hurt me. I felt it," before she started to cry all over again.

Sitting up on the couch, Robert pulled her back into his arms. For a moment, he was terrified. Someone had hurt her and every time he touched her, she relived it. He held her tighter.

"Everything's okay now. I won't hurt you," he whispered reassurances.

When she stopped crying, she pulled out of his embrace and reached for her purse. Inside she found a tissue and wiped her eyes. "I'm sorry. I don't know what's happening to me."

"Baby, you said somebody hurt you. Was it your ex-husband?"

She wiped her eyes, and blew her nose. "No. Lately, I've been seeing these images of a little girl being raped." She glanced up at Robert.

He hesitated, taking a deep breath. "Were you that little girl?" He asked, as his gut twisted into a bigger knot.

"I think so," she said, swallowing back a sob.

SIXTEEN

Her words hit Robert in the head like a ton of bricks. She was telling him that someone had raped her as a child. The expression on her face registered as much shock as his.

"Deirdre, can you talk about it?" He needed a firm grasp on what she was telling him.

Tears rolled down her cheeks again. "I don't know how to express what I feel." She wiped the tears away with the back of her hand.

"Just tell me what you saw."

"A few nights ago, I had a dream about a young girl being raped. When I woke, I realized I had been crying in my sleep. I feel as if I'm that little girl." She held her hand to her chest.

"What makes you think it's you? Do you see her in your dream?"

"Not her face. But my body hurts during the dream. And just now . . . I saw him raping her and experienced the pain again."

"Who was he?"

Deirdre shook her head and closed her eyes. "I don't know. I can't see him."

They sat on the couch in silence for a few minutes. Robert held Deirdre close to him and stroked her hair. He didn't know what to do for her. She was the counselor. All he could do right now was hold and comfort her. From the stunned expression on her face he could tell she hadn't comprehended the entire ordeal herself. He reached down her back and zipped her dress back up.

Her heart slammed against her chest at such a rapid speed, she was sure Robert felt it, too. She took several deep breaths in an attempt to calm her nerves. What happened tonight frightened her. Could she have been that little girl? She brushed her fingers across the scar on her forehead. This would explain all the blood in her dream.

She hoped Robert didn't think she was off her rocker. Right now she was especially appreciative of his comforting arms. The way he cradled and caressed her, made her feel better.

"Robert, I'm sorry. I don't know what to say."

"What are you apologizing for? You just discovered something very traumatic tonight. You don't have to apologize to me about anything."

"Thank you."

"What are you going to do?"

"I'm not sure. I guess I have to figure out somehow if that little girl is me or not."

"But you feel certain it's you?" he probed.

She hesitated before answering. "Yes I do."

"Deirdre, I bet what happened to Sheila is affecting you more than you think. Do you think maybe you're seeing her in your dreams or flashes?"

The necklace she found after Sheila's rape triggered her memory, and was responsible for all these thoughts. "No, it's not Sheila. It's a young girl, and she's crying. I cry for her as I sleep. It's definitely not Sheila."

Robert looked at the clock on the mantel.

"It's almost eleven o'clock," he pointed out.

"Thanks. I'd better get ready to go." She straightened up, trying to pull out of his embrace.

"Hold on." He kept his arm around her and held her tighter. "I wish you could spend the night. All I want to do is hold and comfort you like this, all night long."

Deirdre sighed. "That would be nice." A warm comfortable feeling came over her as Robert kissed her on the forehead.

"Maybe some other night," he added gently.

"Yes, I'd like that," she whispered.

* * *

The next day Deirdre's body felt the punishment of sitting up so late. Thank goodness her parents had gone to bed when she got home. She was tired and her eyes were puffy from crying. She didn't want her mother to think Robert was the reason for her swollen eyes.

This morning she managed to get through the first three sessions without falling asleep. Now, she planned a light lunch to make sure she stayed up the rest of the afternoon.

Leaving for lunch, she picked up her purse. When she opened her office door, Susan was on her way in.

"Cathy's on the phone."

"Okay thanks."

"Deirdre, she sounds pretty bad."

There goes lunch. "Thanks Susan."

Deirdre returned to her desk and picked up the phone. "Hello Cathy."

"Hi Deirdre. Uh, I called to tell you I have to end my counseling sessions. I might be moving away soon."

"Are you sure that's what you want to do?" she asked skeptically.

"Yes, ma'am. I'm afraid I can't afford another session so I wanted to let you know."

Deirdre was afraid this would begin to happen. When her clients read about the rape in the paper, she knew they'd call her. She hoped, however, that they wouldn't panic.

"Cathy, I feel we need a close-out session. You can pay me whatever you can afford, don't worry about the money."

"Uh . . . I uh . . . I don't think I can make it."

"Would this have anything to do with something you read in the paper?" A sense of doom fell over Deirdre.

"Well, I read about that lady being raped. But, that's not why I can't come back. Uh, like I said, I'm about to move so I need to get things together."

"I see. So, where are you moving to?" Deirdre didn't believe Cathy was on the move again.

"Miami, Florida."

"Well, I wish you luck and I hope you like Miami."

"Thank you. And thanks for listening to me when I needed someone."

"Sure. Cathy, do you need me to find you a counselor in Florida?"

"No, I won't need one. I'm fine."

"Okay, honey. Take care."

Deirdre hung the phone up confused. Cathy had left Florida and swore never to return. She had expressed how much she liked Brunswick and had finally found a place she could call home. There was something fishy about her phone call.

Cathy was the first client to quit. How many more would follow? To exonerate her office, they had to catch that rapist.

She picked up the phone and called Officer Duncan. She had to know how far along he was on the case.

"Hello, Officer Bill Duncan," he answered his phone on the first ring.

"Hi Bill, it's Deirdre."

"Hello Deirdre, what can I do for you?"

"I'm calling to see if you're close to finding out who raped Sheila?"

He sighed. "Nothing yet, I'm afraid. We followed a few leads that led nowhere. The guy seems to have disappeared."

"I need to let you know about something that happened to me that morning."

"What's that?"

"When I left for work, I had a flat tire. That's how come I wasn't in the office when Sheila arrived. I didn't think much of it at the time, but my father said it looked as if my tire was punctured."

"Really."

"Yes. I stopped by Leroy's for a new tire. He probably has my old tire if you want to check it out."

"I'll stop by and do that."

"I hope it helps in some way."

"That's right, it might. Any time you think of anything, give me a call. Have you talked to anyone who might have seen something?"

"No."

"Well, don't worry. We'll catch him."

"I hope so. This stuff has to stop, before I lose all my clients."

"You've lost some clients?"

"Only one so far. I'm keeping my fingers crossed."

"Well, leave everything up to the police. We'll have this wrapped up in no time. I assure you."

Robert's words from last night rang in Deirdre's ear. Bill talked a good game, but hadn't solved a crime in years. She hoped since her and Bill went way back, he'd try his best to help her out.

"Okay, but let me know if I can do anything to help myself. I don't care what it is. I want this craziness to stop."

"Have you talked with Robert Carmichael?" he asked firmly.

"Yes, I have. But what does that have to do with the case?"

"Just be careful how much you tell him, that's all. I'd appreciate it if you informed me of any new information before talking to him. It's hard to solve a case when all the details get spelled out in the evening paper."

"Bill, he doesn't print everything I tell him. We've spoken about that."

"Don't be so sure. Trust me, I know him a little better than you do. He's a very ambitious man. I think he'd do anything to land a job at one of those big-city papers again."

There was absolutely no love lost between those two. She found herself poised in the middle, wanting to trust both of them.

"If I learn anything new, I'll be sure to let you know first." She ended the conversation and prayed Bill was indeed on her case.

* * *

As the day wore on, Deirdre's luck worsened. Damon dropped a bomb on her the minute he walked in.

"I appreciate you trying to help me work through some anger issues, but I have to tell you, I don't feel like I need it any longer."

Deirdre hadn't expected Damon to quit, but she wasn't too surprised. Every session with him was like pulling teeth.

"We've only worked on your anger for four months now." She hated to see him quit when they'd only scratched the surface of his problems.

"I know, and I feel like that's enough. Last weekend I sat down and talked with my fiancée. She's agreed to move forward with the wedding plans."

"So, her initial concern is gone?"

"I've worked on it some, and that's all she asked of me. I've never mistreated her. It's my dealings with other people that she wanted me to work on."

"Are you sure about this Damon?"

"Yes, I am. I kept my appointment to let you know."

"Do we need to close things out today?"

"Sure, we can." He shrugged.

"I'd like to go over the issues we've discussed, and point out some items you've agreed to work on."

Damon sat back in his seat. "Okay, I can deal with that."

Two clients quit in one day. Deirdre hoped that wasn't a sign of things to come. She prepared for her last session of the day and hoped no one else called to quit.

"Deirdre, after I close these files out, do you want to read them, or should I file them away?" Susan asked when she entered Deirdre's office.

"Let me look over them first."

"You don't think they quit out of fear, do you?" Susan asked.

"Not Damon. But Cathy, I'm not too sure about."

"Shoot, I looked around good before I got out of the car this morning myself. Since they haven't caught this guy you never know if he'll strike again."

"My God, I hope not. Do be careful."

"Have you heard from Sheila yet?"

"Not yet. Her husband still won't let me speak to her."

"Man, that's too bad."

Knock, knock . . . There were several knocks at the front door.

"I'll get that. It's probably Geneva." Susan went back into the reception area.

Seconds later, Deirdre closed Geneva's folder and stepped around her desk to greet her. This morning Geneva had a little pep in her step. She looked chipper and in good spirits.

"Good afternoon, Deirdre."

Deirdre held the door open for her as she sauntered in swinging her purse and smiling. "Hello Geneva, you're in good spirits this evening."

"Oh, I'm doing fine for an old woman." She took a seat across from Deirdre's desk.

"I'm sure the weather helps a lot. It's beautiful out today isn't it?"

"Yes it is. And I've been getting a good night's sleep again."

"Oh, sounds like the prank calls have stopped?"

"Yes they have. When I reported it to the phone company, they stopped."

"That's great. I know the police said the calls were coming from a pay phone. Maybe they located the phone and watched it. It was probably kids with nothing to do but go through the phone book making prank calls."

"I don't know what they did, but I'm sleeping through the night now, and I'm thankful for that."

"That's wonderful. I can tell you're getting plenty of rest; your skin looks great."

"Well, thank you. And I wanted to tell you how sorry I was to read in the paper about that young lady being assaulted here."

"Thank you Geneva. It was very sad."

"But I decided, that won't scare me into avoiding your office."

That's what Deirdre needed to lift her spirits. "Thank you Geneva. There's nothing to be afraid of, but always be cautious."

"I do." Geneva set her purse in the chair next to her.

"That's what I like to hear. I'm not about to let anyone run me away from this office." Now if Deirdre could only get her other clients to feel the same way.

SEVENTEEN

Saturday morning Mia, Deirdre, and her mother went shopping. Deirdre promised to help her mother find a dress for their pastor's anniversary. Last night, Deirdre dreamed about the child being raped again. This morning, she promised herself to ask her mother about any childhood incidents.

They weeded through a rack of clearance dresses hoping to find something Anna loved.

"Mama, can I ask you something?"

"Sure. What is it?" Anna held a dress out and looked at Deirdre for approval.

"Uh . . . uh. That looks too old." Her mother returned the dress to the rack.

"Did anything happen to me when I was a little girl?" She held her breath waiting for an answer.

"A lot of things happened to you. For starters, you bumped your head. Then you fell out of the swing in the backyard. All the things that little boys get into, you got into."

"Mama, I mean anything traumatic?"

Anna pulled out another dress and held it in front of her.

"God, that's awful. Put it back." Deirdre cringed.

Anna looked down at Mia who held her doll in one hand and gripped her mother's hand with the other. Mia shook her head agreeing with her mother and laughing.

Anna returned the dress to the rack and her attention to Deirdre.

"Honey, why are you asking questions like that?"

How much of her dream did she want to share with her mother?

"Well, I remembered a necklace I used to have that Granny gave to me. Do you remember it?" She saw the blank expression on her mother's face.

"Yes. It was a gold necklace with a ruby stone. Your grandfather gave her that necklace. You lost it in a fight, I believe. Anyhow you came home telling us somebody ripped it from your neck." She stopped and turned to face Deirdre. "And that was an expensive necklace, that meant a lot to your grandmother." She returned to the dress. "It nearly broke her heart when I told her what happened," Anna added

"I didn't lose it, sounds like someone took it from me."

"Whatever, it was gone. That was a family heirloom."

Deirdre was so nervous. Her mother hadn't mentioned anything about her being raped. What was this fight she'd gotten into? She didn't remember losing the necklace in a fight.

"Are you sure that's how I lost it?"

"What do you think?" Anna stopped and asked.

Deirdre looked her in the eye before turning back to the dresses. "I don't know. But I remembered the necklace."

"Come with me while I try these on." She held out two dresses she'd picked out.

She followed her mother into the dressing room and decided not to mention the incident again, until a better time.

When they returned home and walked into the house, the phone was ringing. Anna ran to answer the kitchen phone while Deirdre took Mia to the bathroom. Deirdre walked into the kitchen and heard her mother trying to explain something to Barbara.

"If you called home every now and then you'd know what was going on. You know we can't afford to call Chicago every time you turn around. Daddy and I are on a budget." Anna waved Deirdre over as she crossed the room.

"Here, let her tell you herself. That's the only reason you called anyway." She held the phone out to Deirdre and turned up her nose.

Laughing, Deirdre answered the phone. "Hey Barbara, what's up?" Her older sister and her mother always fought.

"You, from what I hear. How come nobody called to tell me about all this mess you're going through?"

"Well, I figured you talk to Mama from time to time and . . ."

"Get off of it, you know that woman won't talk to me. She won't even call me when somebody in the family dies. So what makes you think she'd keep me informed about anything else?"

"Barbara, maybe you should call her sometimes."

"Like her phone's broken," Barbara's voice rose. "Deirdre I used to call them every Sunday, then I lost my job. Did she start calling me—noo. She expected me to keep calling her."

"Okay, okay, sorry I brought it up." She didn't want to start bickering with Barbara, since it was so easy to do.

"Aunt Lucille called and told me you're having trouble on your new job. Something about a burglary?" Concern laced Barbara's question.

Deirdre pulled up a seat and made herself comfortable. "Well, it started with a burglary. Now we're talking rape."

"Rape! Who got raped?"

"One of my clients. Barbara, it's so frustrating. Bill Duncan is working on the case, but they haven't arrested anybody yet."

"My goodness, this is serious. Bill's a good cop, he can find the guy. Once people start talking, he'll surface. You can't keep too many secrets in Brunswick."

"I hope you're right."

"But, I'm sure Mama and Daddy are taking good care of you. Treating you like a little princess while you're there. When do you plan on moving out anyway?"

"They don't treat me like a princess, why do you keep saying that?"

"Yes, they do. Ever since we were kids, they babied you all the time. I'd be surprised if they let you move out. Has Daddy offered to remodel the house so you can stay?"

"Girl, I don't know what your problem is, but I'm getting tired of that attitude. Why can't we have a civil conversation?"

Barbara hesitated before answering. "We can. The kids miss Mia. When are you bringing her for a visit?" she asked softly.

Deirdre hated to fight with her sister, but Barbara never gave her a choice. "Not for a while. I'm trying to get the money together for a down payment on a house."

"You mean that ex-husband of yours or Mama and Daddy haven't given you enough money for that?"

She wanted to reach through the phone and strangle her sister. "I can come up with my own down-payment money, thank you."

"The bum doesn't have it, and you're too proud to ask your parents. I get it."

"I'm hanging up now."

"Oh, stop it. I'm just playing with you. Take care of yourself. Remember, if you need me, just call, I'm here. Don't be like your mother."

"I'll remember that, thanks."

After hanging up, Deirdre went upstairs and found her mother trying on her new dress.

"Well don't you look good." She walked into the bedroom and sat on the edge of her parents' bed.

"Thank you, honey. I guess I'll keep it." Anna looked into the mirror.

"Mama, was I raped when I was younger?" Deirdre asked point-blank.

Her mother turned and stared at her like a deer caught by headlights. After a few seconds of awkward silence she moved to take off her dress.

"You got into a fight with some boys. They tore your coat, and you said they took Granny's necklace."

"But did they rape me?" Deirdre persisted.

"Why are you bringing this up now?" Anna balled up her new dress and stuffed it back into the shopping bag. She nervously pulled her clothes back on.

"Because I had a dream about a young girl being raped, and I think I'm that little girl. Am I right?"

"Deirdre that was in the past, and you need to forgive and

forget. Look at you." She gestured from Deirdre's head to toe. "You're a grown woman now, with a little girl of her own."

"Mama, you didn't answer my question: Did they rape me?" She insisted on an answer.

Anna opened her closet door, and threw the shopping bag inside. She then walked toward the bedroom door, stopping to look back at Deirdre.

"No. Now I'm going to cook dinner." She left the room.

Deirdre sat there stunned and confused. If her mother had known she'd been attacked, why did she never discuss it? Or, why had she never mentioned it to her? And why was she dreaming about a young girl being raped? She needed to see the child's face.

Gus slammed the door to the hotel room behind him. Susan walked over and threw her purse on the bed, before sitting. This weekend wasn't going so well.

"I can't believe you'd ask me to do that, Gus."

"Why in the hell are you acting like it's such a big deal." He threw his car keys on the dresser and went into the bathroom.

"It is a big deal. My job will be on the line. What if she finds out I did it?"

"Quit talking stupid, how is she going to find out?" He stuck his head out of the bathroom.

"I'm not stupid. And you don't know if she'll find out or not. She might. Then what will I do? Who's going to take care of me? I need this job."

He walked over to Susan, and sat next to her. With his hand cupping her chin, he forced her to look at him.

"Don't you love me?" he asked in a caring voice.

Susan closed her eyes. "What does that have to do with it?"

"It has everything to do with it. If you loved me, this wouldn't be an issue. You'd do it for me."

He let go of her chin and she lowered her head. "I can't," she said, barely above a whisper.

He stomped over to the dresser, and snatched up his keys. "That's okay, I don't need your ass anymore anyway." He threw the door open and pointed.

"Get out."

Saturday night Deirdre's parents' went out with friends. Deirdre let Mia stay up late while they popped popcorn and watched, *The Lion King*.

They sat downstairs in the den cuddled together on the couch. Halfway through the movie, the phone rang.

"Hello."

"Hello Deirdre, it's Sheila," she said anxiously.

Deirdre jumped up in her seat almost spilling popcorn all over the couch. "Sheila, I'm so glad you called. Hold on a minute." She left the popcorn on the couch with Mia, and walked upstairs with the cordless phone.

"Sheila how are you?" she asked nervously.

"I'm okay. I can't talk long. My husband went to the store."

"I've tried to call you several times, but he won't let me speak to you."

"Thank you, I know. He's very upset with me right now. I'm afraid I can't continue our sessions, under any circumstances."

Deirdre lowered her head and bit her lip. "I understand. Are you going to see another counselor?"

"He won't let me. We'll handle this ourselves."

"Sheila you should get into a rape crisis center and talk to someone. If you're worried about him finding out, they can protect you."

"You don't know him. I can't go there either."

Deirdre lowered herself onto the top step. Sheila's husband was a monster, and she needed to get away from him.

"I wish I could help you. I'm so sorry," Deirdre expressed.

"It's not your fault." She moved the phone away from her and a muffled sound came through the phone.

"Sheila, are you there?" Deirdre asked standing up.

"I have to go. My husband's home." The phone went dead.

Deirdre pulled the receiver back and stared at it. "Bye." Her heart ached and she couldn't do anything about it. Sheila was in an abusive marriage and too afraid to get out. She'd never mentioned the extent of the abuse to Deirdre. However, she didn't have to, for Deirdre to know how bad it must be.

Deirdre headed back downstairs then stopped after she heard a knock at the door. She pivoted around and ran back up the stairs. First, she looked out the front window to see who was at the door.

"Who is it?" she called out.

When she didn't get an answer, she tried again, louder. "Who is it?" Still nothing.

Maybe she hadn't heard anything at the door. She opened the front door, and peeked outside.

"Hello." She looked from one side of the porch to the other. A piece of paper on the ground caught her attention. She picked it up. A rustling sound in the bushes distracted her, but she didn't see anything. Probably a cat, she thought.

After she closed and locked the front door, she flipped open the piece of paper. It was a copy of an old newspaper article, blown up.

Local Teen Abducted and Assaulted

A twelve-year-old girl was abducted, and assaulted yesterday in the wooded area behind PeeWee's Market. Investigators said the teenager was apparently walking home by herself at 5:30 P.M. when she took a shortcut behind the store. She was dragged farther into the remote wooded area and raped. After the abduction, the teenager found safe haven at a nearby house.

Authorities declined to elaborate about the teenager's condition. No suspect has been named to date.

Horrified, trembling legs gave way to her body. She flopped down on the living-room floor. No name was mentioned in the article, but it had to be her.

She folded the paper back, and stood up. A shiver ran through her body. Whoever placed this on her porch, might still be outside. She stuffed the paper in her pocket, and went to peek out the window again.

Afraid for Mia and herself, she ran around the house making sure everything was locked up tight. Then she ran downstairs to check on Mia. She'd moved from the couch to the floor, staring at the television.

"Come on honey, you're too close to the television. Get back up on the couch." She helped Mia up onto the couch with her.

She was frightened now, actually for the first time. An overwhelming feeling of fear engulfed her. She tried to shake it off and concentrate on the movie, but she couldn't. Her heart beat double-time as she reached over for the phone. She had to call Robert. His line rang and rang until she hung up. Quickly, she decided to try Belinda.

The doorbell rang, and she jumped up from the couch again.

"Mommy ouch." Mia hit her mother's leg after almost being thrown to the floor.

"I'm sorry honey." She stood up, then set Mia on the couch. "Stay right here, honey. Mommy will be back."

"You're not gonna see the movie."

"I know honey, we'll watch it again. I promise." The bell rang again.

Her heart pounded with every step she took. When she reached the front window, she peeked out and saw Bill Duncan. She opened the door.

"Bill, what's up?"

He walked inside. "I've got some good news."

"Great, what is it?"

"We caught your thief earlier today."

She was speechless. All she could do was place her hands over her mouth and take a deep breath.

"It was an older child from the community center, just as you suspected." Bill pulled out a small pad and read from it.

"At four o'clock this afternoon, we acted on a lead and searched the house of Warren Parker. They found a few of your case files in the house also."

She walked over and sat in a living room chair. "Thank goodness. Does that mean this mess is over?" She looked up at Bill.

"We're not sure if he's connected to the rapist or not. I'll let you know as soon as we find out."

"Thanks, Bill. I really appreciate you coming by tonight."

"I started to wait until Monday, but I know how important this is to you." Standing in the foyer, he looked around the room. "Your parents have a nice place here."

"Thank you. I can't wait to let Mr. Hamel know you caught the thief and it was someone from the center. He told me over and over he didn't think it was any of the children."

"Well, he was wrong."

"Bill I could kiss you. This is such good news."

"Well, I'm just glad we caught him." He turned and stepped out the door. "You take care, and have a nice night."

"I will. Don't forget to get back with me."

"Oh, I won't. Don't worry." He smiled and put his hat back on before walking down the stairs.

She closed the door and rested against it. They'd caught the thief, but what about the rapist?

She went back downstairs and tried Robert's number again. This time he answered.

"Hello," he answered in a rush.

"Robert, it's me. I've got good news." He sounded out of breath.

EIGHTEEN

"Deirdre, Hey. What's up?"

"I'm sorry did I catch you at a bad time? You sound like you've been running," she said.

"No. I just came in, and I heard the phone ring. I wanted to answer it before the service came on."

"Oh. Well, Bill Duncan dropped by with good news. They've caught the thief. It's a kid from the center, as I suspected."

"Bill came by there tonight?"

"Yeah, he said he wanted to let me know as soon as possible."

"Did he say anything about the guy who assaulted your client?"

"No, they're still working on that."

"Well, at least you know the two crimes aren't connected."

"Yeah, I guess so."

"You don't sound convinced?"

"Someone stole our petty cash out of the file cabinet last week, and I didn't report it."

"Why not?"

"You know Mr. Hamel. He's always looking for more reasons to close this office."

"How much money are we talking?"

"A little more than fifty dollars."

"I know you didn't keep that money out somewhere, so who had access to it?"

"Me and Susan."

"How well do you trust her?"

"Completely. She pointed out to me that the money was missing."

"You're going to tell Bill about it, aren't you?"

"Yeah, I guess I better. I didn't think about it when I had him on the phone." Deirdre started to tell him about the note she found on her porch, but changed her mind. She needed to talk to her mother first.

"Deirdre, I'm glad you called, because I wanted to ask if you would let me take you and Mia on a picnic."

Deirdre looked down at Mia and hesitated a moment. She'd definitely love that. "When?"

"How about next Saturday. We could use a little fun, what do you say?"

Her main concern was Mia getting attached to Robert. She seemed to like him so far. Maybe he would take her mind off her Daddy some.

"Okay, that sounds like fun."

After hanging up, she pulled the note from her pocket and tried to decide when to talk to her mother. Obviously, she knew about it.

After church Sunday morning, Deirdre pitter-pattered around the house trying to find the right words to say to her mother. She was scared of the truth, or what she believed to be the truth. Everybody in town seemed to stop by their house after church. Her mother cooked a big dinner and had the pastor and his family over for dinner. After dinner everyone went to the park to watch the boats and relax. Deirdre sat in the park watching Mia and realizing today wasn't a good time to approach her mother about the rape.

Later that night, Deirdre had a date for dessert with Robert. She hoped they'd go out for ice cream, even though she didn't need it. Their friendship was developing into a relationship with promise. Every minute she spent with him was filled with joy. She looked around at the men in the park and realized how much

she wanted Robert, not only as a friend, but as a lover. He turned
her on in ways that William had never even come close to. When
he kissed her, she lost all sense of time and place. They were in
their own little world of luscious lips and scrumptious kisses.

He watched her as he slipped on a new pair of latex
gloves. This one would be more fun than the last. Now
he'd take his time and complete the job.
He got out of the car, gently closing the door. She hadn't
spotted him yet—good. Now he would have plenty of time.
She gathered her grocery bags from the car and took them
inside. When she came out for a second handful, she almost spotted him. He ducked behind the hedges and froze.
Never before had he been spotted, or stopped from complet-
ing his task. And he wasn't about to start today.
Once she had all the groceries inside, she closed the back
door. The sun was setting, so he knew she was in for the
night. A light in the kitchen came on. He moved closer to
the house.
He stood outside and looked in the window. "Sorry Ms.
Levine, I'm afraid you've just lost another one."
He eased around to the front door, and rang the bell. After
several seconds the door opened slowly, and an elderly
black woman opened the door.
"Well, hello there," she greeted him in a warm and friendly
manner.
"Mrs. Shaw, I need to speak with you for a moment."
"What's it about?" she asked smiling.
"The Brunswick Counseling Agency, and Deirdre Levine."
She opened the door even wider and stood aside. "Why
sure, come right in."
He wiped his feet on the mat and grinned as he stepped
through the entrance.

* * *

Monday morning Robert came in to the office early to get a jump start on his day. Since meeting Deirdre he'd cut down on working all night and all weekend. He loved having her to spend his free time with. He even looked forward to spending time with her daughter, Mia. The two of them were a perfect package. He was a lucky man to have found her.

The phone rang interrupting his thoughts.

"Yeah, Robert Carmichael."

"Want an exclusive?" A harsh muffled voice came from the other end.

Robert flung his feet off the desk and stood up. It was him again. That same muffled voice. What was it this time?

"Who is this?" he asked, knowing full well he wouldn't get an answer.

"Guess not."

"Hey! Hang on. Of course, I want an exclusive. I'd just like to know who I'm talking to?"

"The person who's gonna make your career."

"How so?" Robert's heart pounded faster, this was the first time he'd spoken to this guy for so long. This had to be bad.

"You'll find it at the end of Parker street. The small white house with green shutters. But hurry. That is, if you want the exclusive." The line went dead.

"Damn." Robert slammed the phone down and grabbed his car keys. It was time to tell the police about his mysterious caller. He hoped this exclusive didn't have anything to do with Deirdre.

Turning down Parker Street he saw several police cars. He proceeded and pulled right in front of a small white house with green shutters. The house was surrounded by police cars. Right away he looked for another reporter and didn't see one. Okay, he had an exclusive here.

He showed his ID and asked for Officer Bill Duncan. Bill gave him a sharp look as he gave instructions to another officer.

"Robert Carmichael, you must have a sixth sense or something. How come you always manage to show up before any other reporter?"

"You might say a little birdie called me. What happened here?"

"You'll have to tell me about that little birdie. I'm dying to hear. But right now, I've got to deal with this mess."

"What you got here?"

"A murder."

"Anybody I know?"

"Yeah, everybody knows her. Geneva Shaw."

Bill got called back inside, so Robert walked over to a few neighbors gathered on the other side of the crime scene tape.

"Isn't it a shame," one women commented with her arms crossed, shaking her head.

"It's devastating," a man added.

"Do you know if she lived alone?" Robert asked, hoping to get some information from the neighbors while he stood around.

"Yes, her husband was deceased."

"Geneva wouldn't hurt a fly, and somebody walked into her house and took her life. I doesn't make sense I tell you."

"Sure doesn't, what is this world coming to?" The neighbors discussed how Geneva was such a good neighbor.

Minutes later, Bill Duncan and several other officers walked back outside. Robert tried to get as much information out of them as he could.

"Robert, let me ask you something?" Bill looked at him out of the corner of his eye.

"Yeah." Robert knew the only way to deal with Bill was head-on, since Bill had developed such a disliking for him.

"How come whenever something happens that involves that counseling center, you're always Johnny-on-the-spot?"

Confused, Robert glanced around at the other officers, then back at Bill. "What does this have to do with Deirdre?"

"Geneva Shaw was one of her clients."

Robert sighed and looked away for a moment. *My God, what's going on?* He had to tell Bill about his anonymous caller.

"Bill I need to tell you about a call I received this morning."

"Please do." Bill eyed him narrowly.

* * *

"Who found her?" Deirdre asked, barely able to speak. The news shattered her heart into a thousand pieces. Her eyes were filled with tears. Geneva dead—how could that be?

"A neighbor." Bill Duncan sat on the other side of Deirdre's desk. His hat in his hand out of respect, and his head lowered.

"What were they doing there?"

"She says she went by to discuss something she read in this morning's paper. The front door was cracked. She pushed it open and called out, but didn't get an answer. Out of fear, she ran home and called us."

"God, I can't believe this, Bill. Who would want to hurt Geneva? You know her, she's the sweetest little old lady there is."

"I know. I can't imagine it myself. Trust me, I've got a couple of my best men on it. They're checking with all her neighbors and we'll come up with something soon."

"I hope so." She looked at him with pleading eyes. "You've got to find him. He can't get away with this."

"We will." He stood to leave. "I'm going to have to ask you some questions about her."

"I can't tell you much, you know. Our sessions were confidential."

"I understand. We're beefing up our investigation. Right now, everyone's a suspect."

"You're kidding?"

"No I'm not. And I'd like to wrap this up before Robert prints everything in one of his damned articles."

"Robert! Does he know about this already?"

"He was the first reporter there, as usual." He put his hat back on. "Deirdre, I hope you're being careful around that guy. You know how I feel about him."

She hesitated a moment. "Is Robert usually the first reporter on a scene?" If so, that proved how good he was, she thought.

"Not always. However, when it comes to this office, he's always one step behind my men. I'm surprised he didn't show up before we did. Just take care of yourself, okay."

"I will." At a time like this, she wasn't about to get into a discussion with Bill about Robert. Their problems were theirs and not hers.

After Bill left, she didn't have the strength to see anyone else. Standing at Susan's desk, she asked her to cancel all appointments for the day, and apologize for her. Seconds later, Mr. Hamel walked in.

"Deirdre, I heard about Geneva Shaw." He walked over to her and tried to put his arm around her shoulder.

Reluctant to let him touch her, she pulled back and held up her hand. "I'm okay really. Thank you for your concern."

He stepped back. "Well in light of what happened, I think we need to talk. In private." He glanced at Susan.

Susan returned a smile and grit her teeth until they disappeared into Deirdre's office.

Deirdre knew why he'd come by this morning. A client's death was entirely too much for him. Once she'd heard the news she'd prepared to go home for the day anyway.

"Come on in, and have a seat." She motioned to a seat across from her desk, then sat in one opposite him.

"I'm afraid you know why I'm here. We have to close the office."

She nodded. "I understand." And she did. She only wished it hadn't happened.

"We'll close the office for a week or so, and let Officer Duncan do his job. I'd like to consult him before reopening if it's okay with you?"

He was asking her advice? He'd never done that before. "That's fine with me. I've been in constant contact with Bill Duncan myself. He was here this morning."

Mr. Hamel reached out and touched her hand sitting on top of her desk. "Deirdre, I really am sorry to hear about Geneva. I've known her for years."

She looked into his eyes, and saw the genuine concern. Maybe he wasn't responsible for all the problems with her office after all. Maybe deep down she wished it was him, only so he'd be out of her life and unable to cause her any more grief.

"Thank you Mr. Hamel. She's going to be missed. She was a real sweet woman."

"She missed her husband so much. Now, I'm sure they're together." He smiled as he turned and left the office.

Deirdre sat there thinking about what he'd said. Yes, that's how she had to view things. Geneva was with her husband now. They were reunited and happy again. That was the bright side, if there was a bright side.

The downside however, was that Deirdre's career was doomed. In Brunswick, she'd probably never have her own agency. If so, who'd come? After all the bad publicity that she'd managed to acquire, no one would seek her out for help. She had to be realistic with herself. After the police caught whomever was responsible for the rape and murder, the town would talk about it for years. She had no idea what type of work she'd do after the office closed for good, and she knew that was on its way.

A soft knock at the door caught her attention. She looked up to Susan's weary eyes. For the last couple of weeks she hadn't been her usual cheerful self. Maybe she was having man problems, Deirdre concluded.

"Yes, Susan."

"You have a visitor."

Deirdre sighed and shook her head. "I can't see anybody else. Please tell them I'm unavailable."

"But, it's Robert."

He was about the only person she wanted to see. He might be able to give her some more information on Geneva that Bill hadn't. "Okay, show him in."

She didn't even bother to get up when Robert walked in. It was a habit she had developed and did for everyone who walked into her office. She stared up at him trying to control her emotions as best she could.

He closed the door behind him, then kept walking until he stood next to her.

"I'm so sorry." He reached down for her hands, and pulled her to her feet.

She couldn't hold it in. She cried until she couldn't cry any longer. Between sobs, she expressed how much Geneva meant to her. How she had grown so attached to the woman, and loved her like a grandmother.

Robert caressed the back of her head and held her close to him. He kissed the top of her head wanting to kiss the pain away. He pulled her away from him and looked into her eyes.

"Are you going to be all right?"

"No, I'm not all right. I lost one of my dearest clients, and Mr. Hamel's closing the office for a week or so." The tears returned and she began to cry again.

Robert was there to offer his comfort and support. "Deirdre, I didn't know about that. Damn, I am sorry."

"Robert," she sniffed and wiped her eyes. "I can't believe she's gone. This is too much."

He squeezed her hands in his before he let go and helped her into her seat. "How did you hear about it?"

"Bill came by and told me this morning, right after he left her house. He was as shocked as I was."

"Yeah, maybe so." Robert took a seat across from her desk.

"Robert I know you don't like Bill, so let's not go there."

"Okay, I'm sure he was concerned. I hope they catch whoever did this to her. I talked to a few of her neighbors."

"Yeah, what did they say?" she asked through her sniffles.

"Nothing in particular, but I'm going back to question a few of them."

"Are you going to report this?"

He lowered his head, then looked up at her. "You know I have to, it's my job."

"I know, but I still don't like it. She was my client and friend. This hurts like hell." She crossed her arms over her chest, acknowledging the pain.

"That's why I came over as fast as I could. I had to make sure you were okay. Especially after that first rape triggered your dreams and things."

Deirdre looked at him confused. "What do my dreams have to do with Geneva being murdered?"

Robert's eyes searched her face for a sign that she knew, but he didn't find it. He wanted to give Bill a swift kick in the behind. If he was man enough to run over here and give her the bad news, he could have at least given her the details.

"Deirdre, Geneva was raped, then murdered."

NINETEEN

Deirdre sat at the kitchen table with both hands over her mouth. Her mother brought her a cup of tea, then sat at the table with her.

"What's happening to our little town? You never used to hear about things like this happening in Brunswick. And to Geneva Shaw of all people." Anna shook her head.

The more her mother talked, the sicker Deirdre became. She was so sick to her stomach, she didn't think she'd make it through what she had to do tonight. Confront her mother. She'd already let Vita keep Mia for a few hours. Her father was at her uncle's helping with some project.

Here she sat with her mother in the kitchen, and the article in her purse.

"Honey, can I get you anything else?"

Deirdre looked up at her mother with heavy eyes. "Mama, when Robert told me someone raped Geneva I almost fainted."

Anna got up from the table and went to look out the back window. She stared out the window with her arms crossed over her chest. Deirdre sensed she was about to tell her something, but maybe needed a little prodding.

"Mama, I want to show you something." Deirdre reached across the table for her purse. She pulled out the piece of paper, and slid it across the table.

"I found that on the front porch Saturday night when you and Daddy were out," she continued.

Anna returned to her seat at the table. She picked up the paper and open it slowly. As she read over the words, one hand covered her mouth.

From the expression her mother projected, Deirdre knew the article was about her. She had been raped. Her mother folded the paper back up and slowly slid it across the table to her.

"Mama, I need to know if that's about me. I've been having dreams about a little girl being raped. She has blood all over her face and she's crying. I even cry in my sleep some nights. I can't stand when somebody touches my neck. It sends shivers through my body, and scares me." She took a deep breath and watched her mother's face.

"I have to know, is that girl in the article me?" She asked one of the hardest questions she'd ever asked.

Her mother placed both hands on the kitchen table and pretended to smooth out the plastic mat. Anna couldn't look Deirdre in the eye. Silence hung in the air like a roomful of balloons. Deirdre waited patiently for the response that she deserved.

"That happened a long time ago. They didn't mention your name, so no one knew. That could have been any twelve-year-old girl."

"But it wasn't Mama, it was me." Deirdre's voice shook.

"You told me you had a fight." She didn't look up at Deirdre, but stared at the table mat instead."

"Mama, I also found this." She reached inside her purse and pulled out the necklace, holding it up to her mother.

Her mother stared at the necklace in disbelief. Deirdre started to lay it on the table, when her mother reached out for it. Deirdre dropped the necklace into her mother's palm.

"This was my mother's necklace," Anna said as if in a trance. Her eyes fixed on the ruby stone.

"Is that the same necklace she gave me when I was a little?"

"Yes, it looks like it. Where did you find it?"

"Someone placed it on the floor of my office the day Sheila was raped. And you know what scares me?"

"What?"

"If I'm the girl in that article, then that necklace was snatched from my neck. And maybe the guy who raped me placed the necklace in my office. If so, he knows me and knows where I work." A chill ran through Deirdre's body as she reached for her cup of tea. Her hands shook so badly, she set the cup back down.

"They never caught him. He wore a mask that showed his eyes and mouth, so you couldn't describe him for the police. You were in shock." Anna stared at a spot on the linoleum as she talked.

"The police think he was an older high school boy. But without a description, they couldn't do much," she added.

Nausea washed over Deirdre as she listened to her mother talk. She felt as if she were in quicksand. Now she was sinking fast with nothing to hold on to, but a dream.

"Mama, how come you never talked about it?"

Anna turned to Deirdre, her features softened and sad. "You were such a happy child until that day. It happened during the summer break. When school started, instead of sending you to Neptune High, we enrolled you in Lincoln High School and moved across town. Afterward you forgot it. It was as if it never happened."

"But I never saw a counselor?"

"We didn't know nothing about no counselors back then. Sister Green from church tried to talk to you, but all you wanted to do was watch television and play. She couldn't get you to talk about it. A little while later, it was all forgotten."

"Well, somebody hasn't forgotten it." She pointed at the folded newspaper article and the necklace laying on the table.

"Who would do this?" Anna asked, as her eyes filled with tears.

"I don't know. Anybody could have copied the article from the library, but the necklace. Who had the necklace all these years? And why did they keep it?"

"My God, that was such a long time ago. Why can't they just let it go?" she said between sobs.

Deirdre got up and walked over to her mother's side. She leaned over and hugged her mother as they cried together.

"I'm so sorry I didn't tell you the truth earlier. Baby, I didn't want you to have to relive that. You had nightmares for weeks after that incident."

Deirdre pulled out another chair and sat next to her mother. "Mama, I'm having those nightmares again. We can't ignore it this time."

Robert finally got his sister, Bernice, on the phone. After they discussed the latest breaking news he asked her about Omar.

"Mama tells me he's looking for a job?"

"Yeah, finally."

"You know he never called any of the leads I gave him," Robert admitted angrily.

"You don't understand. He can't let you get him a job. He has to do it for himself. Omar has been trying to get out from under your shadow for a long time."

"He's not under my shadow," Robert stated, confused.

"Yes he is. Mama's always asking him why can't he be more like you. When you were in Philly working, she hounded Omar. What was he going to major in? Why weren't his grades better? She pressured him so much. Then when he came home, things got worse."

"Bernice, Omar's just lazy."

"He's not lazy. He feels beat down. After Daddy died, you became the man of the house. Omar didn't feel like he had a place. Mama expected you to do everything. He couldn't find a place for himself."

"He never mentioned anything like that to me."

"And you think he's going to?"

"I guess not," he confessed.

"Of course not. He has to find a job on his own. But, I do think his new girlfriend inspired him."

"So that's it."

"Yeah, you know the power we women have over men." Bernice laughed. "She's a really nice young woman too. Maybe too nice for Omar. So, I hope he gets his stuff together."

"Yeah me, too."

"The next thing you know, he'll be moving out."

"And it's about time, don't you think?"

"Yes. Say, I hear you have a new girlfriend, too."

"Who told you that?"

"Mama. You haven't introduced her yet, but we know you've been seeing that counselor over at the Brunswick Community Center."

"Yes I have, and I know you've got something to say about it."

"I'd be afraid of her if I were you."

"What are you talking about?"

"Women are getting raped over at that office and things. From what I hear, they've been having nothing but bad luck since she started."

"That's not true. She was there six months before the first break-in with no incident at all," he defended Deirdre.

"Yeah, well everybody's talking about that place. You sure picked the most popular girl in town. But, I'm glad to see you picked somebody."

"Thanks a lot Bernice," he said nonchalantly.

Knock, knock. "Robert, can I speak with you a moment?"

He looked up and saw Dean standing in his doorway. "Bernice, let me get back with you."

"Robert, I want you to find out what happened to that old lady."

"What do you mean?"

"I want to know who killed her and why. It's got to have something to do with the calls we're getting."

Dean was asking for something Robert didn't want to do. He didn't want to report another story that had anything to do with Deirdre's office unless it was positive.

"Want me to call somebody down at the police station and see what I can find out?"

"Nope. Not this time. We need to work this story. I want you to get out there and find out whatever you can."

Robert hesitated before answering. "Uh, Dean if you don't mind can you give this assignment to somebody else. I've got a conflict of interest with this one."

"How so?"

"I've been seeing Geneva Shaw's counselor. And I don't think . . ."

Dean cut him off. "Then don't interview the counselor. You can talk to everyone else she knows. Robert, I want you on this story. This is the type of investigative work I hired you for."

Robert looked at his boss wishing for the first time he'd chosen another profession. Or, that he'd been assigned to sports like Wayne.

"I can count on you right?" Dean waited with his hand pressed against the door frame.

"Yeah, I'll get right on it." Unless he took on every challenge that came his way, he'd never get a job with a bigger paper.

After Dean left, Robert stared out into the hallway. Maybe he could do some good with this article in some way. He could probably get some information that the police couldn't. People were more reluctant to talk with police than reporters, and he used that to his advantage every time.

However, if he started snooping around asking questions Bill Duncan might not like it. Knowing he had it in for Robert wouldn't make things easier. If Bill could pin any of this on him, Robert knew he would. He'd have to be careful who he talked to.

What he needed was a little help, and he knew where to get it. He jumped up from his seat and walked down the hall to Wayne's office.

"Knock, knock." Robert said as he walked into the huge office that held all three of the sports reporters. Wayne's desk was in the back of the room.

"Hey Rob, what brings you this way?" One of Wayne's co-workers asked.

Robert pointed to Wayne's desk. "Just came around to see Wayne here."

"Okay, you guys have a nice evening. I'm blowing this Popsicle stand." Wayne's co-worker shook Robert's hand on his way out.

"What's up man?" Wayne asked looking up from his clean desk.

Robert leaned against the desk next to Wayne. "I need your help."

"Sure, what can I do for you?"

"Several weeks ago, you said you knew a private investigator who was very discreet if I ever needed one."

"Yeah."

"Well I'm in need."

"Got a hot story?"

"I've got a story that could blow up in my face if I get too close. So, I need some anonymous help on this one."

Wayne flipped through his Rolodex. "Hey man, don't say another word. I've got her number right here."

"Her number?"

"Yeah, and she's the best P.I. I've ever run into. I've used her myself a couple of times. Because she's a petite black female, no one ever suspects her of being a P.I."

Robert chuckled. "That's great."

Wayne jotted the name and number on a piece of paper. "I read about one of Deirdre's clients this morning in the paper."

"Yeah man, it's getting pretty bad. Dean's put me on the story and I wish like hell he hadn't."

"Here you go." He handed Robert the piece of paper. "Why is that? You've been following all the incidents there so far haven't you?"

"I have, but I've also started seeing Deirdre, and I think this is a conflict of interest."

"Man you know Dean, the closer to the story you are the better, he thinks. He's hoping you can get some inside information that somebody else can't get."

"Well, I don't like it. It makes it hard to pick her up for dinner when I know what I have to write."

"Michelle can help you out. She lives over in Jacksonville, and does a lot of work around the coastal isles."

"Thanks a lot, I'll give her a call."

"Say, if you don't mind me asking, what makes you think this thing could blow up in your face?"

"Bill Duncan's had it in for me since high school. We weren't exactly running buddies. Then I move back in town after all these years and who's the police chief, Bill Duncan. My first story is about one of those young girls raped over on St. Simons Island. Unfortunately, Bill didn't like the fact that I said the police were dragging their feet on the investigation."

"Yeah, I can see why he'd not like that. He hates for anyone to criticize his work."

"Since then, he's been digging into my wife's death. Of course, being the husband, I was a suspect. The police in Philly ruled it an accident, but Bill has it stuck in his mind that I killed her."

"No shit!"

"Yeah, and he throws it up in my face every chance he gets."

"Man, I didn't know Bill was like that."

"Yeah, that's why he's on my case all the damn time."

"Good luck with Michelle. Maybe solving this will get Bill off your butt."

"I hope so."

Deirdre let Mia play on the floor in her office while she checked her e-mail. Since she didn't have a job to report to, she decided to work on her Web page and answer all her mail a little earlier than usual.

The first thing she noticed was an e-mail from GypseyRose. That was the same ID that sent her an instant message a couple of weeks ago. She opened the mail.

DON'T TRUST ANYONE. NOT EVEN THE PEOPLE RIGHT UNDER YOUR NOSE.

Who was sending her these notes? Did they know who the

rapist was and wanted to tell her? This time she had an e-mail that she could respond to. She hit reply and asked . . .

WHO ARE YOU? CAN YOU HELP ME?

She sent her note, and waited around to see if the person was still online. While waiting she read all her e-mail and responded to it.

She couldn't get the words out of her mind. People right under your nose. The rapist or killer was right under her nose? But whom?

One of her clients, Mr. Hamel, Robert, or maybe whoever sent her this note? Whoever was responsible for the article and the necklace, that's who. She picked up the phone to call Bill Duncan. She should have already told him about the necklace and the article.

Bill promised her he'd come by as soon as he could to get a look at both items. They were extremely busy at the moment. When she hung up, she called Belinda. She needed someone to bounce ideas off. They met at The Palmer Gallery on St. Simons Island while Belinda checked out some new photographs.

"So why didn't you tell the police about the Internet messages?" Belinda asked.

"I'm not ready to tell them about that yet. Whoever it is might know who the killer is and lead me to them."

"Did you ever think that it might be the killer?"

"Yeah, I thought about that, but why would a killer send me little messages like that?"

"I don't know. What did the last message say again?"

"Not to trust anyone. Not even people right under my nose. Now that sounds like they know who it is, doesn't it?"

"Yes, and you should have told Bill about that. Girl, the next message might say, 'I'm coming to get you,' or some craziness like that. Aren't you scared?"

"Yes, I'm scared to death, but I've got to try and help myself. I've tried to think of everybody right under my nose, and there are too many people. It could be one of my clients, or anybody at the center, or who knows who else."

"Are the police close to finding anybody?"

"No, all Bill Duncan keeps doing is telling me to be careful around Robert. They don't like each other."

"That's because he's suspicious of Robert."

Deirdre turned to her friend in surprise. "You know about that?"

"Only what Kenneth told me."

"Spill it girl. Tell me what you know."

"Well, first of all Bill is carrying around some stupid grudge from high school. After Robert moved back, Bill found out about his wife's death. He called Philly and got all the details."

"Everybody knows about his wife's death and how he turned to alcohol afterward. He told me all about that himself. That's how he lost his job and ended up back here."

"Well, Bill's hell-bent on proving something none of us believe, mind you."

"What?"

"He thinks Robert killed his wife in cold blood before he drove that car off the embankment." Belinda glanced at Deirdre before turning the next corner. She checked out the photographs on that wall.

"That's ridiculous. The police in Philly would have come to that conclusion."

"I don't know, I'm just telling you what Kenneth told me. Bill thinks Robert started drinking out of guilt. You know, they were getting a divorce. I hear it was a messy situation. Then she conveniently dies."

TWENTY

Saturday morning Robert took Deirdre and Mia to Neptune Park for a picnic. Deirdre let Mia bring along one of her neighborhood friends.

He stood up and looked over at the swings. Mia and her friend were taking turns pushing each other on a swing. Shoving his hands into his back pocket, Robert wrestled with his thoughts. He wanted to tell Deirdre about being assigned to investigate Geneva's death, but he couldn't. She'd already read the article he did on her death. That had to be damage enough.

"Robert, can I ask you something?"

He turned and faced her. "Sure."

"What's the real deal between you and Bill Duncan?"

He sighed. "Do you really want to know?"

"Yes, I do." She walked over to the table and pulled ears of corn out of a Ziploc bag. Robert walked over and helped her wrap them in aluminum foil.

"He broke up with a girl in high school that I started dating, and it pissed him off. Every chance he got, he tried to get back at me. Even as adults, he hasn't let up. It's ridiculous."

"He thinks you killed your wife?" She had to come straight out and ask him. Doubts were lingering in the back of her mind, and she wanted to squash them.

"I know what he's doing, and it's not going to work. He's holding that over my head so I'll quit being critical of the police in my articles. I didn't kill my wife and he knows it."

"I haven't told you this, but he keeps warning me to be careful around you." She felt silly even admitting that she listened to what Bill had said. But after talking to Belinda the other night, she had to hear it from Robert.

Robert looked at her as he placed the corn on the grill. "What does he think I'll do?"

"I don't know. He doesn't trust you."

Robert finished putting everything on the grill and grabbed her hand. "Come here, let me talk to you." They sat on the park bench facing the children on the swings. He straddled the bench and faced her.

He reached out for Deirdre's hand and caressed with it while he talked. "We were driving down the highway when a car pulled out on us. I swerved to avoid a collision, and lost control of the car. We went off the side of the road, and down an embankment. Karen didn't have her seat belt on, and was thrown from the car. She landed on her head, and died instantly."

"My seat belt saved my life. I wasn't hurt."

"I'm so sorry."

He held up a hand in protest. "Let me finish. Karen's family blamed me for her death. She had filed for a divorce and pretty much bad-mouthed me with her entire family. The things she said weren't true, and I still loved her. I would have never done anything to hurt her."

"You must have felt awful?"

"I did. For two years I felt awful. But I've made peace with myself about her death. I know it wasn't my fault now. And not even Bill Duncan can make me feel as if it was."

"Robert, I believe you." She reassured him.

"Good. I wanted to get that out of the way in case you were wondering, or had doubts."

"What? Me doubt you?" She pointed to herself smiling. "Not for one minute."

"Eh . . . yes you. I know you and Bill are friends."

"I remember Bill from when I lived here years ago, but we aren't exactly good friends. If getting that out makes you feel better, then I'm glad you did." She wasn't about to admit it, but she was so glad he'd shared that information with her. The words, people right under your nose, kept coming to mind. And Robert was one of those people.

The children came running back from the swing and wanted to play miniature golf. Robert charmed them into eating first, then promised to beat the shorts off both of them.

Deirdre watched Mia whenever she was around Robert. The two of them got along so well. Could he get Mia to stop crying for her Daddy on Sundays? She hoped so.

While they played a game of miniature golf, Robert asked Deirdre about her job.

"What are you going to do now that the office is closed?"

"First, I'm going to get away for a little while. I'm taking Mia up to my sister's in Chicago for a week. With any luck the police will have caught somebody when I return."

"What if they haven't?" he asked, looking at his golf ball.

"Then I'll have to meet with the board. I don't blame them for closing the office, but maybe I can persuade them to move me into a new location until this settles down."

"Have the police given you any more information?"

"No. And I don't see how something like this can be kept secret in such a small town. You would think somebody would have let it slip by now. Everything else in this town gets out. If you want to know who's sleeping with whom, just ask around."

Robert chuckled. "Oh, life in a small town. Yes, bad news does travel very fast."

"I found something on my doorstep the other night."

"What?" He missed his putt, then viewed her with concerned eyes.

"An article. It was about a little girl raped more than twenty-two years ago. When I showed it to my mother, she admitted it was me."

Robert almost dropped his golf club. He had figured all along she was the little girl in her dreams, but hadn't wanted to tell her so. Being raped wasn't an easy thing to deal with.

"I'm sorry Deirdre, but now that you're sure, you can start

the healing process. Did you say someone placed the article on your doorstep?"

"Yes. I just opened the door, and there it was. It appeared out of thin air just like the necklace." She tried to hit her balls in line with Robert's, so they could stay close on the miniature field.

"What necklace?" He leaned against his golf club and eyed her.

"The day Sheila was raped, I found a necklace on the floor of my office. It was the necklace my grandmother gave me when I was a little girl. Or, it looks like the same necklace."

"Did you tell the police?" he asked with a sense of urgency.

"Not yet, I just confronted my mother. I'm going to tell Bill though."

"Deirdre, you've got to be very careful. I didn't know all that was going on. Don't wait too long, let the police know everything." Now he was glad he'd been assigned to investigate the rapes. Maybe he could help her after all.

"I'm extremely careful. Susan and I have been arriving at work at the same time. Mr. Hamel asked Alfred to come in a little earlier lately also. Things at the office had been back to normal, until Geneva's death."

"What time is the funeral tomorrow?"

"Three o'clock," she answered, sounding blue.

He shook his head. "Want me to pick you up and take you?"

She looked at Robert surprised. "You're going?"

"Yeah, I thought you might need my support."

She walked over and gave him a kiss. "Thank you. I'd love to have your support tomorrow. I'm going to need it."

A couple behind them had caught up, and were patiently waiting. They hurried through so Robert could play another round with the children. The rest of the afternoon was spent throwing Frisbees and chasing the children around the park. On the ride home Mia and her little friend were fast asleep. Robert had to help carry one of the children into the house, so Deirdre could put them down for a nap.

Afterward, he stood in her parents' doorway not wanting to

leave. They had been spending more time with each other, but still not enough in his book.

"Robert I want to thank you for such a fun day. You were wonderful with the girls."

"I'm glad everybody had a good time. I thoroughly enjoyed myself. We'll have to do that again soon."

"I'd like that. We can talk about it when I get back from Chicago."

"I'm glad to see you're really taking some time off. You deserve it. Let the police do their job and find this guy."

"Robert, I've done all I think I can. I read over every client's case file to see if any of them would be capable of rape or murder. I've talked to everyone at the community center and surrounding businesses. Nobody seems to have seen anything. This guy kind of comes and goes like he's invisible."

"You know the police really should have put someone here to watch your house," Robert commented and glanced around.

"I don't need that. Besides, my dad's here. If anybody comes through that door uninvited, he believes in shooting first, and asking questions later."

"I like your father. He's a smart man."

They looked at each other without saying a word, but knowing what was on the other's mind. Robert stepped closer, closing the distance between them.

"I'm going to miss you while you're gone, you know that?"

"And I'll miss you, too. I won't be able to read your articles in the mornings." She smiled at him.

"Is that all you're going to miss, my work?" he asked in a playful tone. Simultaneously, his hand slid around her waist pulling her to him.

"Not quite. I'm going to miss these." She tiptoed and kissed him softly on the lips. "And these." The next kiss gently touched his eyelids.

"Hmm . . . sounds like you're going to miss me."

* * *

When Deirdre and Mia got off the plane in Chicago Sunday morning, Barbara and the kids were there to greet them. They hugged like two sisters that were very close.

"How did Mia take the flight?" Barbara asked.

"Oh, she was fine. A couple of coloring books and she's too busy to think about being on an airplane."

"Great, well let's get home so we can cook dinner."

"Barbara, I hope you don't plan to work me to death while I'm here," Deirdre said in a playful manner.

"You still scared of a little work?" Barbara called the children as they walked down the terminal.

"I've never been afraid of work."

"Oh that's right, you had Mama and Daddy to do your work for you."

Deirdre sighed. "I hope the whole week's not going to be like this."

"Like what?" Barbara asked sarcastically.

"Like our entire life."

The first couple of days were just like that. Deirdre couldn't deal with tiptoeing around Barbara's house another day. She had to confront her sister, or go home. This was supposed to be a vacation.

The kids were downstairs playing video games, something Mia didn't have at home. Barbara's husband had gone to work, so Deirdre took this time to confront her sister.

"Barbara we need to talk."

"About what?" Barbara asked nonchalantly.

"About you and me. Either you're the meanest sister there ever was, or you don't like me for some reason."

"Girl, what are you talking about?" Barbara was ironing the children's clothes for the movie they were going to attend that afternoon.

"We can't carry on a conversation without you getting smart with me. You're jealous about my relationship with Mama and Daddy. And I thought you'd have a hissy fit when I went off to college in California."

Barbara set the iron down with a loud thump. "Well, now that you mentioned it. I am tired of you always getting such preferential treatment. When we were little, you would have thought you were some type of princess or something. Everybody treated you with kid gloves. 'Barbara, Deirdre's tired, can you do the dishes tonight? Deirdre's not feeling good Barbara, can you put the laundry away?' " she mimicked her mother's voice.

"Barbara that's not fair."

"How come it's not? I did all the work around the place, and you got all the attention. They treated me like a stepchild. Hell, worse than that. You treat a stepchild better than my own parents treated me. I couldn't wait to get out of high school and away from that place." In frustration, she picked the iron back up and continued ironing.

Deirdre had figured everything out. Now that she knew what she did about being raped, she knew why her parent's were so careful with her. She wanted to apologize to her sister, but she wasn't sure if it would be enough.

"So, little princess, that husband of yours didn't want to take care of you, so you ran back home to Mama and Daddy," Barbara said in an unsympathetic tone.

Deirdre grabbed an apple out of the fruit bowl on the table. If it were Barbara's head, she would have squeezed it until juice ran out. Her sister had a way of making her so mad.

"Barbara I found something that I think you should know about." Reaching inside her pants' pocket, Deirdre pulled out the article. She walked over and laid it on the ironing board.

"What's that?"

"Read it."

Barbara stopped ironing and picked up the piece of paper. She opened it and read the contents to herself. Deirdre watched the blank expression on her face and realized she didn't know anything about the rape.

After reading the article, Barbara looked up and shrugged her shoulders. "That's sad, but what's it about?"

"That was me." When she said the words, she wanted to cry all over again.

"You're kidding me, right?"

"No, Mama verified it for me."

Barbara backed away from the ironing board and sat at the kitchen table. Her eyes filled with tears as she read the article again. "How come I didn't know about this?" she asked as she folded the paper back up.

"I don't know. I didn't even remember it until recently. I guess I blocked it out of my memory. Then when one of my clients was raped, I began having nightmares."

"Where did you find that article?" Barbara wiped the tears from her cheeks.

"Somebody placed it on the front porch one night."

"You don't know who?"

"No. And that scares me."

"Have you told the police?"

"Yes, I've told them everything and they're looking into it."

"Deirdre I had no idea." Barbara placed her hand over her mouth. "So Mama and Daddy knew all along?"

"Yes, but Mama said I forgot about it, so she did too. She told me it was in the past and I shouldn't worry about it."

"Is she crazy? Something like that can affect your entire life."

"And it has in a way. Now I understand some things about myself that I didn't before."

Barbara started crying again. "Deirdre, I'm sorry about all those princess remarks. I didn't mean anything by it."

Deirdre walked over and hugged her. "I know it. Besides, I never felt like royalty anyway." She pulled back and looked at Barbara so she would know she was joking with her. They embraced again and laughed through their tears.

Barbara pulled a fruit salad out of the refrigerator, and they sat down and talked things over. In the last ten years they hadn't been very close. Five phone calls a year maybe, if Deirdre initiated most of them. Barbara had Deirdre fill her in on everything from her divorce to what had been going on at work.

"Now that you know you were raped, what are you going to do about it?"

"What do you mean?" Deirdre bit her lower lip baffled.

"You're a counselor. You know how important it is to talk to someone about things like that. Are you going to see someone?"

Deirdre held her head down. "I know I should, but until I remember more I don't see a need to."

"Deirdre, you don't think subconsciously that had anything to do with your divorce? And the fact that you have always been finicky about your neck? Not to mention other than William you haven't had another man in your life. At least, Mama hasn't told me about anybody."

"I have a man in my life right now. And thinking back, it may have had something to do with the way William and I got along. But most of our troubles were a result of his job. He spent so much time there, and none at home."

"Maybe he stayed in that lab for a reason. You ever think of that?"

A sinking feeling came over Deirdre. William was the only man she had ever made love to. Most of her married life she didn't care for sex, but had attributed it to William's cold behavior toward her. However, she didn't feel that way now concerning Robert.

When Deirdre didn't answer, Barbara changed the subject. "So, tell me about the new man in your life."

"Do you remember Robert Carmichael from Lincoln High?"

"I don't think so."

"I had a crush on him, but I didn't tell anybody. He works for the *Brunswick Constitution*. Barbara he's been there for me every step of the way during all this mess."

"I bet you haven't had sex with him yet, have you?"

Deirdre stared at Barbara wanting to know what she was getting at. "We haven't been seeing each other that long."

"Deirdre, I'm not telling you what to do, but when you get back home, go talk to somebody. You're a counselor, don't you counsel rape victims?"

"I've never had one before."

"Never?"

"I've never felt qualified. I refer them to a colleague of mine."

Barbara stood up and paced the floor. "Mama and Daddy should have put you in therapy when you were a child. And somebody needs to talk to Mama and Daddy, too, about keeping this a damn secret for so long."

"They weren't keeping it a secret. I told you I didn't remember it."

"Well, you remember now. So do what you would tell one of your clients to do. Seek therapy."

Robert walked from house to house to talk with Geneva Shaw's neighbors. A couple of hours later, he didn't have anything. He had one last house to visit. Melva Atkinson lived right across the street from Geneva. Robert found her in her rose garden.

"Ms. Atkinson, hello. Do you remember me from a couple of days ago?"

The elderly woman with silver-blue hair looked over the rim of her glasses at Robert. "You're that reporter aren't you?" She asked, taking off her gardening gloves.

"Yes ma'am, Robert Carmichael. I'm talking to all of Geneva Shaw's neighbors to see if anyone remembers anything else about that day."

She looked Robert over, deciding whether to talk to him or not. After a few minutes of consideration, she walked over and sat in the yard chair she'd placed under a shade tree.

"I've already talked to the police."

Robert followed her and gestured toward the seat next to her. "May I?"

"Sure, go ahead and take a load off."

"Junior, bring this young man a glass of water," she hollered at a young man sitting on the back step.

Robert hadn't even noticed the young man when he walked up. "Thank you. Ma'am I know you've spoken with the police, but there might be something you forgot when they were here, or you've remembered. I want to help the police catch this guy, before he hurts anyone else in this neighborhood."

"Well, I didn't see nothing unusual that day. I tended my rose garden as usual. Later, I saw Geneva leave for the grocery store."

"How did you know she was going to the grocery store?"

"She has this big shopping bag she carries to the grocery store. It's hard packing in all the little plastic bags they try to give you. When she leaves the house with that shopping bag, I know she's going to the store."

"Did you see her when she returned?" He reached up and took the glass of water from the young man. "Thank you."

"No I didn't. I'd gone back in the house to watch my game shows by then. Mr. Carmichael, people don't sit outside as much as they used to anymore. That was the last time I saw her," she said sorrowfully.

"So you didn't see anyone in the neighborhood you hadn't seen before that morning? Any delivery trucks or strange cars driving by?"

She shook her head and grabbed a rag off the table next to her to wipe the sweat from her brow. "Nope. Nothing but a police car that drove through here that morning. And it's good to see them come through from time to time, it makes you feel safe if you know what I mean."

"Yeah, I know what you mean." He gave Melva his card and asked her to call if she remembered anything else. The same speech he gave all the other neighbors.

Robert left Melva's house feeling as if he'd wasted his morning. He'd talked to more than ten people, but hadn't gained one new piece of information. But, he wasn't done yet.

TWENTY-ONE

Robert's next stop was the Brunswick Community Center. He wasn't ready to give up on obtaining the right piece of information he needed. He talked to a couple of the staff workers, but didn't get any new information. Alfred, the janitor, was in the recreation room cleaning up when Robert found him.

"Excuse me, Alfred."

He turned around and gave Robert a hard look. This one would be tough. He worked for Mr. Hamel and wouldn't tell anything Hamel didn't want told.

"Yeah," he said, absently.

"If you have a few minutes, I'd like to ask you a few questions."

"I talked to the police a couple of times now." He turned and walked away from Robert. "I've got work to do."

Robert had to think quick and get Alfred's attention. "Alfred you like Deirdre, don't you?"

He stopped, but didn't turn to face him. "Yes I do. She's a nice lady."

"I know you didn't do anything. That's not why I want to talk to you. I'm trying to help Deirdre. Can I count on you to help me?"

He turned and looked Robert narrowly in the eye. His dark eyes squinted in confusion. "Help you how?"

Robert looked around the recreation room as he walked over to Alfred. "You told the police you had no idea how somebody got into that back door. But, you're here early in the morning before anyone else gets here. And sometimes you're still here at the end of the day. Don't you lock or unlock that back door when it needs to be?"

Alfred lowered his head and scanned the floor like he'd lost something. "I told you I didn't see nothing." His tone was harsh.

"I'm not saying you did. But, maybe you know how someone could get in and out so easily?"

Alfred finished putting the children's toys away. He sighed heavily and leaned against a table. "A couple of times I came to work and the back door was unlocked. I know I locked it before I left. Somebody either came in here after me, or before I got here the next morning."

"Would one of those times have been when that young lady was raped?" Robert tread carefully with him.

He looked reluctant to answer, but finally said, "Yes."

"Did you tell the police?"

"No." He gave Robert a startled look. "It's my job to lock up at the end of every day. If Mr. Hamel thinks I left the door unlocked, he'd fire me."

"Who do you think unlocked the door?"

"I don't know. All I do around here is my job. I mind my own business."

He rattled on about keeping to himself. Robert gave up on getting anything else out of him. Now he had to find out who unlocked that door.

"Thanks Alfred, you've been a big help."

"Hey, what I said about the back door. You not gonna tell Mr. Hamel are you?"

Robert shook his head. "No, I won't say anything."

Robert's last stop for the day was Susan's house. He'd gotten her address from the Community Center and found her at home.

She answered the door in a pair of extremely short shorts and a tank top. Not much different from the short skirts and snug-fitting jackets she wore at the office.

"Mr. Carmichael, what brings you over to this part of town?" she asked smiling.

"Hi Susan, I came to ask you a few questions."

Her smile relaxed and changed into an expression of worry. "What type of questions?"

"I'm not asking you to disclose anything on Deirdre's clients, only some general information about the office."

"Oh." She stood back so he could enter. "Come on in."

He walked into the living room and sat on the sofa.

"Would you like something to drink?" she asked, gesturing toward the kitchen.

"No, thank you."

"Go ahead and ask away. I'm going to fix myself a glass of tea. It's hot as hell out there, isn't it?"

"It sure is." Robert watched her step into the kitchen, just off the living room. "I've talked to some of Geneva Shaw's neighbors and several workers at the community center. I'd appreciate it if you could think back and let me know if you've seen anything out of order or unusual going on around the counseling office."

Susan returned to the living room and sat in a chair across from the sofa. She crossed her legs exposing more of her thighs.

"Are you writing a story about Geneva?"

"The paper's just trying to help the police solve the crime. That's all."

"Oh, I've already thought about it, and the answer is no. I haven't seen anything out of the ordinary."

"Do you have a key to the back door?"

"Yes, but so do several other people. And I've never used mine."

"Never?"

"No. I keep it in my wallet in case of an emergency, but I've never had to use it. I always enter through the front door."

Robert nodded. So far this interview was going like the ones earlier. "Who do you think left the back door unlocked the morning Sheila Mitchell was raped?"

"It could have been anyone. Probably Alfred. He's very absentminded you know. And he snoops around the office all the time. I wouldn't put anything past that man." She uncrossed and recrossed her legs as she sipped her ice tea.

"You mean he snoops around the counseling office?"

"Yes, and he uses the phone when we're not in."

"How do you know that?" he asked anxiously.

"Once we had a phone bill with 900-numbers on it. They were made late in the afternoon. Long after Deirdre and I were gone home. Who else could have done that, but Alfred."

"How about the stolen money, do you think he's responsible for that as well?"

"How do you know about that?" She stood up and returned to the kitchen.

"Deirdre told me. I'm looking into everything, because all of this may be connected in some way."

"I bet you think I stole that money, don't you?" she asked dumping her drink into the sink

Where did that come from, Robert thought. "I didn't come here to accuse you of anything. I'm only trying to jar your memory and see if you remember anything that might help Deirdre."

"I'm trying to help Deirdre."

"How, by leaving the back door open for somebody?" He had his suspicions about Susan.

She stormed out of the kitchen and toward the front door. "Mr. Carmichael, I'm sorry but I can't help you anymore. Please leave." She opened the door and stood holding it open.

He stood up. "Look Susan, I'm sorry. I didn't mean to accuse you of that. It's just that only a few people have keys to that back door. I'm trying to talk to all of them."

"I'm helping Deirdre in the only way I know how. And that's more than I can say for what you're doing." Her eyes narrowed.

"Is it anything you can tell me about?"

She hesitantly tapped her foot against the floor and looked away. "If I did know something and I told you, you'd print it the very next day."

"No I wouldn't. Susan, you can trust me. You've got to help

her if you can." He walked toward her when he recognized her willingness to talk.

Hands placed firmly on her hips, Susan bit her lip and looked him in the eye. He searched her face for a sign of guilt. Did she leave the door open for someone?

"Susan, do you know who raped Sheila Mitchell?"

This time she didn't hesitate at all. "Of course not. I think you better leave."

Robert left her house knowing she was on the verge of telling him something. He wished he could have been able to persuade her to talk. Now he had to find a way to get it out of her.

Riding down Bay Street, for some reason he thought about his father. Would he have been proud of him? He was determined to do his best work and climb back up the ladder to a better position, at a bigger paper. However, a bigger paper meant leaving Brunswick and Deirdre.

Deirdre arrived back in town feeling better than she had in weeks. The trip to her sister's had given her the strength to make things work for her in Brunswick. No matter what happened, she knew she'd be all right. She'd worked out her differences with Barbara and they were closer than ever.

After she was all unpacked and settled, she checked her voice mail at the office. They were closed, but she wondered if any of her clients might have called.

She had ten messages that blew her away. Her clients were calling to find out when her office would be reopening. The messages helped to make her feel even stronger. Her clients needed her.

Tomorrow morning she'd call Mr. Hamel and see if she couldn't talk them into reopening her office. They'd been closed a week already. It wasn't fair to her clients.

After listening to the messages, she picked up the phone to call Robert. He answered on the first ring.

"Hello."

"Hi Robert, it's me."

"Hey baby, when did you get back?"

"About an hour ago." She detected the excitement in his voice and liked it.

"How was the trip?" he asked pleasantly.

"It was wonderful. I really needed to get away, but I also needed to spend some time with Barbara. And you won't believe the voice mails I've gotten from my clients."

"I believe it. Deirdre you're a good counselor, did you think they'd just let you go away."

"Once the office was closed, I thought they'd just find somebody else. But they're asking when I'm reopening."

"That's great. So, when do I get to see you? Don't tell me I have to wait until your office opens back up?" He asked laughing.

She laughed along with him. "No, I don't think I'll make you wait that long."

"Good. How about tonight? I know this place that has the best food and atmosphere in town."

"Oh you do."

"Yes, and I'm sure you'll love it too. What do you say to seven-thirty sharp?"

"I say, I'll see you at seven-thirty."

Deirdre hung up the phone excited about seeing Robert. Absence did make the heart grow fonder, and she'd missed him terribly.

When she walked downstairs, she found her father sitting in front of the television in his recliner.

"Have a nice visit?" He asked not taking his eyes off the television.

"Yes, I had a great time."

He chuckled. "That's a first. You girls usually fight all the time."

"Yeah, I know we do. But this time things were different. Do you remember what happened to me when I was thirteen?"

Ralph looked at is daughter with apologetic eyes. "Yes, I remember. Your mother tells me that you remember now, too."

She shook her head. "Barbara talked about it. She had no idea."

He sighed heavily and turned down the volume with the remote. "We thought it would be too much for her. At the time we thought we were doing the right thing. You girls were too young to deal with such things."

"Well, somebody else remembers it as well," she said, almost under her breath.

"What's that?"

"Never mind. I'm kind of tired Daddy, so I think I'll go and rest for a little while."

"You work tomorrow?"

"No."

"They haven't officially closed your office have they?"

"No. We're just closed for an undetermined amount of days."

"Fight it baby. Don't let them ruin your career. If I can do anything to help, don't hesitate to ask, okay?"

"Thanks, Daddy." Deirdre wasn't mad at her parents for the way they avoided discussing her rape. They probably didn't know how to handle it, and if she never mentioned it, why should they?

Now that she remembered it, she knew she had to do something about it. No longer could they walk around pretending it never happened.

Later that night, when Deirdre entered Robert's house she smelled a wonderful aroma.

"Hmm . . . something smells wonderful."

"Welcome to Chateau Carmichael's." He gestured toward the dining room.

"The best place in town, huh?" She laughed with her arms crossed over her chest.

Robert turned the CD player on, then went to light the candles on the table. "Yes, ma'am. The greatest food, music and company."

Deirdre sat down at the table and exhaled. "Boy, this is so nice of you. I've never had a man cook dinner for me before."

"I'm no chef, but I do know how to cook." He stood next to her and poured her a glass of wine.

Deirdre shrugged and took a deep breath.

Robert set the wine bottle down and grabbed her by the shoulders. "I think you need a massage more then anything right now." He worked his hands kneading her flesh.

"Hmm . . . that feels wonderful." She closed her eyes and enjoyed his big, strong hands caressing her shoulders.

"You've got a lot of tension in your shoulders. Baby, you need a good massage. Come on." He reached around for her hand. "Bring your drink, dinner can wait."

She grabbed her drink and followed him into the dark living room. He turned on a small table lamp, casting a glow of light in the room. Deirdre took a few sips of her wine waiting on him to pitch all the pillows from the couch onto the floor.

"Here, lie down on your stomach. I'll take that." He took her wineglass and raised it to his mouth, finishing it off.

Without protest she lay down and closed her eyes. Her whole body had been aching for weeks. She wouldn't deny him this pleasure.

Robert moved her hair to the side and straddled her. He lowered himself and kissed the back of her neck. She didn't flinch.

His hands moved down her back pressing firmly into her flesh. Little moans escaped her mouth as she lay there biting her lip.

"Deirdre, take off your dress," Robert whispered into her ear.

She tilted her head looking back at him. He got up from the couch and helped her up. She stood and unbuttoned her dress, letting it fall to the floor. He reached down and picked up her dress, then threw it onto a waiting chair. In her underwear, he lay her back down and continued to massage her entire body.

Deirdre was ready to open up to him tonight. She wanted him to love her. She lay there and let the music take her mind. Her whole body responded to his strong hands. He leaned over and planted soft kisses along her back and shoulders.

"I love your back." He kissed her there. "And, I love your shoulders." He kissed her there, too.

She rolled over onto her back and looked into his passion-filled eyes. Her whole body was on fire. Everywhere he touched longed for the feel of his big hands.

Reaching forward, she began undoing the buttons on his shirt. Without saying a word, he reached down and helped her. Standing up, he stripped out of his shirt and pants. She looked up at his body, and her pulse quickened. This is what she wanted—him.

Instead of them going to his bedroom, he pulled her to the floor in front of the empty fireplace. Robert had to have her tonight. He'd spent too many nights dreaming about her, and wanting to feel her body against his. The minute her dress touched the floor, he was moved to undeniable arousal.

He grabbed several pillows he'd already thrown onto the floor and placed them under her. Her precious body responded to his every touch. Tonight he would deny her no longer.

"Deirdre, I'm so hungry for you," he said huskily, and proceeded to kiss her all over again.

"Robert I want you so badly tonight." She tried to catch her breath long enough to speak. His lips moved up to her neck and kissed her there. She felt her body stiffen, and then relax as he whispered to her.

"It's me baby. And I'll never do anything to hurt you."

The soothing jazz and his voice relaxed her body like a drug. They eased out of their underwear and began exploring each other's bodies. He tasted her nipples, and she tasted his. In a matter of minutes he was just where she wanted him—on top of her.

"Deirdre, I want to make love to you so badly it hurts." His voice was still husky.

"Then soothe the pain, baby." She welcomed him as he entered

222 *Bridget Anderson*

her giving himself totally. Not even in her wildest dreams had she experienced such blissfulness.

He gazed down into her eyes as he emptied himself into her. As the first orgasm plunged her, she stiffened, then shivered into a peaceful calm.

TWENTY-TWO

The next day Robert and Deirdre had lunch plans for twelve o'clock. She'd gotten up that morning to call Mr. Hamel and find out when the board planned on reopening her office.

"Mr. Hamel it's been well over a week now and I was wondering if you'd spoken with the other board members yet?"

He hesitated. "We met, then I had a meeting with Officer Duncan. We've decided to wait a couple of days, then reopen your office with a security guard posted in the parking lot."

"A security guard?"

"Yes, we've already hired someone. He started a few days ago."

"Thank you. I've received a lot of calls from clients this week."

"I probably received some of the same calls. I appreciate you touching base with all your clients before leaving town."

"I felt like I owed them an explanation."

"Susan called concerned about her job. I assured her she didn't have anything to worry about."

"Thanks, I appreciate that."

"Deirdre, I know I've given you a hard time since you've been here, and I apologize. I had selfish reasons for not wanting to open a counseling office. All I thought about was the money to be made if we leased the space out. I didn't think about the good a counseling office would provide for the community. I'm very sorry."

What's gotten into him. "Mr. Hamel my purpose for being

here is to do some good. All I ever wanted to do was help people. I thought it was great that the center wanted to supplement fees to help community members seek counseling. Without your help, some of these people would never be able to afford my services."

"Yeah, I know we're doing a good thing. I guess sometimes you can lose sight of the right thing to do." He hesitated and cleared his throat. "Well, after you open back up, maybe we can get off to a better start. In a couple of weeks we'll be moving into our new facility. Hopefully, we won't have the same problems we've had here on the Riverfront."

"Mr. Hamel when I come in, I'd like to talk to you about that."

"Sure, we can discuss that later."

"Well, thanks for the information, and I'll look forward to seeing you in a couple of days."

She didn't want to discuss purchasing the building with Mr. Hamel just yet. Before she could make that independent move, the rapist had to be caught.

After hanging up, Deirdre leafed through the mail that had stacked up in her absence. Bills and junk mail. She glanced at her wristwatch. Fifteen minutes before Robert showed up. The phone rang, and she hoped it wasn't him calling to cancel.

"Hello."

"Deirdre!" Someone whispered from the other end.

"Yes, this is Deirdre." She set the mail down on the table and raised the volume on the phone.

A soft cry came from the other end. "He's going to kill me. Please help."

"Who is this?" She hoped this wasn't some prank caller.

"It's Cathy."

"Cathy! I thought you left town? Who's going to kill you? Where are you, honey?" Cathy sounded out of breath and scared to death.

"At home, but I've got to leave town. I've got to leave before he finds me."

Deirdre's heart pounded and she grabbed a piece of paper and a pen. "Cathy what's your address. I'm coming to get you."

"No, you can't. He'll kill you too."

"Give me your address."

"Number 20, Vine street. Deirdre, please don't come. I'm leaving town. I'm next. He's going to kill me next."

"Cathy, what are you talking about? Who tried to kill you? Did you call the police?"

"No, don't call the police, please. He'll kill me if you call the police."

"Just sit tight, I'm on my way."

Deirdre asked her mother to watch Mia, while she made a run. She didn't want to let her know what she was doing. She jumped in her car and drove as fast as she could over to St. Simons Island, where Cathy lived. What had stopped Cathy from moving to Florida?

Vine Street was easy to find, and number 20 was a duplex. Deirdre got out of the car and ran up to the front door.

She knocked several times, but Cathy didn't answer. From previous sessions, she knew Cathy could be suicidal. If anything happened to her, Deirdre would never forgive herself. She tried the doorknob, and it gently turned and opened.

Anxiously, Deirdre looked over her shoulder up and down the street. When she didn't see anyone, she pushed the door open.

"Cathy, are you in here," she called out several times without getting an answer. Curious, she walked into the tiny living room and pushed the door up behind her.

She walked down the hallway looking around still calling out. "Cathy, are you back here. It's Deirdre." Opening a door she guessed to be the bedroom, she found clothes all over the bed, and the room in shambles. Her pulse quickened, and she felt as if something was terribly wrong.

Where was Cathy? What had happened to her? She left the bedroom and closed the door behind her. Her hand reached out to open another door, when she heard a noise.

"Excuse me, but who are you?" A tall black man asked standing in the doorway.

Deirdre jumped at the sound of his voice. "Oh, you scared me."

"Sorry, but I hope you can explain why you're running around in my apartment."

She looked up startled. "I thought this was Cathy Benet's apartment?"

"It used to be. She rented from me. I own the duplex."

"But, she called me a few minutes ago, and said she was here."

He shook his head. "I haven't seen her since last Friday. She skipped on me. Left all her junk as you can see, but she's gone."

"How do you know she skipped with all her things still here. She wouldn't leave her television, VCR and all this other stuff would she?" She looked around at the small television sitting on a table. The furniture wasn't in good enough shape to take anywhere.

"She'd missed three months' rent, and she knew she was being evicted. I gave her plenty of chances to give me partial payments. Instead, last week I looked out the window and saw her getting into a car with her suitcase. She didn't even turn off the lights or lock the door."

Deirdre sighed. "Are you sure she left for good?"

"I'm positive. She left the door key in my mailbox."

She looked around and wondered where Cathy called her from if not here. "I'm Deirdre Levine, her counselor. Cathy called me not more than twenty minutes ago, afraid for her life. She said she was here, so I ran over to pick her up."

He gestured around the apartment. "Well, you can see she's not here."

"Is it okay if I look around a few minutes. Maybe I can find something to tell me where she went to."

He studied her a few seconds before shaking his head. "Sure, just don't take anything. I'm going to sell all this junk to get some of my rent money back."

"Thank you."

After he left, Deirdre went over to the kitchen table and leafed through Cathy's mail. There was a stack of bills that hadn't been opened. But nothing to give her a clue as to where Cathy was, or who was trying to kill her.

Robert left his office to go pick Deirdre up for lunch. He pulled out of the parking lot, and drove down Broadway. All morning he'd been thinking about last night. The day he first laid eyes on her, he wanted her. Then last night he'd made love to her. What started on his living room floor, ended in his bed hours later.

He reached a stop sign and pressed his brakes to stop, but nothing happened. The car rolled through the stop sign as he frantically pressed the brakes. All he heard was a grinding sound as he fought to turn the steering wheel toward a grassy area. The car was rolling downhill, and picking up speed.

Suddenly, he saw the embankment approaching and knew he was destined to go over. His foot jammed into the brake, with no luck. The car plowed through a stop sign, missing another car by inches. Robert closed his eyes and prayed, as the car sailed off the embankment and down into a wooded area.

Deirdre left Cathy's apartment with an empty feeling. Where was she? Her landlord hadn't been able to provide any information on her other than the fact that she was a quiet tenant who rarely entertained.

She couldn't remember if Cathy had told her about any friends in the area or not. However, she knew Cathy liked Brunswick.

From a phone booth, she called Robert and found out that he never showed for their lunch date. She called his office and was told that he'd left for lunch, and hadn't returned. Maybe he got held up, she concluded. She decided to keep looking for Cathy and explain it to Robert later.

If she could find a clue as to where Cathy might be, it would be in her case files. She jumped in her car and ran down to her office.

Once inside, she pulled the file and sat down to read at Susan's desk. Cathy had only mentioned first names in her sessions, which wouldn't be much for Deirdre to go on. However, she jotted down the names anyway.

Then she heard something that caused her to stop writing. She froze and listened, but didn't hear it again. She continued to leaf through the notes, then heard what sounded like a doorknob turning. Quickly, she jumped from her seat and looked around for a weapon. Susan locked everything up at night, so there was nothing left out on her desk. She grabbed Susan's radio and pulled the plug from the wall. If nothing else, she could hit somebody over the head with it.

Deirdre eased down the hallway not making a sound. At the back door she watched the knob turn while somebody worked the key. She held the radio over her head, ready to use it if she had to. They were unable to open the door.

"Damned lock."

The voice sounded familiar to her. "Who is it?" She called out, ready to open the door and hit whomever it was.

"Deirdre, it's me Susan."

She relaxed, then lowered the radio. "Susan."

After Deirdre unlocked the door, Susan walked in holding her keys. "Why are you coming in the back door?" *And what was she doing there anyway?* They hadn't opened back up.

"I wanted to see if my key still worked. Deirdre you need to get down to the hospital."

Deirdre's heart stopped. "Why, what happened?" Cathy came to mind and she hoped nothing bad had happened.

"It's Robert, he had a wreck."

"What! Robert?"

"Yes, and I'm so sorry. I came to get you."

Deirdre ran back into the front office and grabbed her purse. Susan followed her. "How did you know I was here?"

"I took a guess. You better hurry and get down to the hospital. I'll lock up here, go ahead."

Deirdre left Cathy's file out and hurried to her car and down to the hospital. She shuddered at the thought of Robert being hurt. Susan hadn't said what happened, only that he'd been in a wreck. Deirdre prayed that he was okay and not seriously injured.

She ran into the emergency room petrified. A nurse helped her find Robert's room. When she stepped in, she saw a small older woman sitting in a chair.

"Hello," the woman addressed her.

"Hi, I'm looking for Robert Carmichael."

"Deirdre."

She heard him call her name, and walked farther into the room. Robert sat on the side of the bed, smiling at her. She ran over to him and smothered him with kisses. He laughed and flinched when she touched certain places.

"Oh, I'm sorry, are you hurt?" She backed away.

"Not really, just a few scratches. They're letting me go in a few minutes."

"What happened?" she asked searching his face for scars.

"My brakes went out, and I drove off the side of the road. But I'm fine."

"Thank God." She hugged him again.

"Deirdre, I want you to meet my mother."

She turned around.

"So, this is the counselor lady." Pearl shook her head.

"Hello, Mrs. Carmichael." Deirdre walked over and shook her hand.

"Well, honey, it's nice to finally meet you. Robert, you'll have to bring her over to the house for dinner."

"Yes ma'am." He reached out and took Deirdre's hand when she returned to his side.

"Well, you seem to be okay, so I'm going home now."

After his mother left, Robert told Deirdre all about his accident. She told him about Cathy's call and Susan coming to get her.

"How did she know about the accident?"

"I don't know. When she told me I took off, and never asked her."

Deirdre drove Robert home, then stopped by her office to pick up her notes about Cathy. Everything was just as she'd left it on Susan's desk. When she got home, she called the police and told them everything Cathy had said to her.

Robert hung up the phone after talking to his mechanic. Someone had cut the brake line on his car. He needed to report this to the police, but doubted if they'd do anything about it.

Instead, he called Deirdre to check on her.

"Hey baby, is everything all right?"

"Hi. Yes, I'm fine. I can't wait to get back into the office in a couple of days."

"Good. I spoke to my mechanic just now. Somebody tampered with by brakes."

"You're kidding!"

"Wish I was. Deirdre, I'm working on something and I need to ask you a few questions."

"Sure, what?"

"I need to know everything that went on before Geneva's death. Is there anything you haven't told me?"

She hesitated a moment.

"Deirdre please. Somebody is after my life now, and I need to get to the bottom of this."

"Well, I've been getting messages over the Internet."

"What type of messages?"

"The first one said, 'Watch your back.' Then I got one that said, 'Don't trust anyone. Not even the people right under your nose.'"

"Why didn't you tell me this before?"

"I don't know, I haven't even told the police. Before I was sure whoever it was would lead me to the rapist, but now I don't know."

"What was the ID?"

"GypseyRose. I tried to search for them on the Internet, but there's no information on that ID."

He pulled out the report from the private investigator and

flipped through until he found the Internet ID, GypseyRose. "Deirdre, thanks I'll get back with you real soon."

He didn't want Deirdre to know he'd hired a private investigator, but now it looked like things were coming together. He needed to pay somebody another visit.

When Susan opened the front door, she didn't look at all surprised to see Robert. She appeared to be expecting him.

"I guess you want to come in." She lowered her head.

"If you don't mind. I'd like to ask you a few more questions." She looked nervous and her eyes were red as if she'd been crying.

"Come on. I owe you some answers." Susan wrung her hands as Robert followed her over to the living-room couch.

"I guess you're wondering how I knew about your accident?"

"Yeah, but first I'd like to know about GypseyRose."

Stunned, Susan looked into his eyes and covered her mouth. She dropped her shoulders and fell back onto the couch. "How did you find out about that?"

"Why did you send Deirdre those messages, Susan? Are you protecting the guy you opened the back door for?"

"I never opened that back door," she protested. "He stole my key a while back. But he returned it long before Sheila was raped."

"Who are we talking about?"

She lowered her head and mumbled his name. "Gus. He got a hold of my key somehow and gave it to a friend of his."

"He what?" Robert hadn't expected this.

"He works for some guy who wants to buy the building instead of Deirdre. They've been trying to sabotage her office to force her out. When the community center leaves, they're hoping she leaves with them."

"He told you that?"

"No, but I heard him talking to someone on the phone once. And he's asked me to do things from time to time, that I couldn't do."

"Like what?"

"Steal files, give him client information. Once he even asked me to leave the front door unlocked. But I couldn't do that."

Robert sat back rubbing his goatee. "Why didn't you go to the police?"

Susan had started crying. "I couldn't. You don't know Gus. If I told the police, he'd kill me. Or, have the guy he works for kill me."

"But he raped two women, and murdered one. How could you not go to the police?"

"He didn't do that. He promised me he had nothing to do with that."

"Where can I find him?"

"I don't know. We broke up a few weeks ago, and I haven't seen him since."

Robert stood up and paced around Susan's living room while she went into the bathroom. When she returned he'd made up his mind. "Susan, you have to take this information to the police. Deirdre's life could be in danger. Your friend obviously knows who murdered Geneva. If the police find this Gus fella, they can find the killer."

"I know. I never meant to hurt her. Believe me, I wanted to tell her a long time ago, but he threatened me. And now I can't find him."

"Is this the same guy who cut my brake line?"

She shook her head. "I suspect he is. He asked a lot of questions about your relationship to Deirdre. But, I've got a friend at the police station, that's how I knew about your wreck."

"So when are you going to the police?" He cornered her.

"I'll call them tonight." She began to cry again, this time sobbing harder. "I'm so sorry."

Robert was so upset, he was unsympathetic to her tears. Because of her withholding information, Deirdre's or his life could be in danger.

"Susan, I find it hard to believe these guys would kill just to force her to leave the building. There has to be more to it than that. What does Gus do for a living?"

"I don't know. But, I think it's illegal whatever it is."

Robert stared at her. "What makes you think that?"

"Because he never seems to be working, but he always has a lot of money. I think he deals drugs for the guy."

TWENTY-THREE

"Deirdre, I'm so sorry. I never meant to hurt you or anybody else. After Robert left my apartment the other day, I made a few calls and found Gus. He stays in Jacksonville most of the time. I told him that I was going to the police, and he can't hurt me. Then, I hung up the phone and called Ralph, my policeman friend."

Deirdre stared at Susan sitting across from her desk in disbelief. How could she have done this to her? She had put so much trust in Susan. She'd given her access to everything confidential in the office.

"Did you tell the police everything you're telling me now?"

"Yes, I did. I gave them Gus's address, not that he's there. I believe he's moved," she said sorrowfully.

"Susan, how could you have given him confidential information about my clients?" Deirdre pleaded. "I explained to you how important that was when I hired you."

Susan wrung her hands and apologized over and over. "I don't know. He tricked me. Deirdre, we had a perfect relationship. He brought me little gifts all the time, and told me he loved me." A single tear rolled down her cheek.

"Please forgive me, I'm so sorry," Susan continued.

"So, who placed the necklace in my office?" Deirdre asked.

"What necklace?" Susan asked through sniffles.

Deirdre eyed her suspiciously. She no longer trusted her to tell the truth. "I found a necklace in my office the day Sheila was raped. He didn't tell you anything about that?"

"No. He didn't mention anything about a necklace. All he wanted was information on your clients so he could scare them into not coming back. And he promised me that's all he did."

Deirdre leaned forward with her elbows stretched out on her desk. "So, you're telling me you don't know anything about the necklace or the article?" If she did, it meant she knew about her being raped.

Susan stared at her with a puzzled expression on her face. "No, he never showed me a necklace or said anything about a newspaper article."

"Susan you know what you've done is grounds for termination?"

She lowered her head and sighed. "Yes, I only pray that you forgive me and keep me on. But, if you don't, I'll understand."

"I don't see how I can. You've broken the breach of confidentiality. I'm going to have to let you go."

It hurt Deirdre so much to fire Susan, but she had no choice. Afterward, she contacted Mr. Hamel to let him know she'd be looking for a new secretary. She contacted all the clients she could and rescheduled their appointments. If she had to, she could run for a week at the most without a secretary, but she had to get someone soon.

Going through her office mail, Deirdre opened a letter from the bank. Great news, her loan had been approved. Elated, she picked up the phone and called Robert.

"Robert, great news."

"What's that, baby?"

"I'm reading a letter from the bank right now, and my loan has been approved. This building is as good as mine."

He applauded her. "That's wonderful. Have you already talked to a Realtor?"

"Yes, weeks ago. Now I need to talk to Mr. Hamel. In less than a month the community center will be all moved out, and I can start remodeling. I think I'm going to lease this side of the building out. The center portion is more than enough for a few offices."

"You've thought of everything, haven't you?"

"This is a big step for me. A colleague of mine is going to join me, and we'll be looking for one more person. But, I've dreamed of this for a long time. There's other programs I'd like to start also. Volunteer-based at first, but I'm looking to build them into something more."

"When do you plan on starting all this?"

She sighed. "As soon as Geneva's killer is caught. I don't feel like I can do anything until then. Susan came to see me this morning."

"I figured she would. How did it go?"

"I felt so bad. She apologized for everything, but I still had to let her go. And we were such a perfect team, that's why I'm still in shock."

"That's too bad. I hope you find somebody good and trustworthy. Is your day booked?"

"No. I've got a few things to take care of before I leave. My first appointment is tomorrow at ten-twenty."

"How about dinner tonight?"

"Make it lunch and you've got a date. I had a bad dream last night, so I didn't get much sleep. I'm crashing early tonight."

"For a date with you, anything. I'll see you at about one o'clock. How's that?"

"Perfect."

Deirdre finished creating her ad for the paper when the phone rang.

"Hello, Brunswick Counseling Agency."

"May I speak to Deirdre Stanley-Levine?"

"This is her, may I help you?" She had to strain to hear the party on the other line.

"Ms. Levine, my name is Ray Jones and I desperately need to talk to you."

"What is this about Mr. Jones?"

"I need a counselor. And if I don't talk to somebody soon there's no telling what I'll do to myself. I need to talk to somebody, now." He pleaded with her.

"Would you like to set up an appointment?" Deirdre couldn't believe her luck. Just when most of her clients seemed to be leaving, she could still pick up new ones.

"Yes, yes, I have to talk with you today."

"I'm sorry I don't have any time for today, but I can set you up for tomorrow morning."

"No! I have to see you today. Is there any way possible you can see me for a few minutes this afternoon? I'm begging you."

"Mr. Jones I'm sorry but . . ."

"You see, I'm new to the area and my counselor in Nashville said I should call you as soon as I got in town. I'm in desperate need of an emergency session."

She hated to turn anyone away. "Mr. Jones what would you be seeing me about?"

"I've been wrestling with suicidal thoughts."

"Well—if you can make it at one o'clock I can see you." She glanced at her watch. That gave her enough time to finish her business and grab a sandwich from across the street. She'd have to reschedule with Robert.

"Thank you so much. I'll be there at one o'clock on the nose."

Deirdre hung up and tried to catch Robert. He wasn't in the office, so she left a message canceling their lunch date. She didn't like seeing new patients that she knew nothing about. Especially, without Susan or a secretary to help with their paperwork.

After she grabbed a quick lunch, she went into Susan's desk for blank copies of all new client paperwork. She attached the paperwork to a clipboard and left it on the desk for Mr. Jones to fill out before she talked to him. She wanted to know who his therapist was in Nashville.

A knock at the door startled her.

She looked up to see Bill Duncan at the front door.

"What does he want?" she said aloud. As she walked to unlock the door, she thought it might be good that he showed up. After all, she didn't know the first thing about this new client.

She pushed the door open and let him in. "Hey Bill, I hope you've got more good news for me."

Officer Duncan took off his hat and walked in. "Well, Deirdre, I see you're back in business." He looked around the office.

She closed and locked the door. "Yes, I've officially re-opened."

"Where's Susan?" he asked walking over to Susan's desk.

Deirdre sighed. She rested one hand on her hip and the other she ran through her hair. "Believe it or not, I had to fire her."

"That's too bad. What did she do?"

"Well, for starters she gave out confidential information." She walked back to her office. "Come on in." He followed.

"That's a shame."

"But you should already know that." She turned and looked at him. "Didn't she come down to the police station and turn the guy in?"

"What guy?"

"Her ex-boyfriend. She said he forced her to give him information on my clients. When I talked to her this morning, she said she called the police and told them everything. I'm surprised you don't already know about it."

He shook his head.

"Damn! I thought maybe you guys would be close to catching somebody with her information. I hope she didn't lie to me again. Bill, I can't believe she turned on me like that."

"You know what they say, don't trust anyone. You never know who's for you or who's against you."

A chill ran through Deirdre's body. She locked eyes with Bill and nodded. "Yeah, I guess you're right." Bill had sat down and made himself comfortable. She glanced at her watch, ten minutes before her new client showed up.

"I'm sorry Bill, but what did you come by for?"

"You know Deirdre, it's good to see you doing good for yourself after all these years. I mean, I never would have known you were going to grow up into such a woman."

Where was he going with this conversation. "Thank you, Bill. You've done pretty good for yourself, too."

"Not quite." He stood up and walked over to a small bookshelf she had on the wall. "You see, I've been wrestling with these suicidal thoughts." He turned to face her. "And I really need to talk to a counselor."

Deirdre stared, and pointed at him. "You're Mr. Jones?"

He fingered the books on the shelf and laughed. "No, I'm not Mr. Jones. You see, there is no Mr. Jones." He returned to the chair in front of her.

"Bill, I don't understand. Why in the hell did you call me saying you were Mr. Jones, some suicidal guy?"

"I wanted an appointment."

Confused, she shook her head. "Then why didn't you just call and ask for one."

"This is the only way I could find out if you received my gifts."

"What?" Baffled she leaned on the desk and asked, "Bill, what in the hell are you talking about?"

"The necklace. Did you get it? I left it here for you." His eyes fixed upon hers leering at her.

Her mouth fell open. Her whole body went numb. Fear robbed her of her speech. She slowly sat back in her seat.

"I know you got the article. I stuck around to make sure you got that one." He reached into his breast pocket and pulled out a pack of cigarettes, lit one, then blew the smoke into the air.

"Why?" That was the only word she could utter.

"Why? Because I never thought you'd come back here. I never thought I'd see you again. How much did you remember? I knew you wouldn't remember me, but I knew you'd remember that necklace."

"How did you get my necklace?" Deirdre asked as she sat there trembling in her seat.

"It wasn't easy. You did put up a good little fight. But you were never any match for me." He threw his hat on the desk. "And you never will be."

She jumped in her seat, then looked around for something to throw at him. Before she could find anything, he dropped his cigarette and ran around her desk. He grabbed her by the arms.

She fought him off with every ounce of strength she had. He twisted one arm behind her back. The pain shot though her so fast she immediately froze.

"That's right, be a good little girl." He stood behind her and whispered in her ear. "Don't put up a fuss like that white lady. What's her name, Sheila. Yeah, she put up a good little fight, and I almost had to kill her." He laughed in her ear.

Deirdre wiggled trying to get him to let go. He'd raped Sheila. Her eyes welled with tears. This was their rapist.

"And Geneva, now that was a treat." He laughed

She wanted to explode. Instead, she pretended to be too exhausted to move. The minute he loosened up on her arms, she reached for a paperweight on her desk and spun around with all her force, hurling the object at him. The paperweight landed at his temple, causing enough pain for him to let go of her completely and grab his head. He cried out in pain.

Seizing the moment, Deirdre pushed him out of the way and ran out of her office. As she reached the front door, she saw the light of day. She could get away from him. Then, she heard a click.

"Hold it, unless you want to die right here." His breathing was heavy and short.

With her hand on the lock, she turned around and saw a gun pointed at her. Petrified, her hand trembled on the lock wanting with all her might to unlock the door and run for her life. Instead, she lowered her hand. She'd have to find another way out of this.

"That's a good girl. Come on back over here, and let's finish what we started twenty-two years ago. And this won't be a sloppy job. You see, I hate sloppy work."

Knock, knock. She jumped and let out a yelp when someone knocked on the front door. Robert stood on the other side of the door.

"Touch that lock, and I'll blow the both of you away. Get over here, quick." He motioned for her to sit in one of the reception area chairs. Moving past her, with the gun on her, he made his way to the front door.

Knock, knock. Robert knocked harder this time.

Bill looked at Robert standing on the other side of the two-way glass door. "Should we let him join our little party? Yeah, why not. I've wanted to kill him for as long as I can remember."

He stood back and unlocked the door. The minute Robert stepped inside, Bill grabbed the door, and locked it back.

"What's going on?" Robert asked looking from Bill to Deirdre confused.

Bill held his gun up to Robert. "Have a seat pretty boy. We were just about to start our counseling session."

Robert threw his hands up. "Hey, what the hell!" He opened his arms as Deirdre ran to him.

"Okay you two. Start walking, back into Deirdre's office. Now," he yelled at them.

Deirdre held the tears back as they did what he ordered. Robert gripped her by the shoulders, and helped her into a chair.

"Bill, I don't understand what's going on here. You don't need to hold that gun on us." Robert tried to talk to him.

"Shut up. This is one story you won't be able to write about. You see, I don't plan on letting you come out of this one alive. No exclusive for you tonight, Mr. Carmichael." He said, disguising his voice.

"What the hell." Robert jumped up from his seat. Bill pulled the trigger on his gun and pointed it at Robert's head. Robert slowly sat back down.

"You see, I had a nice surprise already for Deirdre here." Bill moved behind her desk, and picked up the phone.

"I don't like surprises," she said.

"Oh, you'll like this one." He dialed a number still holding the gun on them. "I'm inside. You know what to do." He spoke to someone on the other end, then hung up.

Robert held Deirdre's trembling hands. "Bill, I don't know what this is about, but if you're doing this to get back at me, please let Deirdre go."

Bill laughed and cut his eyes at Robert. "I could care less about you. When I finished with that girl in high school, she was yours for the taking. Hell, anybody could have had her, she was nothing more than a common whore, anyway."

He turned his gaze toward Deirdre. "Believe it or not, I helped you. You didn't want to be a whore like your sister, did you? You should be thankful for what I did." He smiled, and winked at her.

"You sick bastard." She spit out and rolled her eyes at him.

Robert realized what was going on, and reached over to comfort Deirdre.

Bill laughed again, even louder. "How's that little scratch over your eye?"

Deirdre felt the hair on her neck stand when he looked at her. If she could burn a hole through him with her eyes, she would. Nausea washed over her and she knew she'd hurl her lunch any minute now. She only wished she'd do it on him.

"So, it was you who raped all those women? You're the guy the police could never catch?" Robert asked.

Bill walked from behind Deirdre's desk to the door when he heard a sound in the hallway. "Damn hard to catch yourself, if you know what I mean. But they deserved it. All of them. Nothing more than dirty whores."

He turned back to Robert. "Oh, Robert sorry you won't be able to get this exclusive, but another one of Ms. Levine's clients has bit the dust."

Deirdre's heart sank. *God, what has he done?* She had a feeling she knew who it was.

"I'm so sorry you missed her," Bill turned to Deirdre.

Robert looked from Deirdre to Bill. "Who's he talking about Deirdre?"

She squeezed her eyes together, and bit her bottom lip. Why was he hurting all these innocent people? "Bill, why are you doing this, she never hurt you."

"I wanted to help her, too, but it was too late. But, she never should have fought back. I hate when they fight back."

Robert turned to Deirdre.

She started crying hysterically. "My God, he's killed Cathy."

TWENTY-FOUR

Robert looked into Deirdre's eyes wanting to do more to comfort her. He couldn't do anything right now, but waited for his chance to make a move on Bill. Why he hadn't suspected him before, he didn't know. It should have been obvious, when he wasn't busting his balls to solve any of the rapes.

"Okay you two. Separate, now." Bill waved his gun at them. "Deirdre, get behind your desk. It's time for the party to begin."

A man stepped into the office with a duffel bag in his hand. "We're about to have a very private, confidential session, if you know what I mean." He noticed Robert, surprised. "And we're making it a two for one."

"Gus, cut the crap and get to work. Him first." He pointed at Robert.

Gus opened his bag and walked over to Robert with a rope in his hand. "Hands out front where I can see them."

"Bill. Look, this isn't necessary. All you have to do is lock us in here and you can get away. Hell, lock us in the bathroom, but you don't have to do this."

"Don't tell me what to do. I'm in charge of this show."

Robert struggled to keep Gus from tying the rope so tight.

"Hey man, I might not have enough for both of them."

"Just tie his ass up, make it enough." Bill walked back over to Deirdre.

She'd stopped crying and refused to look at him.

"You never should have returned little lady."

"Bill, I thought we were going to have a party first." Gus

smiled at Deirdre. "I've heard so much about Ms. Deirdre, I was looking forward to this."

Bill walked over and stood in front of Robert, while Gus tied Deirdre up. "Yeah, I had planned a nice little final celebration, but right now I just want to get the hell out of here. These two want to be together so bad. I'll let them be together for one last time."

Robert yelled obscenities at Bill, who took his gun and smacked it across Robert's face. Deirdre cried out begging him to stop.

After tying Deirdre up, Gus pulled the phone cord from the wall, and left the office. Bill stood in the doorway. "Well, I guess I'll call and give somebody the exclusive on this one. Boy, what a shame. A terrible fire burned down the center with two people inside." He put his hat on, and tipped it at Robert. "Sorry old boy, you won't be getting this call." Laughing, he pulled the door shut, and locked it.

"Ray, thanks for coming with me to talk to Deirdre. I just didn't trust Bill Duncan." Susan sat in the police car with Officer Ray Fields. She'd confided everything in him and they were on their way to Deirdre's office to warn her about Bill.

"Well, when you told me about Gus, I knew that was the guy I'd seen Bill with. I'm not sure what they're up to, but we'll find out. Your theory does explain where all that evidence money went to a couple of months ago. We've been missing other things from time to time. All during Bill's shift. Don't worry, he'll be checked out thoroughly."

"Thank you. I know Deirdre doesn't trust me, but I was so scared of Gus I didn't know what to do."

Ray reached over and patted Susan on the leg. "Don't worry about him. I'm glad you called me. We'll get him, and Bill, too."

They pulled into the community center parking lot, and Susan almost jumped from the car.

"Ray, look. The center's on fire! Stop, we have to help them."

He threw the car in park and picked up the police radio. Susan opened the car door and ran out. "Susan, hold on."

At the smell of smoke, Deirdre managed to open her desk drawer and move her fingers around inside.

"Come on baby, see if you can find anything." Robert cheered her on as he scooted his chair around her desk.

"I'm trying. Oh, God, we're going to burn up in here." Tears filled her eyes making it hard to see what was in the drawer.

"No we're not, baby. Just take your time, Deirdre and open another drawer."

"I'm trying." She took a few deep breaths to calm herself. When she pulled open her top right drawer, she fingered through the pens, ruler, and finally, "Scissors," she screamed.

"Good baby, hand them to me. Come on I can move my fingers better than you." His hands were tied in front. A stupid thing for Gus to do, but Robert was glad he didn't know any better.

Deirdre gripped the scissors with her index fingers and scooted over to Robert. He took the scissors and cut her roped wrists. Free, she cut him loose.

They ran over to the door and Robert touched it. It was warm, but not hot. Only a small amount of smoke had trickled into the office. There were no windows in the office, so that door was the only way out.

"Okay, baby. We're going to have to run out of here and find a way out. Let's hope the whole office isn't on fire." He kissed her on the forehead, and she hugged him before he opened the door.

They crouched down as far as they could, walking into the hallway. The front office was set ablaze. The room was filled with smoke that was rapidly moving back in their direction. He grabbed Deirdre's hand and pulled her in the other direction toward the back door. When he tried the knob, it was locked.

"Is there another key somewhere?" he asked holding his hand over his mouth.

"No."

"Okay, stand back." He rammed the door a couple of times with his body, it buckled a few times, then finally flew open. Smoke filled the back room. Grabbing Deirdre's hand, he pulled her to the floor. On her knees, she lead the way to the back door. Their coughing grew worse, and Deirdre started to panic.

Robert took off his shirt and gave it to her to put over her mouth. Just as they reached the back door, Deirdre jumped up screaming and choking. Robert reached in front of her searching through the smoke and saw a man's body laying in front of the door.

He grabbed Deirdre and pulled her close to him. "Who is it?" he asked.

"Alfred, the janitor." She began to cry.

The smoke thickened, so Robert grabbed Alfred's body and moved him from the back door. He reached up and unlocked the door, swinging it open. He grabbed Deirdre's hand and pulled her outside. He pulled her to her feet as they ran from the building coughing.

"Oh God, Robert." She fell against him. "We almost died in there. And Alfred, why did they kill Alfred?" Deirdre alternated between sobs and coughing. Standing in the back of the building, she could see that the entire community center was on fire.

Robert pulled her into his arms, holding on tight.

"Deirdre, Deirdre."

She heard Susan calling her name. "Susan." She let go of Robert and ran into the parking lot. He was right behind her. She found Susan, and a police officer in the parking lot.

"Are you guys okay?" the officer asked running up to them.

"Yes. We're fine. But the janitor's at the back door. He looks like he's dead.

"I've called the fire department. Stay right here." Officer Ray went into the back of the building to investigate.

"Deirdre, I'm sorry I didn't go to the police when I said I would. But, I don't trust Bill Duncan. I told Ray everything and he's told his superiors. We think Bill is behind some of this."

Deirdre shook her head. "I know Susan, that's who set this fire."

A fire truck came screaming down the street. More police cars showed up at the same time. Everything got chaotic. The community center staff had already come running out of the other side of the building. No children were on the premises at the time.

Deirdre and Robert explained to the police everything that had happened to them. Half of the Brunswick Community Center had been burned to the ground. But Robert and Deirdre were thankful to be alive. Nothing mattered but their lives. Deirdre wanted to go home right away and be with Mia.

A couple of days later, Robert called Deirdre to tell her the police had caught Gus, and were close to catching Bill. She asked Robert if she could sit down and tell him the story of her repressed memory of the rape. An article on the subject would help other women. She also called a therapist for herself.

The community center would be moving into its new facility in a week, and had dedicated a building to Alfred. Mr. Hamel offered Deirdre office space if she wanted to continue her services, but she declined his offer. After what had happened, she felt a stronger urge to be on her own. Deirdre researched into purchasing her own building. She still had the approved bank loan.

Robert took Deirdre and Mia on their last picnic for the summer a few weeks later. Robert gave Deirdre the good news.

"I found out something this afternoon that I've been busting at the seams to tell you." He pushed Mia on a swing with Deirdre sitting in the swing next to her.

"What? Tell me?"

"The police have reopened the investigation on several of those rape cases. Bill Duncan is the prime suspect."

"You're serious?" She almost jumped from her seat.

"Yes, and they've located him."

"Where Robert?"

"In Miami. It should be on the news tonight. They're bringing him back."

She wiped at the tears beginning to fall from her eyes. "He belongs in jail."

"And I've got more good news." He smiled at her.

"My, you're loaded tonight. Tell me." She held on to the chain and began a slow swing.

"I had a business meeting today at the Almherst complex, in this new office for three. Great reception area with two entrances. They're looking for someone to pick up the lease on the building. It's not on the market yet, but I think you can have it if you want."

"Robert, no. I don't believe you." She beamed, getting out of her swing.

"Actually, it's yours if you want it."

She ran around and hugged him. Mia's swing slowed down. "Robert, thank you so much." Tears flowed from Deirdre's eyes.

"Can you stand one more surprise?" he asked.

"Normally, I don't like surprises, but I feel as if I'm going to like this one."

He pulled her into his arms. "I want you and Mia to come live with me."

Deirdre pulled away from his arms. "Come live with you?" she asked curious.

He reached into his pocket and pulled out a small box. "Yes, at least until we make it official."

She stared at the box with her mouth wide open. "What's that?"

"My intent to make you Mrs. Robert Carmichael." He opened the box.

At the sight of the ring, tears rolled down Deirdre's face. She took the ring out, and Robert put it on her finger.

"Will you marry me, and make me a happy man?"

Mia ran up to them, pulling on Deirdre's skirt. "Mommy are you okay?"

Robert picked Mia up with one hand, and held Deirdre in the other. "Yes, Mia everything's all right. I think?" He looked at Deirdre.

"Yes." She kissed Robert, then looked at Mia. "Baby, everything's wonderful."

ABOUT THE AUTHOR

Born and raised in Louisville, Kentucky, Bridget Anderson moved to Atlanta, Georgia in 1987 and began her writing career. She holds down a full-time job, along with her writing. When she's not writing, she's enjoying her other passion in life, traveling.

Dear Reader:

Thank you so much for the purchase of my latest novel. I hope you've enjoyed *Soul Mates, Moonlight and Mistletoe,* and *Rendezvous* as well, I appreciate you taking the time to let me know what you think of my work. Every time I receive a letter from a reader, it makes my day. Please include a self-addressed, stamped envelope for a speedy reply. Or reach me via e-mail at Goldexp@aol.com.

Bridget Anderson
P.O. Box 76432
Atlanta, Georgia 30358

COMING IN MAY . . .

SUMMER MAGIC   (1-58314-012-3, $4.99/$6.50)
by Rochelle Alers

Home economics teacher Caryn Edwards is renting a summer house on North Carolina's Marble Island. She was certain it would give her a chance to heal from her ugly divorce and career burnout. What she didn't bargain for was handsome developer Logan Prescott who would unexpectedly be sharing the house with her.

BE MINE   (1-58314-013-1, $4.99/$6.50)
by Geri Guillaume

Judie McVie has worked all her life on Bar M, her uncle's sprawling Mississippi ranch. When he died, they were sure he'd left them the land. But mysterious loner Tucker Conklin appeared with the will in hand, claiming the ranch. She'd do anything to hold onto her family's legacy . . . and he'd do anything to capture her heart.

MADE FOR EACH OTHER   (1-58314-014-X, $4.99/$6.50)
by Niqui Stanhope

Interior designer Summer Stevens is hoping to escape Chicago and throw herself into work at a Jamaican beach cottage owned by the wealthy Champagne family. But focusing on business proves to be a challenge when she meets her devilishly attractive employer, Gavin Pagne.

AND OUR MOTHER'S DAY COLLECTION . . .

A MOTHER'S LOVE   (1-58314-015-8, $4.99/$6.50)
by Candice Poarch, Raynetta Mañees and Viveca Carlysle

No woman is as loved or as loving as a mother, and our authors help honor that special woman. "More Than Friends," by Poarch, "All The Way Home," by Mañees, and "Brianna's Garden," by Carlysle, are three short stories of extraordinary mothers in search of love.

Available wherever paperbacks are sold, or order direct from the Publisher. Send cover price plus 50¢ per copy for mailing and handling to BET Books, c/o Kensington Publishing Corp., Consumer Orders, or call (toll free) 888-345-BOOK, to place your order using Mastercard or Visa. Residents of New York, Washington D.C. and Tennessee must include sales tax. DO NOT SEND CASH.

LOOK FOR THESE ARABESQUE ROMANCES

AFTER ALL, by Lynn Emery   (0-7860-0325-1, $4.99/$6.50)
News reporter Michelle Toussaint only focused on her dream of becoming an anchorwoman. Then contractor Anthony Hilliard returned. For five years, Michelle had reminsced about the passions they shared. But happiness turned to heartbreak when Anthony's cruel betrayal led to her father's financial ruin. He returned for one reason only: to win Michelle back.

THE ART OF LOVE, by Crystal Wilson-Harris   (0-7860-0418-5, $4.99/$6.50)
Dakota Bennington's heritage is apparent from her African clothing to her sculptures. To her, attorney Pierce Ellis is just another uptight professional stuck in the American mainstream. Pierce worked hard and is proud of his success. An art purchase by his firm has made Dakota a major part of his life. And love bridges their different worlds.

CHANGE OF HEART   (0-7860-0103-8, $4.99/$6.50)
by Adrienne Ellis Reeves
Not one to take risks or stray far from her South Carolina hometown, Emily Brooks, a recently widowed mother, felt it was time for a change. On a business venture she meets author David Walker who is conducting research for his new book. But when he finds undying passion, he wants Emily for keeps. Wary of her newfound passion, all Emily has to do is follow her heart.

ECSTACY, by Gwynne Forster   (0-7860-0416-9, $4.99/$6.50)
Schoolteacher Jeannetta Rollins had a tumor that was about to cost her her eyesight. Her persistence led her to follow Mason Fenwick, the only surgeon talented enough to perform the surgery, on a trip around the world. After getting to know her, Mason wants her whole . . . body and soul. Now he must put behind a tragedy in his career and trust himself and his heart.

KEEPING SECRETS, by Carmen Green   (0-7860-0494-0, $4.99/$6.50)
Jade Houston worked alone. But a dear deceased friend left clues to a two-year-old mystery and Jade had to accept working alongside Marine Captain Nick Crawford. As they enter a relationship that runs deeper than business, each must learn how to trust each other in all aspects.

MOST OF ALL, by Louré Bussey   (0-7860-0456-8, $4.99/$6.50)
After another heartbreak, New York secretary Elandra Lloyd is off to the Bahamas to visit her sister. Her sister is nowhere to be found. Instead she runs into Nassau's richest, self-made millionaire Bradley Davenport. She is lucky to have made the acquaintance with this sexy islander as she searches for her sister and her trust in the opposite sex.

Available wherever paperbacks are sold, or order direct from the Publisher. Send cover price plus 50¢ per copy for mailing and handling to Kensington Publishing Corp., Consumer Orders, or call (toll free) 888-345-BOOK, to place your order using Mastercard or Visa. Residents of New York and Tennessee must include sales tax. DO NOT SEND CASH.